CONTENTS

THE DEECIT

a novel

R Michael Purcell

ISBN:
ISBN-13:

DEDICATED TO ALL COVID19 SUFFERERS

CHAPTER ONE

The only thing Beverly knew was that Senator James Quincy missed the Blaze's last tour because of COVID19. She knew there was more to it and she was in LA to find out for herself. Standing under the massive portico in front of the Tom Bradley terminal at LAX, she waited for the rain to stop. Restless and irritable, Beverly was anxious to get home to New York City. Thankfully this was her last intermediate stop. She was concerned about her good friend and song writing partner who had not responded to her emails, text messages and phone calls. Not like the James Quincy she knew.

The taxis, Ubers and LYFTs were lined up single file and she decided to chance being drowned by the rain that intensified every minute. Racing toward an Uber, she stood momentarily while the driver threw her bags in the trunk and ushered her into the back seat. With the cold rain dripping down the back her neck onto her shoulders, she found the Laurel Canyon address and gave it to the driver. Beverly used a crumpled tissue from her purse to stem the trickle of cold rainwater.

A motorcycle parked behind the Uber brought back memories of her father, a motorcycle enthusiast in his heyday who rode every Sunday no matter where he was. John Swift was career army and he and his family lived all over the world until Beverly, the eldest of three children, was thirteen. They moved about every year. Beverly's mother was tired of it like one tires of doing laundry or cleaning the house. It was becoming drudgery. Major John Swift retired, they settled in Minneapolis and Beverly finally took vocal lessons that trained her magnificent singing voice.

At every opportunity between stop and go traffic, honking horns and unpleasant gestures, the driver looked in the rearview mirror before garnering the courage to ask a possibly embarrassing question.

"Are you Beverly Swift?" he finally dared to say as he looked at his passenger again in the rearview mirror. She was wet from the rain, her hair clinging to her head like lint, blowing her nose and trying to stay calm for her mission to see Senator James Quincy.

"Yes. Yes, I am." She smiled.

"Wow. I am one of your biggest fans. Are you touring again?"

"Well, we were trying to tour but COVID19 got in the way. We had fifty cities lined up, but only made five," she said, blowing her nose again. "Unfortunately, the virus dampened the crowds, too, and we decided to cancel the tour since there was no telling how long this thing might last," she said. "Excuse me, but I have the beginnings of a cold."

"Not to worry. I would cherish getting a cold from you," he said, realizing that his statement did not come out right. "Sorry, that did not come . . ."

"No worries. I know what you meant." Beverly giggled.

They made small talk about the tour, her music, his favorite song and what she'd been doing since the last tour. When they reached Senator Quincy's house, Beverly reached into her purse and pulled out a CD, then a black marker and signed the face of it. She handed it to the driver.

"Thank you," he gushed. "This is so cool."

He handed her a business card and told Beverly to call him when she wanted to go back to the airport.

"Will do."

James Quincy's home looked like a war zone. Emergency vehicles, an ambulance, several police cruisers and a limousine with the seal of the United States government on the side. The ambulance was just pulling out of the driveway. A young woman, Q's daughter Beverly surmised, was standing at the front door letting the tears roll down her cheek. Beverly stepped out of the Uber while the driver unloaded her bags and walked toward the woman standing by the front door.

"Hello, are you Jordan Quincy?" She nodded. Beverly remembered her from a recent photograph. "And is that Q in the ambulance?" She nodded again.

"Are you Beverly Swift?"

"Yes, Is Q going back the hospital?"

Jordan started to sob.

"No, I am afraid it's the medical examiner this time. Dad passed away this morning," she said. "Complications from COVID19. I called the Senate Majority Leaders office and that's what they said to do."

"What happened?"

"Well, Beverly . . . Can I call you Beverly?"

"By all means."

"He was feeling great and went to a big fundraiser, but no one wore masks. He was glad-handing and having his picture taken with other supporters. A week later, he was back in the hospital."

"When was this?"

"The fundraiser was January 8th and he was back in the hospital three days later. They were about to release him on the 15th when he took a turn for the worse.

They put him on a ventilator and he got better. He came home Saturday and died in his sleep this morning."

Jordan was crying now after recounting the ordeal.

"So sorry. I promised myself I wouldn't breakdown again."

"You breakdown as much as you want," Beverly said. "You're allowed under the circumstances. When is the funeral, memorial service or whatever . . ."

"The funeral is this Saturday and the memorial service is yet to be determined," she said.

"I'll stay and help," Beverly said, blowing her nose. "In the meantime, I need to get a hotel. What's close by?"

Jordan argued that Beverly stay at the house, but she convinced Jordan that she would only be in the way. The last thing she needed was a fifth wheel.

CHAPTER TWO

The crowd for James Riley Quincy's funeral was quite small since it was only for family, friends, a few United States Senators and members of Congress and all the Blaze musicians, crew and roadies. They all loved Jim Quincy. It still made for an impressive crowd, over a thousand, who sat quietly in the Episcopal church Q attended irregularly when he was home. Jordan had been christened there and attended services almost every week and lately twice a week.

After the liturgical prayers, the ceremonial music, the consecration and prayers for the family, Beverly went to the alter to deliver her eulogy. She'd been thinking about all the death there had been from COVID19, now over 450,000. And now James Riley Quincy. She cleared her throat and looked out at the crowd. She would give anything to just be able to sing at this moment.

"I met James Quincy when he was seventeen years old in a dive bar in Nashville, Tennessee. He was an aspiring singer who just wanted to play in a band in Nashville before going back home to Lubbock, Texas, to go to college. Fifteen years later, he finally did go back," Beverly said. "I was sitting on a bar stool making derogatory comments about his cowboy hat when he challenged me to enter the Karaoke contest with him. We went to the alley behind the bar and agreed to sing *'Ain't No Mountain High Enough'*, a popular Marvin Gaye song. It seemed appropriate to sing a R&B hit in a country bar in Nashville, Tennessee that spoke to our aspirations as musicians."

The guests laughed.

"Ironically, the Karaoke machine had the music on it. Marvin told me later that he recorded a lot in Nashville and frequented that establishment a good bit because it was close to the recording studio and he could smoke weed in the bathroom without fear of retribution, racist remarks, being thrown out or beaten up," Beverly added.

The crowd erupted again.

"Well, James Q and I won that Karaoke contest, received $50.00 each and drank the hundred dollars up over the next two days, mostly in my motel room and decided that if we were good enough for the C & W bar in Nashville, we were good enough for the world," she said. "The rest, as they say, is history. Ten gold albums, five platinum albums and success beyond our wildest dreams."

The mourners were on their feet now. Beverly had to pause for three minutes and finally motion them to sit down.

"As you all know, Jim became a United States Senator . . . In the truest sense of the word. To serve his constituents, follow and abide by the Constitution, and do his best for his country. I loved James Riley Quincy on many levels, never romantically, but I loved his courage and his spirit. When he thought something was not right, he tried to fix it, reach across the aisle and talk sense to the other side. This is not the time or place to list all his accomplishments, but it is worth a trip to the Congressional Record."

Beverly paused and wiped the corner of her eye. There was complete silence.

"The way Q practiced politics is not easy anymore since the values this country was founded on don't seem to matter the way they once did. James always said politics was 5% willingness, 5% desire and 90% compromise. But, now it seems to be all or nothing which never works. Q said to me in December, we print fake money and pass it out to the people who least need it or deserve it, pay lip service to equal rights while we throw people out of their homes because they can't pay their rent or their mortgage and blame them because they can't find a good paying job."

Beverly paused. Every eye was glued on her.

"We've created an economy that only benefits the 1%. Slowly, but surely, we take away people's Constitutional rights because they won't wear a mask or get vaccinated and then deny them access to Facebook and Twitter to express themselves because they disagree with the political *soup du jour*."

The mourners looked at the floor in front of them. Some squirmed uncomfortably in their seats.

"Here is what he said about the January 6th insurrection at the capitol, holding his thumb and forefinger an inch apart."

"Any longer and they would've corralled all of us," he said, "That's how I banged the knee. Fortunately, it was only bruised, not broken. We heard that Trump incited the group to take that action at the capitol."

"In my opinion, he is the dumbest son-of-bitch I've ever seen. You know he denied being responsible for the capital invasion and then would not protect anyone who indicated that preparation had been going on for weeks under his orders. Some even had evidence of receiving emails and text messages hinting of such action. He denied it all."

"Jim would have none of this . . . And said so. But, it fell on deaf ears. He knew, in the end, America was stronger than its enemies, foreign and domestic. In the end, right would conquer might and the strong would survive to fight another day and when it all ends, justice will be done. Rest in Peace, James Riley Quincy."

When she finished, Jordan motioned Beverly into the apse nearest the alter.

"Thank you, Beverly. That was beautiful and so touching," Jordan said. "I want to show you something. A text message I received five minutes ago from the medical examiner."

She held up her cell phone.

"Your father did not die from COVID19. He was murdered."

CHAPTER THREE

"Oh, no," Beverly said. "If that's the case, he was probably set up while he was in the hospital and since he was a U.S. Senator, they probably surveilled his room. Call the medical examiner, or better yet, respond to his text and see if he knows how to get any footage of the security tapes."

Jordan responded immediately and turned to Beverly.

"They said they would have to get back to me," Jordan said, holding a large manilla envelope out to Beverly. "Here, dad put this together for you. He said you would understand and appreciate it. It's something he was working on."

Beverly took the envelope and nodded. She dug into her purse and produced a business size envelope, handing it to Jordan.

"There's fifty thousand dollars in here. Your father's portion of the concert tour proceeds," Beverly offered. "The band voted to give him his share knowing he would give it to charity. I'm just sorry it's under these circumstances."

"Thanks. Me, too," Jordan replied. "Are you headed back to New York?"

"Yes," Beverly looked at her watch. "I better call Escobar to pick me up. Let me know as soon as you can about the surveillance footage and feel free to come East if you need a break. It's been a helluva week."

"I may just take you up on that offer. I need to put the house up for sale, take care of his final senatorial duties and . . ."

" . . . And take a deep breath."

They both laughed.

Traffic to LAX was backed up because of an accident and Escobar gunned his black Toyota to move to an off ramp and take an alternate route. Beverly put her head back, trying to relax. She was thinking about her friend Q and say a little, if inconsequential, prayer to get to the airport on time. Her cold was gone thanks to the frantic and emotional week just passed. Traffic stopped momentarily and when it started back up the motorbike next to them back-fired.

Beverly was transformed to the tiny remote beach in New Jersey in 2016 where Dr. Daniel Elliott led her from his SUV at gunpoint to a remote section of sand and beach grass where she was certain she would meet her end. The only two things she could think about were Harris and Haley. Elliott told her not to turn around just as Gunther raised his police grade Glock Special into the air and fired three tines. Pop! Pop! Pop!

Dr. Elliott lay dead on the sand as the former German Special Forces sharpshooter approached his target and a traumatized Beverly Swift. Gunther took her by the arm and led the shaking former rock star, tears streaming down her face, to the car she came in.

Beverly's head popped back up suddenly like it was all a bad dream and she stifled the blood curdling scream as her head neared the temporary plastic screen that separated her and Escobar.

"Are you all right, Miss Beverly?"

"I think so. Just a bad memory touching the front of my brain," she said. "I'm OK now."

There were long lines at check-in and her flight was full. She was grateful she decided to book a first class ticket. Intermittently, protesters marched in small groups to call attention to the tremendous amount of carbon pollution air travel generated at the expense of the environment. Many others ignored the COVID19 call to action to wear a mask, practice social distancing and wash their hands. Everyone seemed to rush the jetway at once as a false sense of security gripped them after a long absence from air travel. On the plane, masks were required and Beverly could hear some grumbling about having their rights stepped on under such an edict. Beverly smiled under her mask and asked for a glass of white wine, which didn't arrive until they were airborne.

She drank it in one gulp.

CHAPTER FOUR

Q's package was various articles, letters, blogs, and YouTube transcripts, mostly about the World Solutions Group. His package started by offering Beverly a hand-written note about what she held in her lap.

"I have prepared this package for my constituents, visitors to my office, job candidates and in some cases, colleagues. What is happening in the world right now is not pretty. The world is in the process of being manipulated, controlled and overrun by technocrats, bureaucrats and the power elite who want to take away your privacy and freedom in the name of climate change, finance, government and technological progress. We can't let this happen. I have included a short video of a speech I never gave because of the unknown and hidden danger that lurks about in this arena. I hope you will look it over. Let me know how you feel about this after you've finished. Q"

As she read through the various documents, many going back to the start of the Trump administration, she marveled at the way Hans Richter was so consistent in his presentation of the problems facing the world, especially his Great Reset idea and how obvious the problems were facing the world. How could anyone disagree?

Beverly wondered . . . Was COVID19 a manmade virus? There have been a lot of deaths attributed to the virus, but very little confirmation amid rumors that hospitals were paid $20,000 a head for admitting each new COVID case, a terrific incentive for overwhelmed and cash-strapped facilities. Beverly didn't deny the existence of the virus, but little was being done to find the root cause and identify the host, if indeed there was anything to be found, seemed to be an important issue.

COVID had been identified primarily as a respiratory disease that preyed mostly on the elderly, but African Americans and Hispanics seemed to be getting the brunt of the infection because of their propensity for high blood pressure, increased heart disease and poor diet. Could the virus be manipulated to attack these minority groups more than other groups?

This raised a whole other set of questions.

Did masking, social distancing and hand washing really make a difference or were they just diversions in a grand social engineering experiment? With everyone sequestered, and then required to stay home, what difference did it make except to buy groceries, prescription drugs and other essential items when you were forced to wear a mask. Everyone had been brainwashed into thinking the masks were essential, even though some studies concluded that wearing a mask had the potential to make you sicker. Q might be onto something.

The pilot announced their final descent into JFK, landing in twenty minutes. Beverly checked her phone. There was one text message from Darden Green saying he would pick her up and that he had wonderful news.

She smiled at the screen.

"Finally, something to look forward to," she said under her breath.

Beverly got her bag quickly. Darden was waiting at the curb.

"Thanks for picking me up. How are Cynthia and the baby doing?"

"Everyone is fine, thank you. How was the flight?"

"Quite easy. The plane was packed, but I think most everyone had carry-on bags," Beverly remarked. "So what is the wonderful news?"

"They have changed the dates for the World Solutions Group meeting in Davos and they want the Blaze to play the final event - for $2,000,000."

CHAPTER FIVE

Jordan missed the phone call and message from Detective Thomas Middleton. He said it was urgent concerning her father. She called right back. His message was three minutes old.

"This is detective Middleton. Is this Jordan Quincy?"

"Yes it is."

"Thanks for calling back so promptly. That's how I knew who it was," he chuckled like it was an inside joke. "We think we have your father's killer. Unfortunately, he's dead, too, but we're pretty sure it's him." Middleton said. "Did you ever see the security footage of a person dressed in OR scrubs hovering over your father?"

"That's great to hear. Yes, I did see the footage and also some footage showing the same man at the elevator where he removed the skull cap to reveal what appeared to be a birthmark on the top of his forehead. Not a common place for such a mark that probably only a few people have."

"Precisely. We think this person has been involved in a few incidents in the Los Angeles area and we are still investigating them, but hopefully this finding will end all that," he said. "I will let you know."

"This is great news. Let me know if I can help in any way," Jordon said.

"Just one more thing. Did your father have any visitors while he was in the hospital?"

"Only one that I know of. Lionel Kittring from Maryland. He was a senior level security agent with either the CIA or NSA . . .One never knows," Jordan said, laughing a little. "My father was investigating the World Solutions Group and Mr. Kittring was familiar with them. They had an ongoing mutual interest."

Middleton was taking notes and paused briefly.

"Thank you Miss Quincy. I'll be in touch. Here is my number in case you need to reach me. 915 770 2100."

It was eight forty-five p.m. when they arrived at Beverly's apartment. Haley and Harris were in bed, but Haley heard the front door open and raced down the hall to see her mommy. Harris wasn't far behind. They seemed to have grown another two inches.

Beverly was always happy to see them. Holding them tight and squeezing them to the point of loud complaints. She asked them about school and friends, so happy to hear they were doing well. She hugged them again for good luck.

Darden waited patiently, understanding more fully now that he was a parent himself. Beverly put them back to bed and poured two glasses of wine. He had the letter from the WSG in his coat pocket and handed it to Beverly.

January 25, 2021

Dear Beverly Swift:

We have delayed the 2021 meeting of the World Solutions Group until late March and request your presence with the Blaze to perform in concert at the last day of the event around April 2. We have set aside $2,000,000 for entertainment for this event. Please RSVP by February 20, 2021.

Sincerely,

The WSG

CHAPTER SIX

When she woke, Beverly called Reese.

"Welcome home. How was the tour? Seemed rather short."

"Thank you. You think it was short because we only played five out of the fifty dates originally scheduled? "Beverly laughed and started to say something about Davos then decided against it. "What's going on?"

"Well, Washington DC is not lovely this time of years, especially after January 6, but we're getting on. President Biden has been so busy signing executive orders that he hasn't had time for much else. Although he did tell me he thought you'd be a good fit at Treasury," he said, catching his breath. "They could use a lively personality. Can you meet with Dr. Yellen on Tuesday?"

"Let me check real quick." She looked briefly at her calendar. "What time?"

"That depends! If you come to town Monday and stay with me, sometime Tuesday morning." Reese laughed out loud. "If you don't come until Tuesday morning, I'd say 2:00. Which sounds better?"

"I could go for arriving Sunday night and seeing Dr. Yellen whenever," Beverly laughed. And then Reese laughed. "We can still make Tuesday if you come Sunday evening. I have to go. Just let me know what time you'll be here."

"I'll let you know tomorrow."

The children were playing in another room and Ms. Denise, the nanny, was cleaning up the kitchen.

"Can I get you something for breakfast, Ms. Beverly?"

"In a minute. Sit down here and bring two cups of coffee, Denise."

She obeyed, but looked terrified when she sat down across from Beverly.

"Are you going to let me go, Ms. Beverly?"

Beverly looked puzzled.

"Oh, no, nothing like that! I'm so sorry. That never even crossed my mind. What I wanted to ask is are you free to travel overseas?"

Denise's sullen face turned instantly into a smile.

"Why, I don't see why not. I just have to renew my passport. Where we going?"

"Switzerland. The band is going to do a concert in Davos around April 2. That's when the children have spring break, so I thought we would all go," Beverly said. "I will pay for everything, except your passport. Have you ever been to Switzerland, Denise?"

Denise smiled. "Not yet. Thank you so much, Ms. Beverly. I would love to go."

"Great. Get that passport right away. If you have one now, renew in person, or you won't have it in time."

"Will do. Thank you again," she added.

"My pleasure. We'll have a grand time."

CHAPTER SEVEN

When Beverly checked her messages after boarding the train, she remembered Q's short, unreleased video of a speech he never delivered. She called it up on her iPad, took earbuds from her purse and began watching the speech.

"I am increasingly concerned about the America I love," he began. "We no longer take any responsibility for our actions, spending trillions of dollars on wars we can't or don't intend to win only to enrich our war machine and the elites who run it. We pump trillions more into the economy through a slight of hand called 'quantitative easing' that keeps the stock market and the housing market afloat while duping our citizens by saying that we are doing just fine," Q said. "We're not doing just fine. And if we don't start being accountable for our actions, we are not going to own the world's reserve currency, but will turn it over to the likes of the IMF, the World Bank, the International Bank of Settlements and many others who have only their own interests in mind. We continue to blame others for our wrong headedness and divert the attention of our fine citizens with masking, hand washing and social distancing while our environment, money and education systems fall apart!"

"Wow!" Beverly said under her breath. *"No wonder he didn't release this speech. I wonder if Jordan ever saw it.* She checked her messages again and there was a lengthy text from her.

"I got this a couple days ago from the Los Angeles County medical examiner . . . And had a brief conversation with a homicide detective. Seems they found father's killer and he's dead. Call me after you've had a chance to look at this."

The attachment was a short video taken in James Quincy's hospital room. The video time/clock said eleven p.m. January 29, 2021. A man was standing over the bed dressed in medical scrubs, head down, fiddling with Quincy's medicine tube long enough to change the drip. Q didn't move and the man made an about face and left.

Beverly returned Jordan's text. "Just looked at the attachment. I will call soon."

Reese looked better than the last time she saw him and he marveled at how good she looked. Reese had shunned the typical political scene in Georgetown, which was way too gentrified and had grown so expensive that half the retail shops had gone out of business even before the pandemic would've forced them out. He joked that only a lobbyist could afford to live there. His new place was in Shaw, a rising neighborhood fit for Washington professionals and current residents. Not far from the White House with more space at a lower cost than most any other part of the city. In keeping with his upbeat demeanor, Reese bought a row house anticipating that he would be in Washington for at least eight years.

"You look great, Beverly. Are you excited about Tuesday?"

"So do you, Reese. Have you lost weight?" Reese nodded. "Apprehensive might be a better way to describe Tuesday," she said. "When you're not in the nation's capital you think it will be a slam dunk, but when you get here your realize how intimidating it is."

"Once we get going Tuesday you'll find that it's not all that bad," Reese countered. "They're just people, some of them quite powerful, but in the end they're just people . . . Rule number one for DC. And besides, you will have tomorrow to gather your thoughts."

"I guess we'll find out. What's my itinerary?"

"Department of the Interior at ten o'clock. They haven't confirmed the new Secretary's nomination, but I think Dee will be there nonetheless. Then lunch at the White House." Beverly raised an eyebrow, but Reese just smiled. "Two is with Treasury and three-thirty with EPA. You'll be exhausted."

"I'll say, but it sounds very exciting," Beverly said, rubbing the palms of her hands together like she was ready for the challenge. "Now, show me this whole place."

"Coming right up."

CHAPTER EIGHT

The next morning, Beverly reviewed her resume and rehearsed the sample questions Reese had prepared. Some of them were standard government employment questions asked of every person who applied for a management position as well as the required and ubiquitous questions about nationality and disability. Since Beverly was only interested in the Treasury interview, she filled out the application for Treasury ahead of time.

Around three in the afternoon, she called Jordan. They discussed the hospital video, the call from Middleton and the tape of the last speech Quincy never gave. Jordan had not watched it and Beverly encouraged her to do so.

"Do you have any idea who that person is on the hospital tape, Jordan?"

"Not a clue. Unfortunately, when you are in the position my father was in, you have a lot of enemies, known and unknown. And, as chairman of the Foreign Relations Committee the enemies list only grew longer. I didn't think any of them were so bad they wanted to kill him, though."

"It may be a moot point if the police are satisfied the right person they found is dead.," Beverly said. "Have you confirmed that identity? Did Middleton ever say whether it was a man or a woman?"

"No, but he spoke as if it was a man, but he never offered any identification."

"Anything in the papers or the news?"

Jordan paused just as Beverly said her name, she said, "No, now that I think about it."

"He could be an imposter. The simple thing to do is call that phone number he gave you and see who answers. Better yet, call the LAPD main switchboard. And, send that tape to Schumer's office."

"I'll do that. Thanks, Beverly."

"One more thing. See if there is any unusual or questionable footage available from any other night. Your dad may have had other visitors."

The interview at the Interior Department was brief, lasting only forty-five minutes, but nonetheless it was a great start for her Washington job tour. A scheduling error put two items on the president's agenda at the same time and Biden had already agreed to the other meeting.

"There is a very nice restaurant at the Newseum and we have time to do that," Reese said.

"Isn't that the one that's really expensive?"

"Yes, but I heard the food is excellent."

"A friend of mine went there for lunch with her daughter and the bill was just south of $300.00," Beverly retorted. "Let's be a little more respectful of your expense account. Besides, I think it's closed."

Reese turned scarlet. "Oh you're right, I forgot."

They ate at Old Ebbitt's Grill.

Janet Yellen was very youthful and energetic in person, something typically not portrayed on television. She was a bit stooped, opinionated and very worried about the huge deficit that the government was digging deeper every day.

"I know I'm a bureaucrat, but these people think that money grows on trees with their Modern Money Theory and the idea that we can inflate away the debt. It's insanity and it all has to balance out in the end. It will make our grandchildren paupers before they're teenagers. Most of these so called experts have never had a real job," the secretary mourned. "Anyway, Beverly, tell me about your interest in working at the Treasury Department."

"Well, Madam Secretary, as it turns out, my final thesis was on US Monetary Policy and the devastating effect it could have on future generations. I agree that our monetary policy is way off-base, that the Fed is running out of options and may wind up doing something really stupid like buying stocks directly through the Fed to continue to pump up the market," Beverly said, sounding professorial and lecturing her host. "We all know that Mr. Powell is a product of Wall Street and what he does in the short run could ruin us long term."

Janet Yellen's expression never changed.

"Agreed and well said. Do you have small children, Ms. Swift?"

"Yes. A boy eleven and a girl nine. They will be left well off as it is, but I still fear how much more they could have if we had a sane and proper monetary policy."

"I like how you think and I'm going to offer you an undersecretary job, but I have a couple people I want to consult first. I will mail you a firm offer," the Secretary said. "I don't foresee any problem or issues and I think you'll find the offer to your liking. Not quite what you've made on tour by any stretch of the imagination, but perhaps generous by our standards . . . And you won't have to sing every night." She smiled. "So, are you familiar with the World Solutions Group?" Beverly nodded. "And, will you sing at staff birthday parties?"

Beverly laughed. "Of course. I know Happy Birthday by heart."

"That's the spirit. When can you start?"

"Just tell me when and I'll be here. I will need some time to get moved to DC." She said.

"Let me suggest just staying put in New York until the end of the school year," Yellen said. "Be easier on your children. Let's see, it's Monday, so I will reach out to you via email and send a formal letter through the mail. That work for you?"

"That will be fine."

"Good let's plan on you starting next Monday, March 1," she said, surprising herself. "How convenient."

"Very good."

Reese could tell that the meeting went well by the big smile on Beverly's face when she came out of the conference room.

"I guess you have a new job?" he said

"So it seems. Dr. Yellen started out telling me she wanted to run my hiring by some others, but by the time we finished she told me to plan to start next Monday. So, I will commute until the children are out of school," Beverly said. "Don't we have one more meeting?"

"Yes, EPA, in thirty minutes. Janet Yellen doesn't need to talk to anyone about hiring someone unless she just wants Biden's opinion."

CHAPTER NINE

Avis Marsden read the New York Times every morning. Not because Fiona worked there, but because he considered it the finest newspaper in the country just like he considered the Financial Times the best 'money' paper going. He read that, too. He had gotten hooked on a series of articles, short and concise, about a homicide spree going on around the country. No one was talking about it, but it was getting worse by the week involving bankers, attorneys, government officials, Federal Reserve executives who were randomly being killed, murdered actually, with minor variations of the same approach each time. And, not much seemed to be being done about it. He ripped that page of the paper out of the rest to discuss with Fiona.

By the time Beverly got back to New York, she had an email from Janet Yellen confirming her appointment as Undersecretary for Special Treasury Investigations at a more substantial salary than she expected with full benefits, four weeks' vacation, health insurance including dental, vision, hearing and special services for women. And, of course, Harris and Hillary were covered by insurance as soon as Beverly accepted the offer.

She accepted immediately. Dr. Yellen suggested that she read up on the World Solutions Group. The WSG and Hans Richter would be the focus of her work starting out.

"Generally, Mr. Richter is highly regarded by companies and leaders around the world but I personally have some lingering reservations about the purpose of his agenda, so you'll need to dig deep. We will discuss your findings at a future meeting and I hope he does not turn out to be a deceitful man," Janet Yellen said. "He's on a mission and sometimes men like him are dangerous and less than forthcoming."

When the children got home from school, Beverly sat them down, along with Denise, and explained what was going on. The children were excited about the move to DC and Denise was apprehensive, having lived her whole life in New York City. Haley and Harris were excited because their mother was excited although not about her interim commuting schedule and absence during the week.

"Now, Denise, I hope you will consider moving to DC when we do finally move. You are as much a part of this family as anyone and the children adore you. I am not completely certain that we will live in DC, but maybe Virginia in a real house with a real yard. I have to think about that, but either way you'll get a substantial raise by agreeing to join us and your mother and siblings will always be welcome. So, please think it over."

Beverly went to her office and took another look at the letter from the World Solutions Group concerning the Blaze's concert in April. She sent Darden an email and told him to accept the offer and send a contract. She knew he could use the extra windfall.

Another email from Janet Yellen's office requesting a biography that they could include on the website and in Treasury publications. She put together a draft of her biography and stored it for later editing. Now, she had to get caught up from all her travels. A root canal was more enticing!

CHAPTER TEN

Darden called to say he had received a signed contract via email from the World Solutions Group and that two hundred and fifty thousand dollars would be deposited into the band's checking account as a down payment in accordance with the agreement by close of business. They confirmed the date of April 9 as the concert date.

"Wow! That was fast," Beverly said. "Did Hans Richter sign the contract?"

"No! It was signed by Gerard Meister, the Executive Director of the World Solutions Group."

"Interesting. I fear that Mr. Richter might not be in good health. He is quite reclusive to begin with, but he's also a big fan of the Blaze," Beverly said, repeating what she told Darden earlier. "Go ahead and take your 10%."

"Thanks. I might just take 5% for now," Darden said. "Did you take the job in Washington?"

"I did. I start next Monday, but won't move until Haley and Harris are out of school, so I will be back and forth in the interim. If I don't mind the commute I may just continue going back and forth. It would be easier in many ways," she said. "I'm taking the kids to Switzerland when we go for the concert. If spring break is over, we'll go first and then perform afterward. If I don't take them after building it up so much they won't speak to me for ten years!"

Darden laughed out loud.

"Speaking of playing, I'm sure the band members would appreciate some upfront money," he said. "To buy their airfare, book the hotel, you know that kinda stuff. What do you think?"

"Yes, email them and let them know we deposited ten grand in each of their accounts and the concert is a go for an April 9 date. We'll book the hotel, but tell them to be in Davos by the fifth. Good move," Beverly said.

She thought of the late James Quincy just then, knowing how much he would've enjoyed playing this gig, especially in Switzerland. Q was an avid skier and would've made the most of the trip. Beverly wiped away a tear.

"Congrats on the job. I'll be in touch soon once all this high finance is complete."

"Thank you. Sounds like a plan!"

Beverly pulled up her biography, made some tweaks and attached a copy of her final thesis, ***"Banking On the Future and Its Impact on the Next Generation."*** She attached everything to the original email request with a short note and hit the send button. Beverly opened her message app. There was a message from Avis Marsden from three days before.

It said call me when you can have lunch. Fiona would love to see you. Avis
PS Congrats on the new job.

She called him back and got his voicemail leaving a lengthy message apologizing for missing his earlier text, some details about her new job and her itinerary for the coming week. She added that he must've been talking to Darden. When she disconnected, he called right back.

"Hello, Avis. Good to hear your voice and I would love to have lunch. Will Thursday work?"

"Hi, Beverly. Good to hear your voice too. Congrats on your new job. That's exciting," Avis retorted. "Yes, Thursday will be perfect. I'm going to invite my friend Lionel Kittring if you don't mind. He has a lot of insight into working for the government."

"That would be great. Wasn't he the fellow who was shot last year by Gunther Schmidt?"

"He's the one. See you Thursday," Avis chuckled. "I was so sorry to hear about Senator Quincy. Did you know your eulogy was reprinted in the Times?"

"No, I didn't! Thanks, Avis. Q was a very special friend. See you Thursday."

"Good enough. Have a good day, Beverly."

"And you do the same, Avis."

"There were a few email messages in her inbox and one in particular caught her eye. It was from Jordan Quincy dated late the day before.

"Do you know the name, Lionel Kittring? I just met him at the Beverly Hills Hilton.
He is CIA and told me he is working with the FBI investigating dad's death. He told me that all the evidence points to murder (old news) He wanted to ask me if I knew anyone that would want to hurt my father. He said he knew you and would be meeting with you in a few days. Call me when you get this email. Thanks, Jordan."

She continued through her emails. Shelly Davis, Janet Yellen's personal assistant sent some apartment addresses for Beverly to look at when it fit her schedule. She suggested a call back to confirm.

"Thanks for calling, Beverly. What's your preference for looking at these places. I have five possible locations, all good neighborhoods."

"You know, Sunday makes sense starting around noon," Beverly said. "Also, can you get me a hotel for the first week. Are any of the apartments furnished?"

"Amen to that. I'll call you back before the day is out."

"Thanks, Shelly."

"No worries."

Beverly got Jordan Quincy's voicemail. She told her that she knew Kittring, but not well, and was meeting with him tomorrow (Thursday). She suggested they talk after that meeting and that she would call her the next evening.

CHAPTER ELEVEN

The restaurant was crowded for a weekday, but Zatayna was a popular place any day of the week. With some hesitation, Beverly moved the lunch to DC because Lionel Kittring was on a tight schedule and needed to catch a plane to Denver right after the luncheon.

Avis made introductions . . . Reese, Fiona and Beverly were all new faces. Lionel of course knew who Fiona was and when Reese was introduced as the White House Director of Communications, he knew he had to be careful about what he said. There were a lot of Trump supporters at NSA. Lionel wasn't necessarily one of them, but he caught a lot of the conversation around stolen elections, the January insurrection and Republican rhetoric in his informal discussions around the office.

They ordered two bottles of wine and made small talk until luncheon orders were taken. Avis asked Lionel about his recuperation and of course everyone wanted to know what happened . . . how, where and why. Lionel loved being the center of attention, but not on that subject. He glossed over the shooting incident and thanked everyone for their concern. Beverly sensed Lionel's edginess and decided the best thing to do was get right to the point.

"Well, Mr. Kittring, we are certainly happy that everything worked out for you," she began. "What can you tell us about the World Solutions Group and Hans Richter?"

A faint smile broke across Lionel's face, an acknowledgment that Beverly had read his mind correctly.

"Yes, Hans Richter and Gerard Meister are the Executive Director and Deputy Director." Lionel recited. "Few people know this about Hans, but he was trained as an engineer and developed a real concern about the environment and the fact that more lip service was being paid to climate change than any commensurate amount of action. He concluded that the only way anyone would pay attention was to bring the very wealthy, be they individuals or companies, together in a forum to discuss the issue and other matters like it. Voila, the World Solutions Group was born."

Everyone nodded.

"What took so long for everyone to hear about it?" Reese said.

"Hans organized it, got buy in from his targeted market and was ready to go all in at the end of the summer in 2001 and then we all know what happened after that,"

Lionel sighed. "The world interrupted his plans. I was working for him back then. He was devastated because he was ready to get started even if the world wasn't, but he pushed on."

"I didn't know you had worked for the World Solutions Group, Lionel," Avis said. "That must've been interesting work."

"It was very interesting," Lionel said, grimacing suddenly as the inside of his head felt like someone had turned it into a bass drum.

"Are you all right, Lionel?"

"Yes, well no, just another of these damned headaches," he said, forcing a meek smile. "It will be gone soon."

"Have you seen a doctor? How long has this been going on?" Beverly said.

Lionel thought a moment and then shrugged.

"It comes and goes, Ms. Swift. It has been this way since shortly after I was shot, but you're right, I should see a doctor. I'm thinking I need to see a specialist," he said. "Do you have any recommendations?"

"Let me think about it. I'll check around," Avis interjected.

Lionel was the perfect person to keep tabs on Hans Richter, although there was no public knowledge to indicate he needed to be watched. That issue was forming its own momentum. America liked to be in charge, but not accountable. The failed wars from Vietnam to Afghanistan were proof of that. Some twenty trillion dollars had been spent with no accountability from the government, the Pentagon or the generals charged with 'winning' those wars. They all sat on their laurels and asses at the Pentagon debating when the next 9/11 might happen.

The United States needed another scapegoat and Hans Richter was the perfect candidate and he wasn't even an American. No matter and all the better. He had all the qualifications to be a bonafide scapegoat. Buttonholing him on climate change was qualification enough.

"Yes, Avis, it was *very* interesting work. Hans was born as Hitler was coming to power and lived the nightmare of Weimar, Germany, as a young Jewish man," Lionel stressed. "His father vowed to get out of Germany as soon as he could and that happened when his doctor father escaped with the family to Switzerland in the dead of winter with the clothes on their back and a suitcase full of nearly worthless Deutsche Marks. Inflation was 10,000% a day at the time."

Beverly gasped.

"10,000% per day? I never heard that before."

"It's something conveniently left out of the history books," Lionel said, chuckling.

"Yes. Germans who immigrated to America tell stories of being paid with wheelbarrows full of money and pushing the loot at a sprinters pace to get to the bank before the money was devalued again. Most of the time they didn't make it."

Avis cleared his throat.

"So, I presume that the Richter's stayed in Switzerland. How old was Hans then?" Reese said.

"He was eight, but his father never let him forget that horrible financial lesson. At his father's insistence, he got educated. A bachelors, masters and two PhD's from European schools . . . One doctorate in Engineering and one in Economics and a Master's in Public Policy from Harvard. You can imagine the connections he made in Cambridge."

Lionel paused to sip his wine.

"What I think he did was very smart," Lionel said. "When he started the WSG, he got these large companies and wealthy individuals to side with him, to donate large sums of money in the name of tackling climate change, hunger, inequality and healthcare, instead of holding a gun to their heads later and forcing them to engage."

"Yes," said Reese. " That old adage that you attract more flies with honey than vinegar. Most other leaders, or so called leaders, are generals who takeover the government and force the private sector to their knees. His approach was indeed smart."

Lionel and the others nodded.

"At that point, Hans had the attention of the world and all its intellectual and monetary ammunition. That's why the Big Reset is so disturbing. He has some of the best minds in the world supporting him and the message he offers is,

"If you want to keep your wealth, better follow me."

"Not to mention his sardonic quote, "You will own nothing and be happy," Avis added.

Lionel looked at his watch, took the last bite of his lunch and stood up.

"Nice meeting all of you and to see you again, Avis. I need to be going. Thank you for lunch and let's meet again soon," Lionel said. "Reese, my kind regard to the president."

Reese nodded and stood up to shake his hand. Beverly stood up and grabbed Lionel Kittring by the elbow.

"Let me walk you to the door. I understand you met with Jordan Quincy day before yesterday? She said you were very helpful and supportive."

"Yes, I did. Unfortunately, I'm afraid her father was murdered. COVID19 was just a convenient excuse," he said. "People like James Quincy have a lot of enemies, known and unknown. But, I told her we would get to the bottom of his demise. Now, please, you will excuse me, I need to get to the airport."

CHAPTER TWELVE

"Beverly, was Lionel's explanation helpful?" Avis said when she returned.

"Yes. This will help as I gather more information on the WSG, something I've heard a good bit about, but not that much about Richter," she said. "Based on what Lionel said, it sounds like people are out to get him. Am I missing something?"

"Not at all, Beverly," Fiona said. "He is something of an embarrassment to American politicians because he has done something they haven't been able to do, at least appearance wise. We have been talking about climate change since before the first Earth Day in the United States, but all we seem to do is toss that hot potato back and forth and point fingers. Only the private sector has really taken up the cause with products, initiatives and action."

Avis was nodding his head.

"Hans Richter has galvanized the players that really count and has consistently brought his message home. The U.S on the other hand has galvanized each side into a public relations campaign like few others over climate change, effectively trying to make it go away. And Trump didn't handle getting out of the Paris agreement well or very gracefully, even though he had lots of support," Avis offered. "Then, when someone does succeed, the knives and PR machines in the United States come out and usually not in a good way. And they're powerful, persuasive and effective."

Avis hailed a cab through the cabstand operator. He wanted to talk more with Beverly about her Treasury appointment, her trip to Switzerland and help her understand what she was getting herself into. When the cab showed up, they piled in.

"Where to?"

"Union Station," Avis said. "Getting back to Richter, I was thinking he wants it that way and planned it that way . . . The attention and criticism, I mean."

Fiona interjected. "We've never had any luck getting an interview with him at the Times."

"He strikes me as a pretty serious man who took his father's hectoring to heart," Avis said. Fiona was nodding. "Do you have a trip planned to Switzerland, yet?"

"I haven't told anyone, but we have been invited to give a concert in April for the delayed WSG meeting. We're going to be the closing event, but I think there will be an official trip in the interim," Beverly noted. "I'm taking the children and their nanny in April. Apparently, Hans and Gerard like our music."

"Nice! Can I carry the instruments?" Avis quipped.

"How's your back? The piano is quite heavy."

They both laughed and the trio jumped out of the cab at Union Station.

"You know, Avis, while I'm here, I think I will go by the office and see if Janet is available," Beverly said as she motioned the cabbie to wait. "You guys want to come with? I'd like your opinion of her."

Avis looked at his watch and then checked the train schedule to New York.

"It's two thirty now. Think we can catch the 5:13 to Grand Central?" he said. "Fiona, will that work for you?"

"I don't see why not," she said. "Up to Beverly. I'm open all day. Why don't you call and see if she's in?"

Avis sighed. "Always the pragmatist."

Janet was out for the afternoon, but Shelly said she had some apartments they could look at if they wanted. She emailed a revised list to Beverly. Two units on M Street, two places in Georgetown and one was on Connecticut Avenue, farther North.

"Start on M Street, then the two in Georgetown and lastly Connecticut Ave. I'll call and stay one step ahead of you by contacting the agent listed for each property," Shelly said. "The two on M Street are listed with the same agent and only a block apart, so that will help."

"C'mon, you two. We're going apartment hunting," Beverly said. "Janet is not available this afternoon."

CHAPTER THIRTEEN

The first apartment on M Street was in an older, updated building and the bedrooms were small and dark. The apartments in Georgetown were on quiet side streets, but the first apartment was again too small with small rooms and a tiny kitchen. "Denise would kill me," Beverly noted, shaking her head at Fiona and Avis. The second apartment was DC's idea of a high rise building (about nine stories) and brand new. It had all the right criteria and Beverly said she was definitely interested.

The driver had a hard time finding the apartment on Connecticut Ave because it wasn't on Connecticut and it wasn't an apartment, but a house. It was on Tilden, near Connecticut. Overgrown and generally unappealing to the casual observer. The real estate agent was there and told Beverly that the owner had recently died and she could buy it for back taxes and a nominal amount to cover expenses and the remainder of the construction work.

The property was a big two story house with a dry, finished basement, built like things were no longer built, five generous bedrooms and six baths, a new kitchen in progress, mostly complete, hardwood floors and a decent backyard.

"Bingo, Beverly," Avis said. "It still needs a little work, but that can be done before Haley and Harris move."

"This is delightful, Beverly," Fiona added. "I think your search might be over."

"Beverly?" the agent said. "Are you Beverly Swift, the singer?"

"Guilty," she said.

"Well, I'll be. Wait until I tell my wife. She will be so jealous."

Beverly reached into her purse and pulled out a CD. "Got a Sharpie? What's your wife's name?"

"Sandra." Douglas handed her a Sharpie and Beverly signed the CD to Sandra.

""Maybe this will ease the pain," she said, handing the signed CD to the agent, "And, I'll take it."

CHAPTER FOURTEEN

The electricity was on in the house, so Beverly and Wyatt Douglas, the agent, went inside. They reviewed the appliances, the HVAC system, electrical and everything else on his checklist. They agreed on who would fix or replace what and the final price for repairs came down twenty-five thousand. She gave him a check for $100,000, for the back taxes, escrow, fees and her portion of the remaining construction. He gave her a receipt.

"What was it listed for originally?" Beverly said.

"Originally it was listed for $450,000, but when she died and we discovered that back taxes were owed, it was reduced to the amount of the taxes owed and escrow. The deceased owner actually started the renovation before she became ill. When do plan to move in?" Wyatt said.

"Well, I think I will wait until the workmen finish and my children and their nanny can move from New York. Late June, I guess," Beverly said. "Are workmen still working here?"

Wyatt smiled. "Yes, they are. They left right before you arrived. I think we should leave their contract as is. You can settle up with the agency when they're done. I will have all the costs up to now for you tomorrow and I will email them to you. In about ten days, contact the DC Tax Assessor's office to make sure they have registered the payoff. These payoffs have been known to slip through the cracks."

Wyatt winked at Beverly.

Beverly heard Reese's booming voice thank the Uber driver. He picked her up like a dance partner and gave her a kiss. Beverly introduced Reese to Wyatt.

"What do you think?"

"Looks great from the outside. Needs a little paint, but otherwise, except for being overgrown, it's great. It looks big."

"It is big. Five bedrooms, six baths and a den/office, full, finished basement and a partially finished new kitchen. Let's look around."

Wyatt followed them around the first floor and then took over the conversation. He explained to Reese what he had explained to Beverly earlier, including the twenty-five thousand dollar allowance and keeping the workmen working. Reese frowned a little.

"Twenty-five K might cover the kitchen. Did you discuss getting estimates for the remaining work like painting and repairing the wood floor?"

Wyatt didn't hesitate.

"I will have that by Friday. All the electrical, HVAC and plumbing is done and inspected. You can see the red tags on the permits in the front window?"

Reese nodded. Beverly took him upstairs and he seemed satisfied that it was in good order.

"What did you pay? Not trying to be snoopy," Reese added.

"One hundred thousand cash for back taxes, escrow and the construction work thus far," she said.

"My God, Beverly! I'm going to have you negotiate my next deal," Reese said. "Good job. Where did you find Wyatt?"

"He was here when I got here," Beverly said. "Here's his card."

"Long and Foster . . . Good company," Reese said, standing at the head of the staircase. Beverly raised an eyebrow. "All seems in order with the real estate company."

"That's a relief. I need to go to the office with Wyatt to sign the paperwork. I will call you when I'm finished and you can buy me dinner." She smiled.

"And you can spend the night with me. It will be too late to catch the train back to New York."

"Deal! Let me call Denise," Beverly said. "Take some pictures and send them to me. I shouldn't be more than an hour."

At the office in Georgetown on Wisconsin Ave, she signed papers until her hand ached. Beverly talked with the L&F broker, Theresa Hammond, while Wyatt made copies, including her check and gathered neighborhood information about schools, attractions, area shopping and transportation. Beverly was thrilled that she could take Metro to work. Wyatt put everything in an envelope and gave her the keys to the house.

"Normally, we would wait until the check cleared, but I think I'm safe in saying that I am not worried about that," Wyatt said with an engaging grin. "Can I drop you somewhere?"

"No, but thank you. Reese is going to pick me up."

Beverly called Reese and he agreed to pick her up at the Long and Foster office. Theresa invited her to have lunch the following day while they raised a celebratory glass of wine. Wyatt went to his office and closed the door.

"You'll never guess who I just sold a house to?" he said into his cellphone.

Don Olson was smiling.

CHAPTER FIFTEEN

At dinner, Beverly asked Reese's opinion of the house.

"Had it been an Open House, there would've probably been at least fifteen bidders and they would've collectively raised the price twenty percent," he noted in a matter of fact tone. "I'd be a little wary of Wyatt Douglas. I looked him up on the DC real estate commission website. He has appeared before the commission several times for ethics violations, but has been cleared each time by none other than Don Olson's attorney."

"The same Don Olson that runs R.L. Thornton?"

Reese was nodding his head. "The same."

"You think he would tell Don Olson who the buyer was?"

"That was the nature of all his ethics violations, so it is not only quite possible, but highly probable," Reese warned.

"What should I do?"

"Change all the locks in the new house and install your own security system after all the current work is done, even if there is a security system. Have the whole house checked for surveillance bugs," Reese said. "Be very discreet. I can get the names of reputable contractors for the locks, security system and bugs. But, you have to be careful in DC."

After they ordered food, Beverly checked her messages, deleting the ones that were spam or junk or captured by her screening service. There was nothing urgent, but the last message was from Janet Yellen asking Beverly to call her first thing in the morning about a trip to Switzerland next week. Beverly called New York to update Denise on the new house and talk to the children. Harris told his mother to bring pictures of the new house when she came home.

"Everything OK there?" Reese said.

"Just fine. Harris wants to see pictures of the new house, but other than that, nothing out of the ordinary."

"Good. Are you concerned about what I told you about Wyatt Douglas?"

"Somewhat, but I'm more concerned that he has ties to Don Olson. I think Olson must mean scumbag in some foreign language," Beverly retorted, only half-smiling. "He has no morals and will do anything to make sure he remains in control of every situation he's involved in. Do you think the contractor at the house has ties to him, too?"

"Possibly. I was thinking that if you want me to move in over there while they finish the work, I can do that," Reese said.

"I don't think you have to move-in, but if you could make your presence known regularly, that would be a big help. I have to admit that I don't know if they're doing things correctly, except maybe the painting," she said. "But, in the meantime if you can get over there a couple times a week, that would be great. I start work next Monday."

Reese leaned closer to Beverly and whispered, "Are you going to stay with me?"

Beverly smiled. "Interesting that you bring that up. Because I am a Grade B executive, the government will provide an apartment for up to three months within one mile of the office," she said. "So here's the deal . . . Half time at the free apartment and half the time at your place . . . OK?"

CHAPTER SIXTEEN

Jordan was going through the desk drawers of her father's home office, ostensibly to find the password for his cellphone and laptop. She surmised that there was important information in his text messages and personal emails. At first things were not going well . . . Lots of hiding places, but zero information.

In a nondescript small leather notepad, the kind they give out at political conventions, she found something worthwhile. As an added bonus, each password was lined through when it had lived it's useful life and the most recent password marked with a hand wrought asterisk. There were two columns . . . One for the cellphone and one for the laptop.

Taking a deep breath, Jordan tried the laptop first, the screen alighting to the melody of "Peace will Come", the first hit he and Beverly wrote together. Confident that she had the right passwords, the cellphone lit up like a Christmas tree when she entered the other password. There were 700 text messages, all of them less than three weeks old. Jordan went to the kitchen, made a pot of coffee and sat at the breakfast bar deciphering the texts. At least every tenth text message came from the same phone number, but did not identify the sender. She cycled through all the texts until she saw one from Lionel Kittring from the same encrypted phone number.

"Dear Senator Quincy, urgent that I speak to you about WSG as soon as possible. I will be in California next week. I trust your recovery is going as planned." Lionel Kittring.

There were ten more texts from Lionel Kittring prior to that one, all with similar messages about the World Solutions Group. James Quincy has become a very vocal critic of WSG and Hans Richter, intimating in private that the WSG was enabling the spread of the COVID19 virus. It could be deduced that Lionel Kittring was trying to change his mind.

Jordan picked up the phone to call Beverly, but decided against it. Instead, she tried the number detective Middleton had given her. After several rings, a recorded message came on informing her that the number had been disconnected or was no longer in service. Jordan texted Beverly with that information. She flipped the switch on the television to catch the morning news. After the weather forecast, the next story was about a double murder in Denver. The details were sketchy, but two men in a hospital room had been murdered the night before. Both men were in the final stages of recovery from COVID19 and their medication drips had been sabotaged.

"That sounds eerily familiar."

But, Jordan did not have any reason to make a connection with her father's death. She tried James Middleton's phone number again.

Beverly got home to New York at one thirty p.m. to an empty house. Harris and Haley were at school and Denise left a note that she went grocery shopping at eleven thirty. Beverly quickly unpacked, made coffee and called Janet Yellen, who was in a meeting, but Shelly said she would call back about three. Denise returned at 2:00 with groceries, two days' worth of mail and box full of pastries from the bakery down the street.

"Did you bring pictures of the new house," she said excitedly as she poured a cup of coffee.

"Got them on my phone. Let's sit down and enjoy our coffee and some of those sinful pastries," Beverly said, laughing. "It won't take long to look at the pictures."

When she opened her phone, Beverly realized that Reese had not sent pictures, so she called his voicemail and asked him to send all the pictures of the DC house ASAP.

"By the way, have you made your decision about coming with us?"

Denise smiled and nodded.

"I am going to move to Washington with you and the children. I found out I have many relatives there, so it will be a good move for me."

Beverly jumped up and screamed, grabbing Denise in an affectionate hug.

"That's the best news I've heard all week. We have some time, so let me know what you want to move. I will get your new compensation together by the end of the month."

Denise nodded and thanked her. Beverly's phone chimed and the other pictures were attached to an apology from Reese. Denise got more excited with each successive image and told Beverly that she was so happy to have this opportunity and to be able to stay with Haley and Harris after the move.

"I'll be ready to drive the moving van, if necessary!" she said, a lilt to her voice, and then she laughed out loud with Beverly.

"Well, Denise, it will take all the driving patience you can muster to get around DC," Beverly confessed. "Fortunately, I don't have to drive there much. Screwiest city in the country to drive in."

At three p.m. the phone rang. It was Shelly calling for Dr. Yellen who immediately got on the line.

"Congratulations, Beverly. I understand you found a house in DC," she said ebulliently. "I know the neighborhood well and I think you will really enjoy it. Great for your children."

"Thank you so much, Madam Secretary. "What's going on?"

"Well, first off, no more Dr. Yellen or Madam Secretary. Everyone in the office calls me Janet most of the time. Every once in a while, I get an expletive deleted!" She laughed at her own joke. Beverly chuckled. "Do you know who Larry Fink is?"

"Can't say that I do," Beverly added.

"He is the CEO of BlackRock Investments and a strong ally of Hans Richter. BlackRock has seven trillion dollars under contract, so people listen to him," she said. "I've set the appointment for Tuesday next week. I will courier your credentials today and you will have them tomorrow. Please let me know if they don't arrive."

"Will do," Beverly said. "I presume that Larry Fink is in New York City?"

"Yes. His office is just off Wall Street. He is expecting you at 10:00; actually his longtime assistant will be meeting with you. A woman named Carol Cross. She is Larry's right arm and knows things about the WSG that would be hard to come by otherwise. They both know the Treasury Department is looking at irregularities in some investments by the WSG in the United States and she will be a good source of information for you."

"Isn't he the CEO who has been writing to other CEO's recently urging them to get involved in addressing the climate change issues and defining climate change as something that will affect all their businesses if they don't begin to act."

"He's the one. Very good of you to be so prescient. Larry keeps a very low public profile, understanding very well how things can be misinterpreted by the media. I will plan to see you on Wednesday next week and again, if your credentials don't arrive let me know immediately. Shelly just gave the package to FedEx."

"I'll be looking for that package and thank you. Have a nice weekend, Janet."

"You do the same. I'll be in Wilmington with the president and First Lady."

'Enjoy that. I've been there and it's lovely," Beverly said. "I was being considered for a couple cabinet posts and he interviewed me there. You'll love it."

"Very well. We can compare notes next week."

"Sounds good."

CHAPTER SEVENTEEN

The next day, the murders in Denver made national news. Only one savvy television commentator mentioned, almost in passing, the similarity between these crimes and the murder of Senator James Quincy. Avis was watching and that suggestion sent alarm bells through his mind. He dialed Richard Dexter, Director of the NSA.

While the phone rang, Avis realized he didn't want to make accusations and decided he would let the director lead the conversation.

"This is Richard Dexter. Hello, Avis. How are you?"

"Hello, Richard. I'm fine, thank ou for asking. Did you hear about the murders in Denver? I wanted to get your insight into them so soon after Senator Quincy's death since I know that his death was considered a murder, too."

"I was watching the news and see where one commentator compared the two. It could just be a copycat situation to make the investigation more difficult."

"Good point. I tried to call Lionel, but the call went to voicemail. Is he around?"

"He's traveling this week. He was in Denver day before yesterday, Salt Lake today, San Francisco tomorrow, then Seattle and Vancouver. Talking with Federal Banking officials except for Vancouver," the director said. "He'll be back Wednesday."

If the director thought there was anything to tie the deaths together, he was not saying or couldn't say. Either way, Richard Dexter was not talking.

"Anything else, Avis? I am on my way to a meeting. Thanks for calling."

"Thank you, Richard. Appreciate your input."

Don Olson paced back and forth in front of his massive mahogany desk. Wyatt Douglas was late and Don was getting impatient and a little anxious. He was beginning to think something happened to his son-in-law. Don grabbed the prescription bottle from his desk and took a white lozenge from it, swallowing it without the benefit of water or any other liquid. The phone rang.

"Don, I am so sorry, but I got hung up in a meeting that lasted much longer than was intended. Gonna have to make it another day. Will Monday work for you?"

Don Olson held his breath to gather his thoughts and keep from exploding into the phone. He never was long on patience and would jump through the phone if he could in order to throttle Wyatt Douglas. His age and stature in the business community afforded him the luxury of mostly getting his way. He let his breath out and took a deep breath in, filling his lungs with air and holding it there until he spoke.

"Tell you what. Will Sunday *work* for you? We can go to my retreat in the Poconos where it is more relaxing to do our business along with a little fishing," Don said calmly. "Will that work for you?"

Wyatt loved to fish, but hadn't done so in years and the thought of it was appealing. He looked at his calendar and he was clear for Sunday.

"Great idea. How do I get there?"

"Book a private flight on Poconos Air. The flight will take you to Pocono, New York and I will pick you up there. Say eleven o'clock? The fish bite all the time so we don't have to be on the water too early. Call my cell if you have a problem, otherwise I will see you Sunday. By the way, are things getting done at Beverly Swift's new place?"

"Yes," he said, knowing that Don was referring to the surveillance equipment.

"It will be ready next Wednesday disguised as a security alarm system."

"Very good, Wyatt. I'll see you Sunday," Don said. "Enjoy the rest of your week."

"Thank you. You do the same."

In the old days, Don would've made arrangements to take Wyatt out. It was easy to make people disappear and could be done anytime. The mountain lakes were deep, there was plenty of fish and other water borne creatures to feed on the bodies dumped into the icy water. Gunther Schmidt, Richard Ellis, MD, and Ted Swift all lived there now in the deep, deep waters of Lake Pocono. Besides, things were working out well with Beverly Swift and sooner or later she would be reunited with Wendy Jackson in those deadly, pristine waters.

Beverly and Denise took Haley and Harris to the Museum of Natural History. COVID19 had made them all feel like hermits and the children needed some fresh air in a new environment. They both loved the museum with all the dinosaur bones, Pterodactyl skeletons, snake skins, fossils and short movies about pre-historic creatures and life during that time. It was also a great way to wear the children down.

Denise could always gauge how tired they were by how much food they ate afterward. They often fell asleep at the dining table, wherever it was. She wore a Fitbit and dazzled the children with how far they had walked in just a few hours - 22,610 steps.

"No wonder they fall asleep at the restaurant," Beverly teased. "But, I'm starved, so where to?"

They took a vote between pizza, burgers or Chinese for lunch and Chinese won. At the restaurant, Beverly amused the children with pictures of the new house in DC until lunch came. Haley and Harris fell asleep in the Uber on the way home.

Beverly and Denise got the children to bed as soon as they got home even though it was only 7:30. Beverly was quite certain they would sleep until morning. They all had a very busy day and it felt good to get out of the house. She would have to begin in earnest on Sunday making the transition to DC. It had been a long time since she held a nine-to-five job and she was both excited and apprehensive.

CHAPTER EIGHTEEN

It was drizzling at the tiny Pocono airport when Wyatt's plane landed. They walked quickly to Don's Jeep Renegade, a toy he loved to drive on the winding mountain roads, largely ignoring the message on the driver's side visor indicating the dangers of driving a top heavy vehicle on winding, hilly and mountainous roads.

"Sorry to be late. I don't like being late for anything."

"No worries," Don said. He was not a demonstrative person, so he elbow-bumped Wyatt and put his bag in the car. "It's about an hour's drive to my place. Are you hungry?"

"Not really, but a cup of coffee would be nice," he said.

"McDonald's all right. The little cafe in the airport has the worst coffee I ever drank," Don said. "Nice people, but terrible coffee."

"McDonald's is fine. I like their coffee."

Don was curious as to Cynthia's condition, how the baby's room was coming along and if they needed anything in the way of money, furniture, baby clothes or anything else. Wyatt said they were fine. Their first child was due on May 30th. Don was very pleased that everything was under control.

Don drove fast around the windy roads, but Wyatt never flinched. He liked to drive fast, too, and the curvy roads only bothered him when Don hit an area without a guardrail. Olson was a skillful driver and handled the top heavy vehicle like a NASCAR veteran. There was no traffic and they were back at Don's retreat and on the water in one hour.

"It's overcast today, so the fish should really be biting," Don noted.

"So, Don, what's the deal with Beverly Swift? Why keep track of her and her family?" Wyatt said. "Is it something to do with her family, her rock and roll days or Ted? Did she double cross you or offend you in some way? I'm just curious and it won't go beyond this boat."

Don let out a long sigh and ignored the questions while he reeled in the first catch of the day. It was a three pound trout that Wyatt photographed and then Don threw back.

"No, the biggest problem with Beverly was her late, obnoxious husband, Ted."

"What was his deal?"

"At heart, Ted was a con man pretending to be an investment banker," Don said, casting his line again. "His saving grace was his charm and athletic good looks, but he couldn't add a column of numbers on a calculator without counting on both hands if his life depended on it. He wanted eventually to lead R.L Thornton and he was impatient, bullying and arrogant. More than the money, attention and perverse masculine identity, Ted Swift was a gigolo."

"How does Beverly fit in to all that? She doesn't seem the type to go for the Ted Swifts of the world."

Don laughed and reeled in, empty handed. He cast again while Wyatt waited for a bite on his line.

"The Beverly Swift you met a few days ago was not the Beverly Swift that Ted swept off her feet," Don said. "When they met, Beverly had just come off a world tour that made her very rich, very addicted and very lost. She had been to rehab and was anxious to start with and maybe a little paranoid. When Ted found out she had around $350 million dollars, he really turned on the charm, called in all his investor markers and went after Beverly like the sun chasing a sunset."

"Wow. That makes more sense since she had that kind of money," Wyatt added. "She a wrote a check for the new house like she was buying groceries . . . A hundred thousand dollars' worth of groceries. I've never gotten a commission check so fast."

"That's Beverly. Have you ever seen her perform?" Wyatt shook his head. "Well, she is a cross between Julie Andrew's voice, Britney Spear's body and Barbra Streisand's gutsiness. She really puts on a great show."

Wyatt reeled in a small trout and threw it back.

"When she met Ted, she was looking for someone to help her invest that kind of money. Of course, Ted didn't have a clue, but he had plenty of people behind him who did," Don said. "Ted knew all the jargon, all the terms, he just didn't know what they meant or what to do with them."

"He was a salesman at heart?"

"You're being kind. A hustler is more like it, but unless you're Bernie Madoff, when you bring that kind of client into the fold, you are the king . . . or queen, as the case may be, and for a while, you can do about anything you want until the next mark appears."

"What did he do?"

Don Olson rubbed his chin just as his fishing pole bent nearly in half. He started reeling the line in, slow and steady. About the time he got the fish to the boat, Wyatt's line started to sing and his pole bent over, too. Don landed a nice speckled trout about four pounds, a keeper. Wyatt reeled slow and steady. He had a northern pike, about ten pounds. A real beauty.

"Now, don't slip your hand into those gills. They're razor sharp," Don instructed. "Use the grappling hook to save your fingers."

Wyatt nodded and laid the fish out in the bottom of the boat. Don took a couple pictures when Wyatt raised the fish vertically.

"You can do what you want with it, but the Northern's are hell to clean and render little to eat," Don said. "Might want to throw it back and keep trying."

"Good idea," Wyatt said, as he threw the fish back in the water. "Now, what happened to Ted?"

Don yawned. "Well, the first thing that happened was Beverly caught him in bed with Ellen Stein. Stupidly, they got drunk and Ted was going to prove to Beverly that he was the boss in the family and could do whatever he wanted. You've probably figured out by now that that's not how marriages work. After Beverly caught them and threw Ted out, he tried to access a large portion of her fortune to no avail."

"Who's Ellen Stein?"

"She was a senior member of the Posse, a working girl if you get my drift, who decided a long time ago that monogamy was not her thing and she literally screwed her rich husband to death . . .Heart attack."

Don chuckled, but Wyatt doubled over laughing.

"You're joking, right?"

"No, I didn't know this first hand, but there are others who did and that's the story they tell."

Wyatt straightened up.

"So what happened to Ellen?"

"Well, first of all, she was crazy for Ted. It got to the point where she would only sleep with him. Ellen was a beautiful woman who maintained her body and her looks to please men and she made a fabulous living doing it. But, she just wanted Ted," Don related, reeling in another catch. "But, when Beverly threw him out for sleeping with Ellen it made him resent her so he arranged an elaborate scheme to stage his own death in a burning car with Ellen in it. He got out of the car, but she didn't, and Ellen burned up."

"But as far as the world knew, they were both dead, right?" Wyatt added.

"Precisely. Ted met two cousins named Gunther Schmidt and Boris Kitlov who had come to the United States to ostensibly team up with NASCAR to take racing back to Russia. Ted set them up with a car recovery business in New Jersey that was really a chop shop for the mob. They used Gunther and Boris to disassociate themselves from the cars they used in hits, robberies, murders and other things like money laundering and extortion. Any time they needed to get rid of a vehicle, they turned to Gunther and Boris. It made Boris and Gunther rich."

The fish were really active now and every cast resulted in a nice catch. They soon had ten fish on ice and Don said he was ready to go back to the house. Wyatt didn't argue.

"So, then what happened?"

"Beverly already knew the remains from the car fire were not Ted's, but she couldn't figure out what he was doing," Don said, easing the boat up to the dock. "She was a serious candidate for president after the IP convention, but Ted was playing the invisible man. Then the strangest thing happened."

Don told Wyatt about the hairdresser who came to Beverly's hotel room to cut her hair and revealed that he had secretly cut Ted's hair the week before when Ted was supposedly in South America. Ted told the hairdresser he was on his way to Russia to investigate Beverly's ancestors after a friend told him that Beverly's real father was Russian.

"Wow! I hope you've written this all down. This is better than a Tom Clancy novel."

"Oh, it gets better!"

"Before he disappeared, Ted tried to blackmail Beverly with old photos of Beverly in compromising positions when she was traveling with the Blaze, her rock band," Don said, chuckling. "Fortunately, she had a computer geek on her team who was able to quash any Internet exposure."

Wyatt got wide-eyed and stared at Don Olson.

"Then, after Ted was killed, it was discovered that his airbag had been tampered with and instead of going off on impact, it was delayed long enough to throw him through the windshield. He actually had been to Russia trying to make the Russian connection about Beverly's birth father. Beverly's mother fessed up about an affair she had with a Russian soldier when she worked in Moscow for the State Department at the end of World War II."

CHAPTER NINETEEN

Jordan Quincy bolted upright in bed and looked at her alarm clock. It was four a.m. She had tossed and turned all night thinking about the unread text messages from Lionel Kittring on her father's cell. She grabbed her robe and made her way to the dark office on the first floor that belonged to her senator father. Jordan retrieved the cell phone and methodically went through each message. Much to her chagrin, many of the messages were disconnected before anything was said. Three messages were intact and had some content. One message in particular grabbed her attention.

November 24, 2020

LK: Did you get the article I sent you about the WSG?
JQ: Yes. Thank you. It changed my mind about them.
LK: So, are you going to support the legislation endorsing them?
JQ: Yes, I believe I will.
LK: Excellent. When is the vote?
JQ: As soon as we come back from holiday break. Mid-January.
LK: OK. I'll be in touch.

Dad was so against the WSG, I wonder what article changed his mind.

She was going to look for it as soon as she had some coffee and a chance to call Beverly Swift.

"Did you get my text about officer Middleton's phone number?" Jordan said.

"No, I didn't see it," Beverly said. "Was it a working number?"

"No, it has been disconnected. At a loss now as to what to do?"

"Let me talk to my friend Avis. He has all kinds of connections in telecom," Beverly indicated. "I'm on my way to a meeting and I will call back as soon as I can."

"Thanks, Beverly. Sounds good. I am looking through Q's files right now," Jordan said. "I have something else to send you. Important. And by the way, did you hear about the double murders in Denver? Very much like dad's situation."

"I'll look for it."

BlackRock's offices were on 52nd Street in the Park Avenue Plaza Building. Larry Fink's office was on the top floor and his firm occupied the fifteen floors under him befitting a financial titan that kept a lower profile. BlackRock was among the top financial firms in the world and didn't see any reason to seek the kind of media attention that other investment firms embraced.

Carol Cross was an attractive woman, who, according to the company's Forbes 500 listing, worked *with* Larry Fink, not *for* him. She was a warm, well dressed, articulate person befitting her role as Assistant Board Treasurer and lead counsel for the firm. Like old money in America, she didn't wear her status or her character on her sleeve. There wasn't a trace of the narcissistic tendencies that bedeviled other women of her stature. Carol was not shy or overzealous.

"I know Janet Yellen sent you down here to see me . . . or more precisely, up here, but Larry said something about the World Solutions Group," Carol said gently. "So, I will let you expand on that. And by the way, he told me to tell you that he apologizes for his absence. He's a huge fan."

That last statement took Beverly by surprise. In her mind, people like Larry Fink enjoyed opera and Chamber music, not rock and roll.

"I'll be sure to bring him an autographed collection of my work."

"If you could, bring two. I'm a huge fan, too," Carol said. "I don't think I have ever been this worked up over talking to someone in my entire life," she gushed.

"Thank you, Carol. May I call you Carol?"

"By all means," she said.

Beverly cleared her throat.

"Dr. Yellen has assigned me the task of finding out as much about the World's Solutions Group as I can from a monetary standpoint," Beverly said, choosing her words carefully. "They seem to exert tremendous influence on world business and political leaders and we understand that Blackrock knows Mr. Richter quite well."

"Well, Beverly . . . May I call you Beverly?" she nodded. "To say we know him quite well is presumptive on your part. Except for a very few people in his inner circle, no one else knows him 'quite well'. As long as our firm has known him, he has always been a little reclusive and I think that stems from just the sheer number of people he has known, friend and enemy alike, and touched during his career. At the beginning of the WSG, like all things new and untested, he drew a lot of criticism," Carol Cross said through her engaging smile. She sipped some water. "It was tough and slow going at the start, especially since he planned to launch the WSG the day after 9/11. Few people took his environmental claims seriously not to mention that he was already in his sixties."

"There has been some criticism of the WSG that they are just a front for billionaires and wealthy companies who pay lip service to the ideals espoused by the group, but then go and do whatever they want without regard to the any of the tenets espoused by the WSG."

"Yes, we've heard that, too, and been the brunt of a lot of criticism along that same line of thinking," she said. "Everyone has an opinion on the environment, good or bad, informed or ill-informed. As a culture with our smartphone accessibility and speed-dials, people think solutions to the environment are, or should be, as simple as making a phone call or snapping one's fingers. When I'm asked, I tell the ill-informed that we didn't get in this environmental mess overnight and we won't get out of it overnight, either. That is Larry's stance, too."

"Mr. Fink wrote letters to your clients and BlackRock investors laying down the law about practicing green concepts in their businesses, didn't he?"

"Not quite that harsh, although I guess he did sound like Vladimir Puten to some of them," Carol laughed. "Or Atilla the Hun. But, we haven't held the companies and some individuals accountable and that's where it has to start, accountability. Like any good steward, he told them that if they wanted to continue benefitting from BlackRock's success, they had to step up to the climate change plate. Larry loves baseball and he uses analogies from the sport often. It is not a matter of money for most of them, but knowing where to start and what to do. They have finally realized that their shareholders won't abandon them. In fact, to the contrary, bottom lines have improved."

"Just two more items, if you don't mind."

"Not at all. I'm open until 1:00."

"A statement saying that in the future, 'You won't own anything and you'll be happy' has been attributed to Hans Richter." Carol giggled.

"Larry told me that was a Hans Richter line taken out of context when someone asked him about the future economic outlook. He said, in fact, that if the world does not solve its environmental, governmental, economic and political problems, You won't own anything. The 'And you'll be happy' came later. He was referring to the fact that no one will be able to afford to own anything."

"And what about digital currency? What are your thoughts on that?"

Carol took another sip of water.

"We know China is experimenting with it as an extension of their social spying system. It will be easier to accomplish in Communist and Socialist countries," she said. "But, it's no secret the U.S. is working on it, too. But, it will be a hard sell here. People know what FDR did to gold ownership back in the 30's, lying about it like Lyndon Johnson did about Vietnam. People need some privacy in their lives and the smartphone has stripped us of most of that already. Digital currency would be the final straw for anyone's privacy in financial transactions and a hard sell in America."

Carol Cross looked at her watch and stood up. “Are we done here?”

Beverly nodded and stood up and extended her right hand.

“Yes we are. Thank you for your time and your wonderful insight,” she said.

Carol walked Beverly to the outer office and shook hands again.

“I enjoyed our conversation, almost as much as I enjoy your music because it is easier and more fun to listen to,” she said. “I look forward to getting that music collection and I know Larry will, too.

Carol Cross looked at the receptionist. “Call my driver to take Ms. Swift home.”

In the Town Car going back to her apartment, she was rolling Jordan Quincy’s words about Denver around in her head when she remembered that Lionel said he was on his way to Denver when he left the luncheon at Zatayna’s.

Beverly dialed her cell phone.

“Melanie. There was a shooting in Denver recently, a murder, and I want you to find out everything you can about it as fast as you can,” Beverly said, almost shouting into her cell. “Call me as soon as you find out anything.”

“Will do, Beverly. Thanks.”

CHAPTER TWENTY

It was Reese's worst day since coming back to Washington and it showed. He was quiet and self-absorbed, visibly shaken by the enormity of the task ahead of him. Beverly wanted to talk about the bogus investigation into James Quincy's death, but decided that it was not the right time.

"And how was your meeting with . . . with . . . good ole what's his name?"

"Boy, you are tired. Larry Fink, one of your Wall Street heroes, if I remember correctly. I met instead with Carol Cross, chief legal counsel because Mr. Fink was called out of town. It was a good meeting and I found out that Beverly Swift, the singer, has two more fans."

"Well, you're right, he is a hero of mine," Reese said. "I've always imagined him to be a bit self-effacing, but confident. Is that accurate?"

"Well, I don't know about *his* confidence, but everyone I met was confident. Carol is very confident, but not lawyerly, and I could tell that what she said is pretty much what Larry would've told me," Beverly indicated. "She was very opinionated about Hans Richter, had good insight into the WSG and I'm sure she said what Fink would've said, she's just the wrong person to ask."

"Why would that be?"

"I don't think any of them knows Hans as well as people think they do, especially Janet Yellen," Beverly said. "She assumes that because Blackrock folks spend a lot of time with Hans Richter that they know him well."

"I can tell you something about Janet Yellen. She doesn't fly too much outside her familiar circle," Reese offered. "If there were three other Larry Fink's in the WSG, she would have you talk to all of them. You have to remember that she was the Fed Chair under Obama because she was predictable and safe."

"What about now? Biden nominated her for the Treasury job from the very start."

"The president has great faith in her, although I have to say, I am not sure it's reciprocal," Reese noted, yawning. "She was an academic, like Obama, and there are certain theories in academia that don't work in real life . . . Like MMT and baling out the country with endless and reckless money printing for the sake of one-upping other world leaders. And, that you can inflate your way out of massive debt. That's what the Germans did after WWII and look what happened to them . . . And the world!"

"Is that a warning?" Beverly quipped. "Janet brought up the MMT and inflation theories when we met for my interview. She is definitely not in that camp."

"Sort of. Janet is like all women in high places. She admires Joe Biden and vice versa because she understands our monetary system, the importance of the dollar being the world's reserve currency and a healthy disdain for central digital currencies and people like Yvonne LeStatt. She naturally wants to discredit and weaken the influence of the Hans Richter's of the world. Dr. Yellen sees it as the American way which is quite Nationalistic and not much different than Trump."

"What's your advice, then? Should I tell her about the meeting with Blackstone?"

"Definitely. She set it up for you, didn't she?" Beverly nodded. "She's probably already been debriefed by Carol Cross, so she will compare your notes with what she was told by her. Just remember, she knows the rules at Treasury a lot better than you do, so when you get the employee handbook, learn it like gospel."

Beverly swigged the last of her beer and set the bottle on the table.

"Thanks for the tutorial. Are you ready to go. I'm whipped."

Reese smiled a bit wickedly. "No argument here."

Beverly was about to turn her phone off for the night when the message indicator lit up. It was Jordan Quincy and the display said urgent.

"Did I wake you up? Sorry to call at such an hour, but I've been trying to solve a puzzle all day and I think you can help," Jordan said. "You know who Lionel Kittring is, right?"

"Yes, I do. He's a senior government official in the intelligence community. High up in either the CIA or the NSA. Why?"

Beverly looked over at Reese whose eyes were fluttering. She leaned over and kissed him good night, easing out of the bed to find a better location to talk. She headed for the bathroom, convenient and quiet.

"I was going through dad's cellphone and there were about fourteen messages between my father and Lionel, the sole subject matter being the World Solutions Group, a group father initially despised but later changed his mind," Jordan said. "Mostly because of Lionel Kittring."

"Well, if anyone could get your father to change his mind, it would be Lionel. He's a master spy and could convince investors to buy beach property in Nebraska." Beverly said. There was a long pause. "Why don't you send me that transcript of the phone log. I also asked my admin assistant to find all there was to know about the

Denver murders. When I parted company with Lionel he was on his way to Denver. I really hope it's all just coincidence."

There was silence momentarily and then Jordan said, "Can we talk tomorrow? Thanks for your help."

"No worries. I'll call you during my lunch hour, between nine and ten your time. Tomorrow is my first day in the office at my new job at Treasury, so I have to get some sleep."

"Congratulations. Talk tomorrow. Good night."

CHAPTER TWENTY-ONE

Melanie told Beverly she had some information on the Denver murders, but she wanted to talk privately in Beverly's office.

"The police investigation is still going on, but the information I got was eerily similar to James Quincy's death," Marlene began. "Same MO, same suspect dressed in OR scrubs and according to the Denver police, the same drug was used to kill all three victims."

Beverly dropped her head. "What did these Denver victims do for a living?"

"Federal Reserve of Denver . . . Both men were high officials, conducting an investigation into the World Solutions Group."

"Do you know if they had any contact with Quincy?"

"No, but I can find out."

"Please see what you can find out, Melanie. Great work."

"Thank you. Great way to start your new career, eh?"

"I'll say."

Beverly was nervous on her first official day at the Treasury office, despite already being immersed in some unexpected duties. At their first official morning meeting, Janet barely mentioned the Blackstone interview or what was discussed. Reese was spot on in that regard, she had already gotten all she needed to know from Carol Cross. She introduced her assistant, Melanie Strong, to Beverly.

Beverly sniggered. "We've talked on the phone."

Janet showed Beverly around the office herself, which was highly unusual and not often done. Time didn't allow for a tour of all five floors (including the basement) and they ended at Beverly's new office. A woman handed Beverly a meeting schedule, instructions on how to access the computer system, which was separate from the rest of the government, a department directory, keycards for the entrance and lobby doors, a metal key for her own office and an invitation to a baby shower for Janet's assistant on Monday next. Beverly laughed at the card's graphics.

"I have a staff meeting on Thursdays and you will be part of that. It starts at nine o'clock in the conference room next to my office," Janet relayed.

"Got it . . . Where is your office?"

Melanie spoke up.

"I'll escort you there in the morning. No worries."

"Thank you, Melanie. See you tomorrow, Beverly."

""Can I ask you a question?"

"Sure."

"Are you Beverly Swift, the singer, whose band was the Blaze?"

Beverly laughed. *I hope this doesn't happen a lot around here,* she thought and smiled at Melanie. "Guilty."

"Wow. I saw all five concerts in DC. What are you doing here?"

Beverly smiled again.

"Spying to make sure my money is safe," she chuckled. "Just kidding. I have my MBA and wanted to stay busy. Please don't give up my identity. It would be greatly appreciated."

Melanie made a gesture to lock her lips. "Mums the word."

"Thank you," Beverly said. "Plenty of people recognize me or my name without being prompted, especially if they're over forty, and I would prefer to keep it that way."

"No worries. If I bring my CD's to work tomorrow, will you sign them?"

"Of course. Now, a little help with the phone system would be greatly appreciated."

The phone system was easier than it looked and employees could do things with this phone system that you couldn't with most others, not that Beverly knew the difference, but Melanie did. Melanie helped her save the most often used phone numbers starting with Janet Yellen, who rarely picked up a call unless it was the president or Jerome Powell.

"She always calls back."

Melanie helped her figure out the programs she wasn't familiar with and download files to send to her personal computer. When it got to be lunch time, Melanie suggested they walk over to the Museum of the American Indian to eat lunch.

"I have never found the exhibits to be great, but they have the best food on the Mall," Melanie said. "The building is huge, but I don't think they got the cooperation of all the Indian tribes to mount exhibits. More than a few tribes are not very happy with the federal government, anyway. The exhibits are few and far between. They're interesting, but not arresting. But, you will love the cuisine."

"I think it is an excellent idea, Melanie. Give me five minutes."

It was a mild, sunny day in Washington, DC and it felt good to walk outside. Winter had been brutal and the early weeks of spring were a temperature rollercoaster. So, it was a perfect day to walk.

Over lunch, Beverly learned a great deal about Melanie Bishop. Almost a PhD in finance, cut short by a cheating husband, a nasty divorce and a two year old daughter caught in the middle. She lived in Maryland and had worked at Treasury for six years.

"You mean to tell me you're almost a PhD and you're only a Personal Assistant?"

Melanie nodded. "But, not all Personal Assistants are created equal," she noted, smiling. "I make a six figure income and when I go back to my dissertation, the government will pay for the rest of it. Personal Assistant is one of the few positions in the government with no job description, pay scale or defined benefits."

"Wow. So when will you resume your dissertation?"

"In June."

When they got back to the office, Janet summoned Beverly to her office.

"I wanted to let you know that I spoke with Carol Cross about your meeting and she was quite impressed with you. She had no idea that it was your first day on the job," Janet said. "I told her that you had a lot of experience meeting people for the first time and reminded her who you were in your former life. Carol said she was a big fan of Beverly Swift, rock and roll queen extraordinaire, and felt more nervous about meeting you than you did meeting her. I told her to check out the October 20, 2010 issue of Time magazine. Isn't that the date you were on the cover?"

"Yes."

"I thought so. I still have the issue," Janet said, laughing mostly to herself. "Carol was a test to see if you could handle someone of her stature before I unleashed you on Hans Richter. I should've known better and perhaps I should've told you in advance, but then your interview might've been contrived because you knew the situation."

Beverly glared at her boss. For whatever reason, she wasn't upset about the setup.

"Actually, I'm happy you didn't tell me because I might've come across as nervous or insincere," Beverly said. "I'm glad it worked out. What now?"

"I was thinking that after the staff meeting tomorrow we could map out a strategy for the meeting with the World Solutions Group. I have a couple people in the office to assist you, Charlene Evans and Tomas Hogan, young and bright researchers who between them speak seven languages," Janet iterated. "They have been doing some advance work on the issues."

"I am going to give full disclosure here. My old band manager, Darden Green, got a letter from the WSG inviting the Blaze to perform at the closing of the forum this year. As you know, it has been pushed back to April 7 through the 9th because of the pandemic," Beverly said. Janet just nodded. "We get a large payday and most of it will be donated to charity since the band members are quite well off. I wanted you to know and suggest we meet with Hans right before the Group meetings."

"Yes and that will give us some extra time to formulate our game plan. Thank you for telling me about the concert," she said. "Who knows! Maybe I'll dance a little."

Beverly sniggered. "That will definitely go viral."

CHAPTER TWENTY-TWO

Beverly suddenly felt very old.

Charlene and Tomas didn't look old enough to be out of high school let alone ranking members of Janet Yellen's senior staff. Charlene had a beautiful ebony complexion and, as Janet indicated before the meeting started, an IQ north of 150. She was taller than anyone else in the room. Tomas, pronounced toe-mas, was tall and rail thin. He wore a dark suit with pants legs above his ankles and a thin, un-patterned dark tie. He looked brainy and severe in his oversized black-rimmed glasses.

Pepper and salt, Beverly thought.

Tomas asked if she was the Beverly Swift who fronted the Blaze. Charlene looked at him like he had gone bonkers, especially when Beverly said yes. He told Beverly that her concert in Berlin in 2012 was one of the best concerts he'd ever attended. Janet raised an eyebrow and Beverly shrugged and said thank you.

"Do either of you play an instrument or sing," Beverly said, looking at Charlene.

"I play the piano and the cello, but I don't sing," Charlene said stiffly.

"I play the guitar some, but not very well. You don't ever want to hear me sing," Tomas offered. "I kill houseplants when I sing."

Everyone laughed and Tomas turned red with self-effacing embarrassment.

Beverly noticed that Tomas didn't look at Charlene when she spoke, focusing on either Janet or herself or he just stared into space. He never looked at her. That was unusual to Beverly's way of thinking and she made a note to speak to Janet about it.

"OK. Thank you, Tomas. Who's the senior person here?"

They both raised their hands. They started working at Treasury the same day.

"So, we're looking into the World Solutions Group, Hans Richter and his influence over COVID19 and the Great Reset," Janet said. "Tomas, since you are the economist, I want you to continue to concentrate on the money and Great Reset as it concerns WSG finances." He nodded, looking right at her. "And Charlene, since you are the Sociologist/Environmentalist, I want you to investigate COVID19, the WSG's environmental agenda and social politics."

She nodded, too.

"There will be a formal trip to Switzerland in April and Beverly may do a fact-finding trip in the meantime. Do either of you have any questions?"

Tomas raised his hand. "What is the time-frame for our next meeting?"

Janet nodded at Beverly.

"Two weeks. After the staff meeting in two weeks." Beverly said.

They stood up, reached across the table to shake Beverly's hand and left the room, Charlene leading the exit.

"Have you got a minute," Beverly said, looking at Janet as the door slowly closed.

"Did you notice that the whole time we were meeting, Tomas never looked at Charlene? Am I detecting some friction here?"

"Yes, I noticed it, too," Janet said. "Tomas is brilliant, confident and very German. He has never cared for people of color, but knowing that he has to work with them, not looking at them is his way of protesting. His grandfather was a member of the Nazi party in wartime Germany and while his father never openly disdained Hitler, he made up for it by serving in the U.S. Army a generation later. Tomas adored his grandfather and the old man filled him with a lot of nonsense about Jews, Blacks and Hispanics, telling him of the glories of the Aryan race. He still has idiosyncrasies even though he has changed tremendously in the time he's been here. When he started, he wouldn't even speak to her."

"I get it. Can I talk to him later?"

"Of course. Anytime."

"I think it went well today," Beverly said. "I'll get busy on an itinerary for Switzerland."

"Good idea. Let's talk tomorrow."

"Will do. But, give me the thumbnail on Charlene. "

"Oh, yes, by all means. She was working at the EPA when Trump was elected. He gutted the agency so much that her job was eliminated," Janet said. "She was referred to me because of her strong math background even though she has a PhD in Sociology and Environmental Science. Her BS was in accounting. She is really brilliant and showed me some of the math behind getting closer to a climate change solution. She was a Godsend."

"Where's she from? She's beautiful and smart, but kinda quiet."

"Originally from Namibia, but she emigrated with her parents when her mother came to teach at Vassar. Her father taught at Brown University, so she is well-heeled in academics," Janet noted. "She worked as a model during college and that's where the poise was instilled. She's quite a young lady. Her folks live in New Haven."

"I'll say she is. Think she might moonlight as a babysitter when I get moved? Haley would love her and I would love the role model."

"Ask her. You might be surprised."

"Her folks still around?"

"Yes. They live in New Haven, Connecticut. George moonlights at Yale and Gale is the Dean of Women," Janet said. "Good folks. Charlene is their only child."

CHAPTER TWENTY-THREE

When Beverly returned to her office, Melanie had messages for her from Tomas, Charlene, Denise and Reese. Seeing those messages reminded her to check her text messages from Jordan and call Avis. The information was all there and Jordan said she had something important to do regarding her father's estate and that she would call later.

Melanie came by, rapping the door with her knuckles.

"Want to get a drink after work? My daughter is with her grandmother for the night."

"Sound like a good idea. Did you find anything more on the Denver murders?"

"No, but there was an attempted murder in Salt Lake City. Same MO and the visiting doctor was surprised by a staff doctor and left the room. The proposed victim was a female worker on vacation there."

"Do you know what she did?"

"She's the admin to the senator from Idaho and a devout Mormon."

"You think she might talk to you if you called her. Having survived the ordeal, she will have some fresh insight," Beverly said. "Tell you what. See if you can get her on the phone and I'll talk to her."

"Got it. I'll meet you in the lobby at 5:00 and hopefully have good news."

"Great!" Beverly opened her phone to Reese's number and sent a text message.

"Let me know about an hour before you leave and I will cook dinner. Tired of restaurant food. Going for a drink with my assistant at 5:00."

Jordan called and left a message to call her back before eight o'clock DC time. Beverly quickly called Avis, but got his voicemail. She told him she needed his help tracking down some information and to call her back as soon as possible.

They were both a little out of breath and anxious to sit down. It was unusually warm for early March and their winter coats were burdensome. They went to a bar that was not a Treasury hangout because as Melanie said, those places have big ears.

"So how was the first day in the office?" Melanie said.

"My day was good, thank you for asking." Beverly said. "Thank you so much for being around to help. Any news from Salt Lake?"

'I found out her name and had nice conversation with here husband. Her name is Lacey and she is in the hospital one more night for observation in a heavily guarded room," Melanie disclosed. "He said she would talk to you tomorrow when they got home."

"You think that will happen?"

"I do," Melanie said. "But, I guess we'll find out."

"Do you think Janet has spies among us?"

"Well, yes, there are spies all throughout the department, in every department across the government, but Janet probably doesn't know who they are. They're not whistleblowers which is serious business," Melanie said. "The whistleblowers are generally known even though the media would like to make you think otherwise. The whistleblowers are the government equivalent of William Calley, Liz Cheney or Michael Flynn who've been trotted out for possible illegal or immoral acts to show the world that our government works even though nothing really ever happens to them."

"No argument there. What do you think of Dr. Yellen . . . Janet?"

"Generally, high marks. You have to take much of what she says to the media or in public with a large grain of salt. She does that to keep up appearances and keep her job," Melanie revealed. "She is genuinely worried about the money printing machine the Federal Reserve has been operating since the pandemic started. Powell has misguided and vested interests since he made his millions as a stock broker. And, he's an attorney."

"I didn't know Powell was also an attorney," Beverly said. "Did you work for Janet at the Federal Reserve?"

"I did. Things were much different then . . . No coronavirus, most people who wanted to work were working and we imagined that there was at least some semblance of racial justice . . . No George Floyd that we paid any attention to."

"Ah, yes, I think Walt Disney coined the term, Fantasyland."

"Exactly," Melanie said. "I better go. Taking the bus home and I need to get my car from the shop. Enjoyed our chat, but please don't share it with anyone. Things have a way of getting back to Janet and they're not exactly a transcript of the original conversation. I'll see you tomorrow."

Over dinner Beverly asked Reese, "Do you think congressmen and women sometimes say things they don't really mean to say to protect their status?"

Reese laughed. "All the time. Ever notice when a government executive, be it a congress person, bureaucrat or other elected official speaks spontaneously. They stumble a lot and pause? That's because their statement or reply is not scripted like it usually is. They rarely say their own words. That's what the various communications departments do."

"So, they really may not believe what they're saying?"

"Exactly. By the way, how was the first day in the office?"

"Not very scripted."

Beverly called Jordan at ten o'clock, DC time. Reese was already asleep, but Beverly was pumped after reading Jordan's text message.

"I have attached some more footage from the hospital security camera. Take a look and we'll talk soon." Jordan

Beverly looked at the new footage a couple times. The video was of the same person in Q's hospital room leaving the room and going to the elevator or some other destination. The intruder was pushing elevator buttons and holding a limp skull cap in their hand. Beverly decided that two heads might be better than one and called Jordan.

"Hello, Beverly. Did you get my additional video?"

"Hi, Jordan. Yes I did. I thought we might look at the last bit of video together. The one where the intruder has removed the skull cap and is at the elevator."

"Got it. Did you notice the dark mark on top of the forehead?"

"Hang on a minute. Let me look. Yes, I see it. Looks like it could be a birthmark," Beverly said. "I am going to blow the image up to get a better look."

"Think you're right. It is a birthmark and we have just reduced the number of suspects down to about five million," Jordan said. They both started to laugh.

"I tried to call Avis, but got his voicemail. I told him broadly what I was after and will send along any advice he has to find out if Detective Middleton is real."

"Appreciate that. Let's talk again after you hear from him."

"Definitely."

CHAPTER TWENTY-FOUR

The following morning, Beverly met with Janet like she would every morning for the first two weeks. The sessions were rather banal as the secretary watched over Swift like a mother hen does her chicks. Janet wanted to make sure Beverly understood the finer points of the Treasury's role in United States government and monetary policy. This lesson was on the IRS and setting straight the many misconceptions about the Revenue service that permeated, mostly negatively, the public at large.

At two o'clock, Beverly's office phone started flashing red and she picked it up immediately. Melanie told her that Lacey Sanders, the latest victim of the scrubs killer, was on the phone. Beverly punched the button again and was connected to Lacey.

"Lacey, may I call you Lacey?"

"By all means."

"Thank you so much for calling us back. Do you have any idea why we called in the first place?" Beverly said.

"Melanie said something about a couple of other similar incidents where the victims weren't so lucky, so I guess you want to talk to me about what happened."

"Precisely. I understand you work for your senator in Idaho," Beverly said and Lacey agreed. "Did you ever meet or know Senator James Quincy from California?"

"Yes, I work for Senator Larkin. He knew James Quincy very well. We were so sad to hear of his passing."

"Thank you. I knew James Quincy for many years," Beverly said. "Can you describe what happened in Salt Lake City?"

"Well, I had COVID19 early on, back in August of 2020. I was taking some time off to do some spring skiing when it felt like I was relapsing, so I checked into the hospital in SLC," she said. "They have a separate ward for COVID patients and the staff is very alert and on top of things, checking the ward about every fifteen minutes."

Thank you. I am so happy to hear you have recovered. Did a doctor dressed in green surgical scrubs come to check on you?"

"Yes. And he started messing with the medical tubes going into my arms when a staff doctor came in the ward like he did every hour and questioned the other doctor about what he was doing."

"What did the other doctor say?"

"Oops. I have the wrong room and left. Never saw him again. The COVID doctor checked all my drips, called the nurse and told her to sit with me until further notice. That was all."

"Did you ever see the OR doctor's face?"

"Nope. He left in a hurry and never said another word."

"How would you describe him?"

"Average build, slightly stooped with a tattoo on his right arm like a coat of arms. Except what he said to the other COVID doctor, he never said anything."

Beverly had never seen Lionel Kittring bare armed, but she made note of the tattoo.

"Well, Lacey, thank you so much for help. Our best to you and your family."

"Thank you, Beverly, and the same to you and your family."

Beverly had typed the interview like an email and sent it to Melanie, asking her to review and then come to her office. Melanie's take on the situation was that it would've helped lot if the intruder had been unmasked. Beverly agreed and added that at least there was a pretty good description of his build and that seems to match previous descriptions.

"I agree. We just have to keep plugging along and wait for the opportunity to get to the bare skin."

Beverly laughed.

As Beverly was getting ready to leave for the day, Reese called to say he had to fly down to the Texas border to personally check things out for the president. Concealing her glee, she asked if there was anything she needed to do at his house while he's gone.

"Everything is in good order. I'll be back in the morning," he said. "Sorry for the late notice. Things are not any better down there as we speak. See you when I return."

"Be safe and have a good trip."

"Thanks. Plenty of food in the freezer."

CHAPTER TWENTY-FIVE

The next morning, Beverly got a wakeup call from Avis Marsden. He apologized for the hour and tried to reconstruct her original question. Beverly reiterated the bogus phone number that apparently was disconnected and raised questions about Thomas Middleton, who he was and what his motives might be. Beverly explained that Middleton told Jordan Quincy that Q's killer was dead.

"I can tell you, Avis, Jordan is just looking for some closure at this point."

"I understand that. Let me snoop around some and I will call you back . . .maybe not for a day or two. Getting intelligence on the death of a U.S. Senator is not easy."

"Thank you, Avis, and I know Jordan thanks you, too."

"Very well. Have a nice day, Beverly."

"You do the same."

There was a text message from Tomas Hogan requesting a brief meeting later that morning if her schedule allowed. He was polite and to the point. She told Tomas she could meet in thirty minutes in her office, shortly after ten thirty.

Tomas confided to Beverly that he had issues working with women and people of color, but did not admit being racist or misogynistic. He had been lying to everyone for so long he didn't know the truth any longer, but he kept that to himself. In Beverly's estimation, it was all a front for him to do the other things he needed to do. There was neither regret or shame in the words he spoke and she didn't push it since he volunteered the information.

"Have you determined when you're going Switzerland?" Tomas said, sitting down across from Beverly. He crossed his legs.

Beverly shrugged.

"Have you ever met Hans Richter before?"

"No, but I have been told he was a big fan of my band when we were touring, but we never played Switzerland."

"That processes with what we know. It also brings up the possibility of ulterior motives. Do you know if he ever attended any of your concerts?" Tomas said, sitting upright now in his chair.

"I don't know. We were hired to perform at the closing of the belated WSG this year and we are scheduled to do that on or about April 9," Beverly said, feeling suddenly compelled to discuss the details with him. "A man named Gerard Meister signed the contract and provided a ten percent down payment. We were told that all of the members of the WSG will be invited along with spouses and guests, but that the performance is primarily for Hans. We did a similar program for King Juan Carlos of Spain a few years back. His people sent down a playlist, we played it and that was the concert. No one was the wiser."

"Makes sense. Would it matter if they moved the venue?" Tomas said, adjusting his back into the chair. "We are not sure what state Hans Richter's health is these days and it may need to be moved closer to his home."

"It can certainly be done, but about five tons of equipment, lights, light bridges, instruments, soundboards and other stuff would have to be moved, too, and it's not something that can be done at the drop of a hat, not to mention the considerable expense," Beverly interjected. "So keep that in mind."

"When is everything scheduled to arrive in Switzerland?"

"Around April first and it will take two days through customs and three to five days to erect," Beverly said. "So, if it all has to be moved, it would be best to do it from the airport."

"Got it."

"Let me ask you a question," Beverly said, leaning forward over her desk.

"Go right ahead."

"Do you think Hans Richter is in ill health or maybe hiding out?"

"Why would he hide out?"

"I understand that some of his predictions, statements and suggestions have not gone over very well with members of the WSG. With all the negative press Bill Gates is getting because of his high standing with the WSG, it may be a reason to lay low," she offered.

"I don't know, but I will be sure to check it out," Tomas said. "But, one thing we do want to try to accomplish in going to Davos early is to contact Hans Richter directly and find out what he knows about the origins of the pandemic, public surveillance, digital money developments and any other information he might surrender."

"Wow! That would cover it."

Beverly smiled and nodded her head. Tomas didn't have the reputation as a gossip or tattletale. People described him as quiet, almost shy. He knew much more.

CHAPTER TWENTY-SIX

Lionel Kittring loved springtime in DC and little else. DC residents and visitors enjoyed plenty of park space and the Cherry Blossoms were about to bloom, a ritual akin to local political campaigns, creating a white and pink landscape beyond compare.

His allergies were killing him and he thought perhaps the main cause of his recent headaches. No matter what, though, he had to press on with his professional duties. That's the way he was. He was unsettled by the prospect of leaving NSA, but it was clear that his new boss, a quiet appointee of Joe Biden, did not see eye to eye with him on how the agency should be run, which groups or individuals should be targeted and how to go about it.

Only a few colleagues saw the writing on the wall going forward, Avis among them, which prompted a meeting on this glorious spring day. They were meeting for lunch at the Kenwood Club on River Road just beyond Friendship Heights. Lionel had walked to Union Station to await Avis's arrival and they would take a ride share to the country club. His head was pounding, he was exhausted from his multi-city tour and anxious about what his future held for him. The train was on time from New York and Avis was walking fast, almost running, to meet Lionel who was waiting in the vaulted Grand Hall, sitting on a bench near Massachusetts Avenue watching the travelers pop off the escalators.

"Am I late?" Avis said, giving his old friend a hug as he tried to catch his breath. "How are you, Lionel? And how is Marilyn?"

"Marilyn is fine, but I have been better, Avis," he said. "I will be history at NSA soon and that's why I wanted to have lunch at the Kenwood Club in Chevy Chase."

"Sounds good. How are the headaches these days?"

"I think they're caused mostly by my allergies. I have one now and the pollen is sky high," Lionel said. "Otherwise, I'm fine."

"Glad to hear it. Let's get going. I'm starving."

Getting a Lyft was easy since it was mid-morning and riders were at work or shopping or drinking Starbucks coffee. On the way to Chevy Chase, thirty minutes by car, they talked about their spouses, the latest on the pandemic, baseball, the new president, their glee over Trump losing every ballot fraud appeal, the weather and a little about next steps.

"So, Lionel, what happened? I thought things were going well." Avis said, sipping his wine. "This is good. Don't normally drink at lunch so you may have to carry me out."

"Or vice versa. Yes, this is the house Pinot Noir," he said. "They have an excellent beverage manager who is also a Sommelier. So, long story short, I was quasi recovered from the shooting when the new Director came aboard. I was working about three days a week in the office and keeping up through Internet chat rooms, email and web links. Then, one morning I went to plug in to the NSA and I had been blocked."

"Wow. What did you do?"

"The first thing I did was make sure it wasn't a technical glitch by checking with my team to see if anyone else was having a problem. I have ten team members, but only three responded to tell me they were not having issues," Lionel said, his eyes welling up with tears. "The next day, Richard Dexter, the new director, un-invited me from meetings I've been going to for ten years. That was last Thursday. I figured out that was his cowardly way to fire me."

"Did you talk to him?"

"I tried email, text messages and a few phone calls, but he didn't respond to any of them. I'm not afraid of him," Lionel said. "But, his actions certainly indicate I'm a goner."

"What are you going to do?"

"My first thought was consulting. I have many outside contacts apart from NSA, but then I remembered our conversation with Beverly," Lionel said. "I am intrigued by her investigation of the WSG. I know the players and I also know that it wouldn't be hard for Beverly and her colleagues to get in way over their heads."

"I did have a voicemail from her yesterday. Let me find out what's going on. I think she would be thrilled to have your expertise especially since you worked for Hans," Avis said. "What's your time frame?"

Lionel smiled. "I resigned this morning."

"Oh. I guess *you are* ready to start something new, then. Did I tell you Beverly bought a house in DC?"

"No. Where?"

"On Tilden, just off Connecticut Ave."

"Who was the listing agent?"

"Wyatt Douglas from Long and Foster. You know him?"

"I do. But, I wish I didn't," Lionel said, sagging into his chair. "More on that another time. Let's order!"

CHAPTER TWENTY- SEVEN

Lionel and Avis took an Uber back to Union Station. Avis shook Lionel's hand and jumped out. It would be a stretch to catch the next train to New York.

"I'll talk to Beverly this weekend and be in touch afterward," Avis said through the window before departing his old friend. "Chin up old chap. This setback may be the best thing that ever happened to you."

"Maybe so. Thanks for your help, Avis, and my best to Fiona." Lionel said, smiling meekly.

His head was pounding inside his skull. The driver sped off to the Smithsonian where Lionel had parked his car. He wrote a text to an anonymous recipient as the Uber driver pondered alternate routes amid the backed up traffic.

"I think we're in. Mission One accomplished. Mr. WD should contact me soon!"

Avis's train was late and he used that time to make a call to a contact at the FBI to get things rolling on the mysterious Mr. Thomas Middleton and the bogus phone number. Jeb Spencer answered on the first ring as was his usual custom. He and Avis caught up briefly as Avis organized the information he had.

"Does the name Thomas Middleton ring a bell, Jeb?"

"It does, but I don't recall why," he said.

"When Senator Quincy was pronounced dead, his daughter was told it was a homicide, not COVID. Later Detective Thomas Middleton, with the LAPD contacted Jordan Quincy and said he thought he had caught the murder suspect, who was also dead," Avis noted. "But when Jordan tried to follow up with Middleton, the phone number he gave her was no longer in service."

"OK. I know many detectives on the LAPD, but that name does not ring a bell, but his name does sound familiar. No matter, Let me check it out and I will call you back in a couple days," Jeb said. "Everything all right with you?"

"That will be great, Jeb. All is good here and I presume the same by you?"

"Yes. Getting married next month. A prosecutor in the DA's office. She makes me very happy."

"Congratulations. We'll talk soon and thanks for your help, Jeb."

"No worries. Great to hear from you, Avis."

Beverly's phone was ringing when she got to her office. It was Avis. He asked her to find out from Dr. Yellen if Beverly could add independent, outside consultants to her team.

"Tell her that this is a person who worked for Hans Richter several years ago and has been a consultant to the president for several years through a top level, don't say secret, agency in government and is available immediately," Avis said. "You can mention his name because chances are she won't know it."

"Thanks, Avis. You're talking about Lionel, I presume," Beverly said. Avis Marsden answered 'yes' quietly. "You'll have to tell me later what happened at NSA, but he would be a good candidate to have on the team. I think I can add members as long as their duties and responsibilities don't overlap, like two people from the same department. Is he leaving his current position?"

"Yes, but not by choice, although he did resign," Avis responded. "Beverly, did you know Lionel was shot last year in DC while investigating the vaccine scandal? Nearly killed him, another Gunther Schmidt special. For obvious reasons it didn't make the papers. He still spends some time recuperating, but Biden's appointee to Lionel's agency thought he was a slacker. Or more likely, very threatened by his presence."

"No, I didn't know all that. I guess Biden's appointee and Lionel weren't meant for each other. Gotta go. I'll let you know what Janet says. I know she will want to see a resume. Have him email it to me." Beverly paused. "Did you know that Gunther saved my life as I was recuperating from the car accident? He killed my doctor who was going to kill me on an isolated beach in New Jersey."

"I think you told me or I read it in the Times, but I had forgotten about it."

"I guess there are two sides to everyone."

"Yes, I think so. Call me later today, if you can. Lionel is anxious to get going. And one more thing. A contact in Los Angeles is checking up on Thomas Middleton."

"Thank you, Avis."

"Thanks for hearing me out, Beverly."

"No worries, Avis," she said. "Thank you!"

Beverly caught up with Janet as she was finishing preparations to go to San Francisco for a meeting with other Treasury secretaries from the G-7 countries. She wasn't in a particularly good mood about it because flying all that way for a meeting with national treasurers from the UK, Canada, Italy, Germany, Spain and China would not be productive or pleasurable. They never were. She gave Beverly the courtesy of answering her questions.

"Yes, Beverly, you can add outside members to your team. You just have to give me a name, a resume', salary requirements and when they can start. I can get them on board in three days that way. Who did you have in mind?"

"Well, I am waiting for his resume', but I know he worked for Klaus several years ago when the WEF was in its infancy. He has strong International credentials and has been working for the last several years at an agency that advises the president currently holding office."

"Sounds like a good choice," she said. "I will be back Monday and we can decide. Good work, Beverly. "It sounds like perhaps this is someone within NSA or high up in central intelligence. That place is getting shaken up daily."

Beverly took a deep breath. "Great. Have a good trip and enjoy the other coast."

"Thanks, I'll try."

CHAPTER TWENTY-EIGHT

Beverly was certain Janet knew who the candidate was, but when Beverly forwarded the email with Lionel's resume, she didn't offer any more information about it. She wondered how easy it was to quit something like the National Security Agency if you resigned. She imagined months of debriefings, a mountain of disclaimers and pledges that had to be executed by the designee in order to leave without being carried out feet first. Walking away from the NSA wasn't like quitting a job with a major accounting firm, bank or university.

Beverly's cell phone was vibrating. It was a message from Reese saying he was back at the White House and would call her after lunch. Her cell phone rang. It was Reese.

"Should've just called in the first place. I have a staff meeting after lunch and it could take a while," he groaned. "How are you? Any problems at the house?"

"I'm fine and everything at the house is, too. Did some work last night," she said. "How was the border?"

"Worse than we thought. Like a sieve, so we've put some new measures in place that will hopefully slow things down so we can catch a break," he said. "Some of the border agents there are not very helpful. They're not following the guidelines and many of them are acting on their own, breaking protocol, lying on reports and sneaking friends and family across the border," he said, "But, they're heavily unionized so firing them would be more trouble than putting up with their shenanigans."

"Can you fire them?"

"I hope so, but it would be a very long, drawn out process. They're union is quite powerful. Not my concern. I can only observe and report," he said. "You mind eating in tonight. I'm really tired."

"Nope. Doesn't bother me a bit," Beverly said. "I'll think of something for dinner."

"We sound like an old married couple. Anything but Mexican for obvious reasons," Reese chuckled. "See you about seven."

Beverly laughed. "OK, dear."

The office phone was blinking and Charlene Evans was on the line, bubbly and upbeat and wanting to make an appointment to see her.

"How about now . . . Or in the next twenty minutes."

"Twenty-minutes. See you then?"

"Works for me."

Meanwhile, Beverly looked up her notes from the meeting with Tomas and Charlene from a few days earlier. All the personnel information was running together.

"Sociologist/Environmentalist, I want you to investigate COVID19, the WEF environmental agenda and social politics." Janet's instructions.

Beverly hoped she'd already found something interesting.

About that time, Charlene was at the door. She was always smiling. Beverly wondered about people who always smiled. Beverly recalled that Eddie, her lover and the drummer in Blaze smiled all the time and always had a faraway look in his eyes, right up until that last snort of cocaine killed him two days after they returned from that last world tour. It was sad because he was a gifted, but obdurate, man.

Charlene worked all the time and Beverly surmised loneliness was a big factor. She distrusted men, having been raped in college by a blind date. She was unforgiving and not interested in men or a social life. Unfortunately, she accepted that as her fate and rather than turn to drugs or anti-social behavior, she turned to her work. Something she inherited from her parents who worked all the time, too. It seemed unnatural for a twenty something.

She sat down across from Beverly, placed her coffee mug on the desk top and handed Beverly a copy of her findings thus far.

"Up until eighteen months ago, there was very little information made public on the World Solutions Group. There was a members-only website that required password access," Charlene said with a firm voice. "Then Gerard Meister became the Deputy Director of WSG and the whole organization opened up."

"Any reason why that happened then?"

"Meister thought social media would make for a wider WSG audience and wider acceptance of the ideas they professed," Charlene offered. "And it did. The membership jumped tenfold. Online articles were downloaded by a factor of 50 and corporate memberships increased by fifteen thousand."

"What's happened to Hans Richter?"

Charlene cleared her throat and took a big drink of coffee.

"There were rumors that he was ill and no longer involved, but his office told me he has been very busy with various programs and sub-programs within the Group," she said. "The WSG has made him phenomenally wealthy and he consults now with the richest of the rich . . . Gates, Bezos, Buffet, Musk, Cook, Bienhof and Jamie Dimon, who is also his banker and financial advisor. "

"So, what's the dirt on him?"

"The phrase, "You will own nothing and be happy!" is attributed to him, but I can't find a direct quote in anything I've researched so far," she said. "It may be from a speech or a book I haven't read, but Russell Brand jumped on that phrase like Hans' uttered it with his last breath. The phrase pissed off a lot of people and it may have been taken out of context by certain factions of the press who are no more accountable than my cat. Whatever other information on the matter there might be is closely guarded and difficult to access. Hans Richter comes across as a very bright guy concerned about the future of the world."

"And what does Charlene Evans think?"

"That there is something rotten in Denmark or Switzerland as the case may be. You know much about the insurance business?"

"Not much. Why?" Beverly said, looking at her watch.

"Before an application is submitted to the insurance company, a senior level person 'scrubs' the policy for incorrect information to make sure it's approved quickly," Charlene said. "Think of Hans Richter as an insurance policy that has been carefully scrubbed."

Beverly raised one eyebrow.

"Now, I get the picture."

CHAPTER TWENTY-NINE

Two days after Lionel left San Francisco, a day early, the chief of police went to see the District Attorney in San Francisco County. There had been two murders in a local hospital in the COVID ward the day before, a Sunday, and Johns Littel wanted to discuss the crimes with Perkins Scott, the DA. Scott had been watching the murder spree unfold from Denver to Salt Lake City, Seattle, Vancouver and now San Francisco. He was delighted when Johns called to ask for the meeting. He thought he might be able to shed some light on what happened.

"Let's get some coffee and adjourn to a conference room away from the phones and office distractions," Scott suggested. "I appreciate you coming over."

"My pleasure, Perkins. We haven't had this much activity with COVID since late 2020."

"Have you been following this apparent string of connected homicides?" Scott said. "Same MO, same surgical dress, same patient type and, except for the case in Salt Lake City, the same outcome."

"Interesting that you bring that up. I just got off the phone with the FBI office here and they were filling me in on the eerie similarities between the cases," Littel explained. "They are also not ruling out the case of James Quincy in California. He was a U.S. Senator."

"I read about that one, but didn't connect it. Maybe he was the prototype?" Scott said. "How is your investigation going?"

"We've looked high and low for a person fitting the rather poor physical description we have. We found the OR scrubs in the parking garage, but no one really saw anything because it happened around eleven pm on Sunday, which I understand is also a trait of this killer . . . Secluded and late at night."

"Precisely. Whoever it is, they know what they're doing."

"What do you suggest?'

Perkins yawned and sipped his coffee.

"I'll stay on top of the research and you stay on top of the crimes," he said. "Inevitably, we will get a visit from the FBI and like always, they will take over."

Littel stood up, killed the rest of his coffee and extended his right hand.

"Sounds like a plan. I'll be in touch as we progress. I'll let myself out."

Perkins gave his guest a thumbs up.

Charlene left, smiling, with high praise from Beverly.

Beverly called Reese Talbot and got his voice mail. She left a message saying she was going to work late because her trip to Davos was coming soon. She asked him to call when he left his office, assuming that at some point he would actually look at her message.

Melanie knocked on her partially open door.

"Have you got a minute for Tomas? And you had a call from Lionel Kittring. He said you had the number."

"Send Tomas in. Thanks for the message."

Tomas looked disheveled and tired, not his normal self. Tie undone, collar open, shirt partially out of his pants, like he'd just run in from the gym. He plopped into the chair across from Beverly and let out a long sigh.

"Excuse my appearance, but I have been at the Library of Congress trying to connect the dots on Hans Richter and the WSG," Tomas said, breathlessly. "Financially speaking, that is. I ran back to catch you before you left for the day and it's warmer out there than I realized."

Beverly noticed little beads of sweat on his forehead.

"I got sidetracked looking into some of the personalities involved. Do you know the name Wendell Bennett or Donald Olson?"

Beverly smiled and said she knew them both, explaining how and describing her association with them in a very sketchy way.

"I understand Wendell Bennett is dead. He had a cardiac embolism in my campaign headquarters in 2016. He had been drugged and collapsed in the doorway to my hotel suite."

Tomas looked surprised. "What about Don Olson?"

"Don took over for Wendell at R.L. Thornton Companies when Wendell passed. In my opinion, Don is a conniving, crooked, selfish asshole who will do anything to make money, legally or illegally, and eliminate anyone who stands in his way," Beverly said, her shoulders shaking as she spoke. "And I'm being kind. If I never see that jerk again it will be too soon. He tried some things with me of a sexual nature when my rock band was just getting started in exchange for backing us."

Tomas raised an eyebrow.

"Apparently, Wendell is not dead. He laid low for a while and then got involved with the WEF, changed his name to Avery Saxton and did the whole criminal recourse spiel . . . birth certificate, passport, Swiss driver's license, fake family history, etc. There is evidence that he and Don are working together to infiltrate the WSG,"

Tomas explained. “And not in a good way.”

“Where did you find this information?”

“Mostly on the Dark Web. There are some reliable resources there, albeit few and far between, so you have to nourish the relationship to get unfettered and accurate information.”

“I guess,” Beverly said. “After Wendell died, there was not another word said about him except from people who thought he’d been murdered to make way for Don,” she said, sipping her cold coffee. “Also, that Don probably did it or was responsible for it, something that is next to impossible to prove. Do you think you can reach Avery Saxton through WSG channels?”

“I am going to try as soon as I leave here.”

“On your way to your office, stop and tell Charlene what you found out.”

“Will do. And thanks for your time.”

“Always. Thanks for the input. Great work,” Beverly said.

Tomas shrugged and grabbed the door handle.

Beverly thought Lionel might be able to shed light on Avery Saxton so she picked up the phone to call him when her cell phone went off softly playing ‘Let It Be’ by the Beatles. It was Reese telling her he’d be leaving the office about seven. She texted him back, ‘Perfect.’

Lionel picked up on the first ring.

“Thanks for calling me back. Have you gotten a decision from Dr. Yellen? I am ready to roll.”

“Not yet. She’s in San Francisco meeting with other treasury secretaries from the G7, but I think she will come through, so be ready,” Beverly teased. “Can I ask you a question?”

“Sure.”

“Do you know the name Avery Saxton?”

“There’s an Avery Saxton at the WSG. I don’t know him, but he does high net worth recruiting for them,” Lionel said. “Why?”

“One of my researchers just told me that Avery Saxton is actually Wendell Bennett, the former CEO of R.L. Thornton who was murdered in 2016,” she said. “R.L. Thornton was the funding arm of my presidential campaign. Do you know anything about Wendell Bennett?”

“Well, when he was alive, so to speak, we kept very close tabs on him. I told Avis that I thought Wendell came to a meeting at NSA about the vaccine issue because there was an incredible amount of money involved.”

“That would’ve been after he was murdered.”

"I think he introduced himself as Wendell Bennett. That would've been last year and if that is the case, it makes sense that he would be concerned about the money if he really worked for Hans Richter then and used his alias. Being dead or alive would've immaterial."

"Would you check, please?"

"I have a week left at NSA, so I will see what I can find out. But, I really want to talk to you about your upcoming trip to Switzerland," Lionel said. "You've got to do everything in your power to see Hans Richter while you're there and you have a lead-in because he loves your music. That's the only way we can buy some time to search the WSG offices."

"Way ahead of you. The concert is on the ninth and I have a meeting with him on the seventh."

"You need to move the meeting to the tenth so we can get in and get out during the concert. If you do it beforehand, he will be preoccupied by the break-in and won't meet with you."

"Right. So it makes more sense to meet with him on the 7th."

Lionel was silent momentarily. "Yeah, you're right. Too much on my mind. Thank you. We'll talk later."

He disconnected the call and turned off the tape recorder. Don Olson was smiling impishly.

Lionel's head was pounding and he just wanted to just go to a neutral corner and lay down. It felt like a boa constrictor was wrapping itself around his neck, squeezing his skull. He closed his eyes and rubbed his temples.

CHAPTER THIRTY

"Hi, Jeb. Thanks for calling. Did you find anything?"

"Probably more than you want or need to know, but we found plenty," Jeb Spencer noted. "Long story short, the phone number goes into an automatic phone log at the NSA in Maryland as well as a copy to the person placing the call. All the call records are encrypted, so no one can recover them without the encryption key," Jeb said.

"I have some contacts at NSA and I'll see if they can help. What about Thomas Middleton?" Avis noted.

"Middleton was a detective on the LAPD twenty years ago. He's dead and has no heirs on the force, so someone was pulling a fast one on Senator Quincy's daughter. There is one more thing."

"Shoot. I'm ready."

"The FBI in San Francisco is putting together an investigative team at the request of the District Attorney, Perkins Scott. There was a double murder there on Sunday nd the chief of police thinks there might be a connection to the murders in Denver, Seattle and the attempt in Salt Lake," Jeb relayed. "And to Senator Quincy's death, too. You will probably get a call. Lionel Kittring is a suspect."

"That makes sense and good to know. I think the investigation is overdue," Avis said. "Thank you so much. I owe you one."

"No worries, Avis. Let me know the next time you head West."

"You bet. Talk to you soon."

"So, is Wendell Bennett alive?" Lionel said, sipping a glass of water.

"Wendell is not alive, but Avery Saxton is very much alive and he has all the papers to prove it!" Don sniggered.

"So what happened when Wendell collapsed in the doorway of Beverly Swift's hotel room? He was pronounced dead at the scene, wasn't he?" Lionel said.

Don rubbed his chin.

"Not exactly. Wendell had a very slow heartbeat for such a big man. We lowered his heart rate even more with Digoxin, commonly referred to as Digitalis, long enough to make it appear that his heart had stopped. The EMS team that showed up worked for me at the time and they went through the motions of reviving him. Any activity that looks right is acceptable. People don't like watching that sort of thing anyway, so we whisked him off to the lowest level of the parking garage."

"Does he work for Hans Richter, now? Avery, I mean."

"Yes, for about two years. He works in client engagement getting more companies to join the World Solutions Group. He has increased membership by some 20,000 by teaching them the pros and cons of environmental economics," Don said, standing up to light a cigarette. "He has done a great job infiltrating the WSG and Hans likes and respects him."

"We've heard that Hans is not in very good health. Can you enlighten me?"

"At 83, he has slowed down, but we should all be in such ill health. He doesn't need to be involved day to day anymore, so he spends much of his time in the south of France," Don said.

Lionel closed his eyes momentarily and grimaced as the vice-like pain in his head tried to subside. Don grabbed Lionel by the elbows and stood him upright.

"Lionel, are you all right? You're white as a ghost. I want Jeffrey to take you to the emergency room to be checked out."

Lionel wanted to protest and say he was fine, but he just nodded and sat back down. The imaginary boa constrictor had gotten the better of him. He pressed on while Don summoned his grandson.

"Is R.L. Thornton a member of the World Solutions Group? You certainly qualify in terms of size and wealth," Lionel said.

"We are now thanks to Avery, but for a long time I didn't see eye to eye with Hans or his tactics and methodology. Then the pandemic hit and the world stopped and I realized as radical as Hans' approach was, it was the only one that could work," Don said, his face solemn now. "By the way, did you have your appointment with James Quincy before he died?"

Lionel nodded. Then Jeffrey burst in, breathless and red as a beet.

"Jeffrey, this is Lionel Kittring, a good friend and ally and I'm afraid also quite ill. Please take him to Mt. Sinai Hospital, now," Don growled. "Tell Mary to get my car ready."

Jeffrey nodded and held up one finger to Lionel to please wait.

"Is this the same boardroom that Gunther Schmidt blew up back in 2016?" Lionel said.

"The very same. The restoration was just completed in December, in time for the annual Holiday party. In fact, in 2020, Gunther worked for me a brief time."

"You know, Gunther is the one who shot you during the vaccine fiasco."

"I'd heard. I still carry a part of him with me . . . his bullets anyway," Lionel said, making a joke. "I also heard he's met his maker."

"He has. Gunther also put me behind this cane, killed three board members and the lovely Gretchen Davis, our corporate counsel," Don said facetiously. "She was the most beautiful woman I ever met."

Jeffrey opened the door and waved to his grandfather without turning around.

"You ready, Mr. Kittring?" he said

"Glad to have you aboard, Lionel."

The door shut behind him. '

Well not quite on board yet, Don. But we're pretty close. I just need enough evidence to hang you or kill you and then it will all be good.'

CHAPTER THIRTY-ONE

The neurologist at Mt. Sinai did a MRI after discussing Lionel's health history and giving him a general exam. They discussed his recent headaches as well as his lifestyle, drinking habits, exercise routine, prescription and street drug use, sexual proclivity and habits. He told the doctor he did not exercise regularly and had not had sex in a good while. The MRI was inconclusive and the doctor gave Lionel a prescription for extra strength Tylenol and told him to reduce his consumption of alcohol, get more sleep and start exercising by walking every day.

"Come back in two weeks and write down your dreams," Dr. Napali insisted. "I know it's a lot to ask, but we can catch any issue now, before it gets out of hand."

"One more thing," the doctor asked. "Is that a birthmark at the top of your forehead or something else?"

'My birthmark is on my right thigh. I'm not sure what you're talking about on my forehead," Lionel said.

The neurologist grabbed a hand mirror and showed the mark to Lionel. It looked like an old bruise, irregularly shaped and brownish red in color.

"Have you ever had any trauma to the head in the last couple years?"

Lionel had to think back.

"I was shot three times in DC last year and may have hit my head on the telephone pole I was leaning against waiting for EMS, but I don't recall. You are the first person to mention it."

"Does it bother you?"

"No. Like I said, I didn't even know it was there."

"Well, let this office know if it does start to bother you, Mr. Kittring. It could be serious or it could be nothing. If you have throbbing headaches, double vision, memory loss or strange dreams, contact me or the neurology department and let us know . . . Immediately!"

He handed Lionel his business card.

Lionel sat back abruptly at the mention of 'strange dreams'. He was already having some of those symptoms, but they were intermittent and never lasted. He decided not to mention any of it to the doctor just now.

"Thank you. I will do that, doc," he said through his dazzling smile. "See you in two weeks."

"Excellent. Have a great day."

"And you do the same."

Lionel asked Jeffery to drop him off at Grand Central Station so he could return to DC. Lionel was somewhat relieved that his headaches were not the precursor to something more serious, but was concerned about the mark on his forehead. He vowed to monitor the blemish and not let it get the best of him. When he arrived in DC, he filled the prescription for Tylenol Dr. Napali had given him.

It was a beautiful afternoon in the nation's capital and Lionel walked the few blocks to his DC field office near the raised portion of I-95. The office, once a road maintenance hub, was tucked against the massive concrete structure that supported the raised portion of I-95. It was perfect for NSA's purposes . . . small, tiny actually, nondescript, functional and relatively quiet although it was under an eight lane highway.

The Cherry Blossoms were budding and people on the street were smiling, not just about the Cherry Blossoms, but the specter that the pandemic was winding down, too. Lionel always stopped and paid homage to the telephone pole where he collapsed that rainy night in 2020, two months before the election, ready to die, just not quite ready enough when the EMS showed up. He patted the pole to acknowledge that it may have gotten the best of him, then inspected the pole for any indication that he had hit his head that fateful night. He didn't find anything, but it had been a good while since the shooting incident.

There were also times when his mind went blank momentarily and he forgot what it was he was doing and why. And, then, there was the lingering irritation of the side-effects from the gunshot wounds themselves. It was the Oxycodone he was sure, perhaps the most dangerous drug openly available by prescription on the market. He often wondered how it ever got approved by the FDA and, of course, there were many unapproved versions available on the street. Lionel was certain the FDA filing told a different story than the drug itself.

He was concerned about the very bizarre dreams he was having the last few weeks about killing his wife, Marilyn, while her sister, Adele, looked on. There were three versions that coursed through his sub-conscious like a newsreel, especially when he'd had too much to drink, which lately was often.

To top it all off, there was the never ending election scandal featuring ex-President Donald Trump. He had his own theories about who was financing Trump's election backlash, but it was a worthless pursuit over a man who thought so much of himself that in his own mind the great Donald Trump couldn't possibly lose an election.

Lionel took two extra strength Tylenol as the doctor had prescribed in order to get some work done. He had some ideas for infiltrating the WSG's expansive digital file system and wanted to coordinate with Beverly to do it during the Blaze concert. He was also monitoring the health of Prince Philip because his situation did not look encouraging. Lionel was a British subject with dual citizenship. The prince's death could disrupt Davos and provide some opportunities related to the break-in.

He got Beverly's voicemail and left a cryptic message that he needed to talk to her ASAP to review some scheduling and events. She called him back in ten minutes. It was 5:45 p.m.

"I'm not comfortable discussing this over the phone," she said. "Is there a private place we can meet?"

"Are you familiar with the Press Club on Massachusetts Ave? We can meet there and have total privacy."

"That sounds perfect," she replied. "I had lunch there last week with my real estate broker."

"Get a cab or an Uber and meet me in thirty minutes. If you get there first, tell them you're meeting me," Lionel said. "I'll be along shortly. The address is 1200 Massachusetts Ave."

"See you soon."

During her cab ride, Avis called with his update on the matters surrounding Senator Quincy's death and the possibly related deaths elsewhere. When Avis finished relaying what Jeb Spencer had found out, there was a long pause on Beverly's end of the phone call.

"Would it be worth a look at Lionel's cell phone? It seems to me he spent an inordinate amount of time in California before Q passed," she said firmly. "And possibly these other places."

Avis rubbed his chin. "It can't hurt. He certainly had a vested interest."

"When we are in Davos seems like the perfect time," she said. "Thanks for the update, Avis. I'll see you soon."

"Yes, you will, Beverly. Ciao."

CHAPTER THIRTY-TWO

Traffic was awful and Lionel arrived twenty minutes late. He had called ahead and told the maitre'd to take good care of Beverly Swift, his guest. When he arrived, Gregor ushered them into a private room outfitted with lounge furniture and a couple of end tables. In the interest of time, Gregor took their order and closed the door. He returned quickly with their drinks and flipped a switch that indicated the room was occupied and locked the door when he left.

"Beverly, it's good to see you again. Did you have any trouble finding this place?"

"No, the driver knew right where it was and Gregor said you had called and then we got into a discussion about my music albums and the band. He knew Eddie, the drummer and the father of my miscarried children," she said. "Those were some difficult years."

"Ah, yes, I bet so. Do you keep up with the Royal Family?" Beverly shook her head. "There is a situation developing in the Royal Family that may have an impact on your concert. What day is the concert scheduled for?"

Beverly sipped her drink.

"It was originally scheduled for the 6th, but it's been pushed back to the ninth."

"Prince Philip, the queen's husband is quite ill and may pass any day. Hans Richter would most likely attend the memorial service as he and the Royal Family are quite close. All a bunch of tea sipping Socialists as far as I'm concerned, but Prince Philip and Hans used to hunt together."

"And what you're saying is that would be the perfect time to step up our investigation. Correct?"

"Yes. I've had so little time to work out the details. I already have the team together, but my biggest concern is doing an end run around Avery Saxton," Lionel chuckled with clenched teeth in a typical British gesture similar to what John Cleese used to do endear American audiences. "I've gotten close to Don Olson to try to catch him in one of nefarious lies and he told me that indeed Avery Saxton and Wendell Bennett are the same person. He works for the WSG now and will be alerted to any potential trouble if Hans goes to the U.K. The way to stop him is not my style, but it may have to be that way. When do you plan to go to Davos?"

"Around April second. Be there with a few other government officials and Janet will arrive around the 6th for three days," she said. "We will also be rehearsing some and getting acclimated, typical concert performance stuff. My children and their nanny are coming, too. Dr. Yellen plans to attend the concert."

"I will be in touch. Thanks for meeting with me, Beverly."

Lionel was watching the news closely for information on Prince Philip's condition. It was March 28th and the Prince had been in the hospital a month once before, home for two weeks and then back in the hospital for what most watchers thought was the final time. The man was like a human battleship and decommissioning him would not be easy, just sad . . . Very, very sad. It was no longer a matter of if, but when.

He was staying in touch with his operatives world-wide as they reported on incidents or situations that would demand the NSA take action. The agency operated mostly in secret, preparing each move carefully so as not to disrupt the order of things in the world too much and always denying everything. There were high profile targets that Lionel directed himself. Nowadays it was related mostly to COVID19 and he had to review the target's situation, their health status, their impact on the global health scenario and what action to take. It fit nicely with the way Lionel Kittring liked to operate.

CHAPTER THIRTY-THREE

Lionel called Avis. "Where are you?"

"On the mall," he said. "Where are you?"

"So you are in DC? Can you come over to my office? Remember where it is? Three blocks from Constitution Avenue going East and then 2 blocks south," Lionel said. "It's really fancy and hard to miss."

Avis started to laugh.

"That's not what I remember, but it was the middle of the night and you were trying to die sitting on the ground against that now infamous telephone pole. How many broken windows from the corner is it?" Avis laughed again. "No worries. I'll find it."

"That telephone pole is still there, too. They haven't moved it to the Smithsonian in honor of me," Lionel said, laughing heartily despite his splitting headache. "Better yet, I have a car and I will pick you up in front of Air and Space in ten minutes . . .make that thirty minutes. We can go to the house in Bethesda," he said. "Marilyn is in Europe and we won't be bothered."

"Sounds good. See you then," Avis said. "What's up?"

"I'm going to need your help. Ever been to Switzerland?"

"No, but I get the impression that I will be going soon."

"There you go. That's my Avis!"

The Bethesda house had not been occupied for three weeks since Marilyn left for Europe. Lionel and Avis went around the first floor opening windows to air it out and Lionel turned on the A/C, grabbed a couple beers from the fridge and set up his laptop on the kitchen table. He set his cell phone down beside the computer.

Avis admired the beautiful mahogany tabletop and asked Lionel where he'd gotten it. He didn't answer. In twenty minutes the place was livable and Avis and Lionel repeated the window tour, closing them this time. Avis excused himself to the bathroom and Lionel took two more extra strength Tylenol. It was a ritual now about every three hours.

"As I told Beverly, although the WSG search has always been planned to take place during the concert, I think, unfortunately, that Prince Philip's present condition is going to afford us an extra measure of protection when he passes."

"Fiona has been following that story closely and said it is not a matter of if, but when."

"Precisely what I said. Hans and Prince Philip knew each other quite well, having hunted together for many years all over Europe, South America and Asia. Rumor has it that the prince loaned Hans one million pounds to launch the WSG, so I can't imagine that Hans would not attend a funeral or memorial service for him," Lionel said, smiling. "Giving us one less thing to worry about because I think his memorial will come about the time the Davos conference ends."

"You have a team together, yet?"

"Your old friend, Xing Ma, arrives in Switzerland tomorrow and plans to meet with Hans on Asian security," Lionel noted. "He will lead the team with two men from NSA, infiltrating the main WSG headquarters and other facilities, the prime target being the data center. Another team will cover Hans' home a few miles from Davos and a third team will search the house in Provence. They will set explosives as they go and use cell phones to signal the charges if it comes to that."

"Whoa, Lionel. Explosives?" Avis said nervously. "You never said anything about explosives. Otherwise, it sounds like things will come off as planned, except for the memorial service, and that will allow more time, if indeed it coincides."

"I got the idea for explosives in case our digital thievery doesn't find anything. If everything goes as planned, we have to be cautious and then figure out how to use any damaging information or blow the place to smithereens."

Lionel was the only one laughing.

"That may be the hardest thing of all. Whatever information we do find will have to be turned quickly because the break-in and theft will be world headlines the next day and will trigger some sort of backlash from WSG," Avis conferred. "I have been thinking about this and if we want to stop the lying, manipulating and fear, it will have to be by fighting fire with fire. I assume your backup plan is a series of explosions to cripple their operation?"

Lionel nodded and scratched his head and then his chin, dropping his elbow on the table to rest his head. He yawned.

"Did you ever see a doctor, Lionel?"

"Yes. Jeffrey took me to Mt. Sinai hospital and a neurologist checked me out . . . MRI and brief general physical. The MRI came back without indicating anything, so he told me to slow down on the booze, get more rest and exercise and take prescription Tylenol," Kittring announced. "And here I am. The doctor did find a spot on my forehead." Lionel pushed his hair away where the mark was and showed Avis. "He thinks it might be where I hit my head on the telephone pole when I was shot, something I don't remember."

"Good deal. I'll help you keep tabs on the elusive spot," Avis said, grabbing Lionel's beer from him. "You can cut down on your drinking starting now." Avis glared at him. "Do you have another appointment with him?"

"Yes, In two weeks . . . Oh shit, we'll be in Davos. I'll have to change it."

"That'll work," Avis shrugged. "All these tech guys are smug and arrogant, but I'm sure they know a few malware types and have pissed off more than a few of them off who would willingly, for the right price, infect the likes of Facebook, Amazon, Apple, Netflix and Google. The FAANG!" Avis said, smiling broadly. "I think this is where the retaliation starts, sending a message and allowing time for apologies, restitution and a whole boatload of anxiety. Got any guys like that?"

"Let's see," he said, sitting back in his chair. He smiled.

"As a matter of fact, I do. When I was recuperating from my gunshots, I needed a quick computer repair. A guy from Geek Squad came out and as we were talking he told me he was Jeffrey Olson, Don Olson's grandson." Avis looked at Lionel like he was speaking Arabic. "Don runs R. L. Thornton and Jeffrey was talking about the Dark Web and all the cool information on there, including instructions on how to shut down a company's computer operations."

"Has he ever done something like that?"

"He has not, and I know there are many well-known hackers who have, but he knew some geeks who had done it and they were going to help Jeffrey do a mock malware attack," Lionel said. "He would be a good place to start. I still have his card and access to a hacker's list from NSA to verify whatever he might tell me."

CHAPTER THIRTY-FOUR

Ryan Snyder was a veteran FBI agent who knew all the rules and generally played by them. He had been assigned the murder case in San Francisco that very quickly became five murder cases. Serial killings was his specialty. His claim to fame was that he solved a John Wayne Gacy copycat murderer in a St. Louis suburb when he was a FBI rookie. He stuck a shovel in the ground in the suspects backyard and hit something solid. It aroused his curiosity and ten dead bodies in shallow graves. That sort of thing tends to stick with you and follow you around.

Born in Ohio, Ryan was a high school All American linebacker who went to Notre Dame on a full athletic scholarship. He studied criminology after his best friend from high school died in a suspicious car accident that the local police never solved. He had been on the FBI's radar ever since he solved the crime three years later after having worked every summer to conclude his friend's death. Ryan Snyder was recruited his senior year at Notre Dame.

Short and completely bald, he still worked out every day, ran twenty miles a week, played golf and still treated his bride of twenty years like they were on their first date. He had been recruited by the CIA, NSA and the FBI. He said the CIA was too wonky and the NSA was too secretive, although he liked the NSA interviewer, Lionel Kittring.

Ryan gathered as much evidence as he could get his hands on before contacting Perkins Scott and Johns Littel. He had looked at all the hospital security footage and agreed with the Perkins and Johns that it indeed could be the same man in each case. The botched Salt Lake killing was the place to start because there might be clues that weren't readily available in the other locations. He was scheduled to go the Salt Lake the following day to meet the other agents investigating the near homicide.

Avis went to the restroom while Lionel called Jeffrey and got his voicemail. Five minutes later, be called back.

"Jeffrey, this is Lionel Kittring. You fixed my computer a while back . . . Yes, everything is fine. I wanted to talk to you about another project,. When would you be available?"

"I'm off today. I can be there in twenty minutes. Will that work for you?"

"Actually, it would. I am at my home in Bethesda, 1825 Mercer Street, where you came before. Just whenever you get here will be fine."

"OK. It will be later this afternoon. I just realized I'm helping a friend move and I'm on my way to his apartment now."

"Later this afternoon is fine, also. Just give me a call first."

"No worries."

Lionel hung up and saw another call coming in from a number he didn't recognize. It was Beverly.

"Did you talk to Avis? He called me earlier to tell me you were meeting with him."

"Yes, he's just getting ready to leave. Do you need to speak to him?" Lionel said. "He's on his way back to New York."

"No worries. I just found this old message from him and wanted to make sure you connected," Beverly conveyed. "Off to see the boss lady. Thanks, Lionel."

"We should talk this afternoon if you have time."

"Can you meet at one. I'll take a late lunch," she said. "Old Ebbitt's work for you?"

"I'll see you then."

Avis came around the corner from the stairway to the upstairs bathroom.

"Mind if I tag along? I haven't seen Beverly in a while."

"Not at all. The more, the merrier."

CHAPTER THIRTY-FIVE

Beverly liked Old Ebbitt's because it was filled with Washington insiders, journalists, old money and brass and wood. Few people knew who she was and she was not bothered by men, or women, trying to hit on her for an autograph, a selfie or a date. She slipped the maitre'd a twenty to give her the most secluded table available.

"Avis, what a pleasant surprise. I thought you were on your way back to the city?" Beverly said, standing up to give hugs. "Glad you can join us."

"Fiona is on assignment today and tomorrow, so no real need to hurry back and I always relish the opportunity to see my old friend . . . and I'm starving." He smiled his killer, 'Have I Got a Deal For You' smile from the old days.

"Me, too."

Lionel intentionally dragged things out until the restaurant lunch crowd was nearly gone even though a few regulars hung at the bar. They weren't interested in what he had to say.

"Are you about ready to go to Switzerland, Beverly? Avis will be going too and I will explain that in a minute," Lionel said, looking over the menu. "They're famous for their crab cakes, Right?"

"Yes," Beverly said. "And corn chowder, hamburgers and steaks, Cobb salad and martinis. I've never had a bad meal."

They all ordered something different. Lionel told the young woman to put it all on one tab and give it to him. Beverly tried to protest, but Avis put his forefinger up to his mouth. When the drinks came, three martinis, Lionel began. He raised his glass and cheered Avis and Beverly.

"Salute! Let me back up a little to put this all in perspective. We are almost 100% certain the Sars-CoV-2 virus was made in a laboratory in Wuhan, China and released accidentally. Not the first time this has happened as the labs there are generally badly managed and poorly staffed," he said, sipping his martini. "Boy that *is* good. You could stay here all afternoon and get hammered and not even know it until you tried to stand up. Anyway, most of the people working these labs have no idea what they're handling and how dangerous the substances are until it's too late."

Lionel took a long drink of his martini.

"The scary thing about that Chinese lab, like so many other so-called virology labs, is that it is not a virology lab at all, but a bio-weapons lab that is developing and studying ways to make viruses that can be used in war . . . or peace," Lionel said. "Ha ha!"

"I'm a little surprised they haven't used them against the protestors in Hong Kong," Beverly added.

Avis smiled abstemiously and took another sip of his apple martini.

"I think they have used a variation of the virus on the protestors, because the COVID19 variant might be a little too obvious," Lionel said. "And, I think there are some very smart people in Hong Kong who know how to counteract it. A few of them our own agents!"

He gulped the last of his first martini and help up his glass.

"Now, regarding the World Solutions Group, as I told you before I worked for Hans Richter back in the nineties and what he started out to build was a methodology to understand and develop solutions for climate change, poverty and racism. But, things have gone terribly wrong. He has either concluded that there are no solutions or he has realized that the billionaire members are the real Deep State and the best thing the WSG can do is shield them. And the problem is nobody knows, so we need to try and find out which scenario it is?"

Beverly and Avis nodded and dug into their food.

"And whether or not that information is at the WSG," Avis noted. "Right?"

"Right. Hans has always been very private and his public persona has been through the WSG and his writings, which have become more radical as time has passed," Lionel said. "You're right about one thing . . . These are the best crab cakes, I've ever eaten. "

Beverly and Avis nodded and kept eating.

"Ah, but I veered off topic. And, Hans is quite angry about it all. He or his executive director, Gerard, aren't going to volunteer anything, so I think the best strategy is to find out for ourselves and that's where Xing Ma and Avis enter the picture," Lionel said. "I'm not sure WSG has broken any laws, but the tenor of the meetings have become very despotic and dictatorial, supporting a dangerous agenda with a dangerous leader and I don't mean Hans."

Avis's mouth dropped open and Beverly dropped her fork.

"We have to know more about the Great Reset because no one else is talking, least of all certain billionaires," Lionel concluded.

"So, who do you think is the dangerous man here?" Beverly said.

"Me!" he said giggling and thumping his chest. "I'm not going to say just yet, but it will become evident soon, I think," Lionel said. "There are more dangerous people involved than Hans or Gerard. People whose public persona and image would never lead anyone to think what they're really up to."

Avis put his fork down and sipped his drink.

"So, we must find out what information the WSG has," Avis noted.

"Although the data collection doesn't hinge on Prince Philip's death, it would make things much easier if he passed during the intended heist. I'm going to contact Hans via email and try to find out his thinking about Philip; whether or not he would go to a memorial service for him. You can bet that it will be closed to the public and not televised."

Lionel felt the vibration of his cell phone. It was Jeffrey Olson.

"I can be there at 4:00?"

"Make it 4:30."

"Good enough."

Lionel looked at his watch.

"Can you believe it. I've had this watch for 20 years and I've only recently put a new battery in it," he said, shaking his head. "And that was just last year."

Avis laughed. "If it were less than ten years old, you'd have put five batteries in it by now."

"I have to go soon. One of our Davos associates is coming by at 4:30 to talk about the data collection."

Beverly nodded her head.

"Let me ask you something, two things actually. Do you think the COVID19 situation is a conspiracy, number one, and number two, will the end of it even get us back to some semblance of normalcy?"

Lionel nodded and grinned, downing the last of his second martini.

"I could drink those all afternoon! Beverly, but, I think we all forget that human beings are animals of a very high order . . . inquisitive, thinking, independent. We still have herd instincts and march to the herd we recognize and accept. I don't think COVID19 was a conspiracy as much as an opportunity that certain people, companies and countries have been planning for a long time," he said. "They just didn't know what it would be. There have been books and warnings and speeches about a coming pandemic for at least thirty years, even Bill Gates has been saying that."

"But not very loudly," Avis added.

Lionel nodded.

"Depending on who you believe . . . The masks, lockdowns, social distancing and hand washing were all mostly unnecessary, the deaths were exaggerated, ventilators over used and medical practices questioned, all in the name of a grand social engineering experiment that a bunch of fucking elite technocrats cooked up," Lionel said, his face turning bright red. He grabbed his head with both hands and looked down at the floor "They decided to see what they could get away with and it was a lot."

"And it was all aided by governments, big tech and big pharma using fake money and fake stimulus to create a needy society that willingly accepted government handouts over working or questioning anything the administration did. Everyone was trapped," Avis said. "It's like everyone has been drinking the Kool-Aid and now it is just starting to hit them."

"Never looked at it that way," Beverly said. "And then, the question becomes, who would they question to get any answers. The ones with the answers are the same opportunists."

"Not to worry. It's broken, but it can be fixed," Lionel reiterated. "It's just going to get messy."

"Lionel, I know you have to leave, but what do you make of the recent murders in several western cities?"

"I'm not sure what you're talking about, Avis. I haven't heard anything," Lionel said. He stood up and stopped a moment, placing a hand on the table's edge.

He smiled and shook his head. "Love those martinis."

CHAPTER THIRTY-SIX

"Avis, is Lionel sick? He doesn't look very good."

"I don't think so. Those ongoing headaches are blindsiding him, but he has been checked out by a neurologist who gave him some medication and advice which included cutting down on his drinking. Something he doesn't appear to be following," Avis said. "His boss called me yesterday but I missed it and I need to call him back."

"You going to Union Station?" Avis nodded. "Let's ride back together."

"Sounds like a plan. You ready to go?"

The police in Salt Lake City had picked up a man wearing green OR scrubs walking along the village green in front of the Mormon Temple. He refused at first to answer any questions until he spoke to an attorney, but when none came to his defense, he opened up about the time Ryan Snyder arrived. Eddie Davis was sixteen years old with a rap sheet as long as his arm for petty theft, stolen autos and solicitation. He'd read about James Quincy's death in the newspaper and decided it would be something different and fun to try. And a great way to become infamous in and out of Salt Lake City.

"You do realize that this crime is a serious charge and will land you behind bars for a long time," Ryan told him. "It appears that you acted alone so you have no one to blame but yourself."

"Well, don't forget about Mr. Beeswax," Eddie replied. "He is my partner in everything."

Ryan looked him right in the eyes.

"Does Mr. Beeswax live with you, Eddie?" Snyder said, not missing a beat.

"Yes. Always."

"What does Mr. Beeswax do, Eddie? Does he have a job?"

Eddie Davis nodded. "Yes, he does. He's my spiritual advisor and crime partner."

Ryan Snyder pulled the arresting officer aside outside the interrogation room.

"Is there judge on duty today, a juvenile judge?"

"Yes, Judge Endicott."

"Take the interview tape to him or her . . ."

" . . . Her."

"And get a court order for a mental health evaluation."

Lionel got out of his car just as a car he didn't recognize pulled up to the curb in front of his house. It was Jeffrey Olson. Inside the house, over coffee, Lionel explained the project. The more he explained, the more Jeffrey's face went from consternation to understanding to enlightenment. He smiled and nodded politely.

"I can't do it, but I know the perfect hacker who can," Jeffrey said. "I can arrange it. He's never been caught and he's not cheap, but he can definitely do this."

"Money is of lesser importance than his ability to do the job. Have you got a name?"

"Not until I talk to him, which I can do tonight. This person is already in Europe and there is a few hours difference. Can I call you this evening?"

"Yes, but timing is important. Maybe we should call together so I can give them all the details," Lionel said. "Can you come back?"

"How 'bout eight o'clock?"

"That works. Can you give me his or her first name?"

Jeffrey scratched his head. "I guess so . . . Mica."

When Jeffrey left, Lionel accessed his NSA account and entered 'Hackers' into the subject line. Two hundred and eighty-five thousand names came up ranked by country of origin, status, arrest record and age. Only three Mica's appeared, a woman and two men. The men were in prison. The remaining Mica was ranked twelfth. Mica Hrbek of the Netherlands, 23 years old, never been arrested and currently not wanted in any country.

Mica looked like she wasn't old enough to be out of high school, yet she held advanced degrees from a university in the Netherlands and another in Germany, ironically the same school where Hans Richter once taught. Lionel formed a broad smile and laughed out loud. She was not only perfectly qualified, but easy on the eye, too.

'Better to be young than old,' Lionel thought. *'She has to be up on the latest technology and techniques.'*

The phone rang. It was his private line into the NSA.

"Lionel, is Marilyn still traveling in Europe? There has been a breach in Paris, the favorite target of Al Qaeda and some others," John Jenkins said. "Have you heard from her recently?"

"Yesterday and she was on her way to Paris. What happened? Another bombing?"

"No, but this time they took hostages as a protest for the Israeli - Hamas conflict. Three Americans included," Jenkins said, trying to be positive. "Can you try calling her and then call me back?"

"Yes," Lionel's voice broke as he disconnected the call, trailing off to a soft sob. He quickly recovered and slammed the palm of his free hand into the dining table three times.

"Shit, shit, shit."

Marilyn's cell rang three times at five minute intervals and Lionel got voicemail each time. He tried a fourth time after ten minutes and she answered on the first ring.

"I was just getting ready to call you back," she said. There was a long sigh on the other end of the phone. "Is anything wrong. Our train was delayed from Munich and I just got to the hotel. I am freshening up to go sightseeing with our group."

"There was an incident earlier today on the Champs-Elysées and hostages were taken including three Americans. The captors are evidently protesting the Israeli - Palestinian conflict," Lionel conveyed. "Have you heard anything about it?"

"Somebody on the train said something about that, but we have not been given any official word. We'll be careful and I will find out what's going on," she said. "There are many more Gendarmes around the hotel than usual and that may explain why. I will call you this evening."

The line went dead and Lionel awoke suddenly and called John Jenkins.

"Hello, Lionel," John said, pleasantly. "Can I help you?"

"I thought you just called me?"

"Not today. Everything all right?"

"I think so. Sorry to bother you, John?"

He called Avis, who kept on top of these things better than Lionel, but it went to voicemail. He asked for a call back and in the meantime, John Jenkins called again.

"Lionel, I hate to be a pest, but are you sure you talked to Marilyn? The reason I ask is that some of the attackers got into hotel rooms by interfering remotely with the wireless lock codes after guests left their rooms and then terrorized them when they returned."

Lionel liked John, but he was known throughout the agency as a nosey pest, worse than a dog with a bone.

"Yes, John, I'm quite sure. She was calm, and sounded a little tired, but I didn't get the impression she was under any undue stress or frightened."

"OK. Well, if you talk to her again, let me know how that goes," he said. "Have you talked to Avis?"

"I just called him and asked him to call me back. I'll let you know," Lionel said and disconnected.

The call waiting was Avis.

"Looks like the Paris attack was a Hamas splinter group protesting the conflict in the Gaza Strip," Avis said. "The protesters are not well armed and are targeting foreign tourists by kidnapping, questioning them and then releasing them after taking their money, watches, credit cards, etcetera. "Avis said. "Is Marilyn all right?"

"Yes, she's fine." Lionel said. "Call jittery John so he will stop calling me. I will talk to Marilyn again tonight."

"Tell her to book the first flight to Geneva or Zurich and wait for you there until you get to Davos. Much safer environs there."

"Will do. When are you leaving for Davos?"

"Day after tomorrow. Talk soon. Got another call."

Lionel checked his watch. It was already 7:45 and Jeffery would be there soon. He wiped the sweat from his forehead with his handkerchief, gulped the rest of his beer and took a deep breath. That he blacked out again concerning the call to Marilyn, but he would have to deal with it later. He needed to do something about the blackouts.

'I'll worry about that when this other matter is over and done.'

He took his empty beer bottle to the kitchen when the doorbell rang. It was Jeffrey Olson and a young woman that Lionel suspected was Mica Hrbek.

"Hello, Jeffrey and hello Mica," he said. They looked at each other, but neither flinched. "Thanks so much for coming. Can I get you something to drink?"

They both declined.

They talked for two hours. Mica was impressive and knew what she was talking about, had a preliminary game plan and was quite willing to listen to any ideas Lionel had to offer.

"One thing that is critical is that the digital theft occur as if nothing is wrong on the user side," Lionel said. "What I mean is the capture of data, logs, files, images and algorithms must not be detected, transferred or captured while anyone anywhere can use the same data, logs, files, images and algorithms."

Mica laughed a little and Lionel gave her a strange look.

"You're talking about a Bot, Mr. Kittring. They're easy to build and can gather whatever information we tell it to gather," Jeffrey said, so as not to upset Lionel.

"Ahhh, I get it now. Thanks for explaining."

Lionel grabbed three beers from the refrigerator.

While Jeffrey and Mica drank up, Lionel went to his home office on the other side of the house, cut them a check from a private, Cayman Island account for $50,000 made out to Mica and gave them each an untraceable Black American Express card for expenses.

"See you both in Davos in three weeks. Stay at a local hotel because the major establishments will be booked solid for WSG. Meet me in the town square at the appointed time," Lionel said. "Use these cell phones. Press @@606 to activate them and leave your personal phones at home. And be very careful. The Swiss are very smart, cunning and ruthless. Be especially careful with overly friendly young men or women. They aren't your friend. I will introduce you to the other team members at our project rendezvous."

"Actually, I thought we might go a little early to scope out the target and get the lay of the land," Jeffrey said.

"Good idea. I will get there as soon as I can," Lionel said. "In the meantime, keep me posted on your progress and let me know if you need anything."

CHAPTER THIRTY-SEVEN

Richard Dexter was British in every way a man of his stature could be. He was tall and only a little paunchy with a perfect tan who wore three piece suits in the summertime. His demeanor was cheery, unusual for a former CIA agent who joined the NSA after working for MI6 through the disastrous end of the Vietnam War. He was curious, intelligent, polite and well regarded by his peers.

"Thank you for coming Avis. I didn't want to do this over the phone."

"My pleasure, Richard. Good to see you again," Avis said. "Sounds like Beverly and I are not the only ones concerned about Lionel."

"Likewise. And you're right about many folks being concerned about Lionel. Did he tell you he resigned from the NSA?"

"Yes."

"He did not resign and he was not fired, but this is the kind of thinking I have been dealing with since he was shot last year."

"Exactly. We have all seen a change in him since then and I think much of it came from the Oxycodone he was devouring for several weeks."

"Well, the bottom line is, we all need to keep close tabs on him because his thinking right now is quite delusional and he is a danger not only to others, but himself," Dexter said. "I found some of his diaries recently and the entries are quite dark."

"Can we meet again soon to take a look?"

Richard pulled up his calendar. "Tomorrow afternoon?"

"I'll be here at one o'clock."

CHAPTER THIRTY-EIGHT

The next afternoon, Richard Dexter and Avis sat in Richard's office looking over some of Lionel's diaries.

"I brought an old diary to give some flavor to what Lionel was thinking back then. This first diary is from 2010, the first year he kept a diary," Dexter said. "It is a daily diary, but many of the dates have no entries which is, I understand, quite normal for someone just starting to journal and the entries are more about socializing, dating, drinking and partying than the affairs of the world."

Avis looked through the entries quickly and had to green with Dexter that it was pretty mundane.

"Did you bring a more recent diary since the shooting?"

"Yes, here is the one from the day after the election," Richard Dexter said, grimacing some. "It's quite enlightening in tone and content."

"How could anyone in their right mind re-elect Donald Trump? We're in for the election ride of a lifetime with myriad lawsuits, court filings, protests and maybe even some violence," Lionel wrote. "Trump will not accept defeat or take this gently or even listen to reason. It will be a dark day for America."

Avis opened another diary.

"The answer lies in getting rid of the oppressors so America can operate as it should. This includes the Feds, certain members of Congress, billionaires, doctors, scientists, the White House and WH staff and many, many others. The time to start planning is now to get rid of the WSG, the IMF, International Bank of Settlements, the World Bank, and all the scoundrel type spy agencies around the world."

The entries were night and day, almost like two different people had written them. Lionel had gone from being a flag waving patriot to a treasonous zealot with entries about the real Donald Trump to the vaccine fiasco to Hans Richter and the World Solutions Group and everything in between. The final entry talked about how bad things were getting and how he planned to do something about it, starting with the scoundrels involved in COVID19.

He shoved the remaining diaries back across Richard's desk.

"Did you notice anything different in the most recent diaries?" Dexter said, return the diaries to a storage box.

Avis rubbed his chin. "The latest diaries are all full. Every page is written on."

Richard Dexter smiled and nodded. "Exactly!"

"How does Lionel get away with saying things like this?"

"It's called the Constitution. Besides, this is nothing more than the rantings of an ill man that is talking through his medication. He hasn't named names or threatened anyone, so trying to do anything about it would get us laughed out of court."

Avis nodded.

"The problem is, Avis," Dexter said. "Lionel has the experience, the skill, the connection and spymaster smarts to pull something off. Keep your eyes wide open."

CHAPTER THIRTY-NINE

Avis sneaked out of Richard Dexter's office to join Lionel in the horseshoe conference room. They were waiting for Beverly, Charlene and Tomas to arrive. Lionel had asked Avis to come early, he wanted to get his input about Jeffrey Olson and Mica Hrbek. The meeting with Richard Dexter was brief and the timing couldn't have been better.

"Do you think Don knows what's going on?" Avis said. "He has an uncanny way of finding things out."

"I don't know. Jeffrey never mentions his grandfather. I do know he and Mica are old enough to make their own decisions, twenty-one and twenty-three respectively," Lionel added. "There was a complete NSA profile on Mica. She's never been caught, no arrest record and no allegiance to the Dark web."

"All I can say is if they get caught, there will be hell to pay. I think you need to make sure Xing Ma sticks close to them," Avis noted. "The one thing in your favor is that Don Olson has no use for Hans Richter."

Tomas held the door for Beverly and Charlene. Beverly gave an overview of the course of action, who the players were that would be diverting attention away from World Solutions Group employees, hacker's responsibilities and how the ending would play out. Lionel explained the situation with Prince Philip and how that could, unfortunately, work to their advantage. He called it their 'Ace-in-the-Hole'.

"The procurement team is being led by a trusted advisor of mine and will be using members of my team to carry out the digital extraction," Lionel reiterated, never mentioning the words theft or robbery. "The digital team leaves tomorrow and will work primarily behind the scenes to infiltrate the data access required and unlock security codes."

There was no mention of explosives as a backup plan and Avis spoke up.

"I will be there, too, helping any of you get what you need when you need it and helping the digital team by running interference for them."

Beverly looked at Charlene and Tomas.

"Tomas and Charlene. You will accompany me to the concert and report on it like any good journalist would. You'll work closely with Avis Marsden throughout," Beverly said. "If I'm successful in getting an interview with Hans Richter, both of you will attend that, too, and record the interview . . . One in writing and one of you digitally."

"OK, everyone, that's all I've got. Anyone have any questions?" Lionel looked at each person in the room.

Tomas raised his hand.

"What happens if someone gets caught? What do we say if one of us is asked about what we're doing, or worse, hauled off and interrogated."

"Good question. If you're caught, you are entitled to one phone call like in the United States, so call me or Avis. Make sure you have our cell phone numbers in your phone. Officially, you're part of the concert press corp and you don't know anything about anything else."

"Don't be heroic and don't be smart as in don't be a smart-ass. Cooperate if push comes to shove." Avis added and winked. "Anything else?"

No one budged.

"Enjoy the trip. Switzerland is a beautiful country and if you've never been, have a look around. Euro pass is very inexpensive. Act like a tourist."

Lionel stood up and walked over to the big mahogany conference room doors.

"Meeting adjourned."

There was a small table next to the doors with black travel bags marked for each team member by name. As everyone left, Lionel handed out their personalized bag, tore off the name tag and shook their hand.

Late that afternoon, Avis got a call from Xing Ma. It was on his NSA line, so he took it.

"Hello, Avis. Calling in to make sure everything is still a go," Ma said. "I was able to get a security guard to give me the nickel tour of the WEF facility so I at least I know where things are. She told me that she would be on duty for the next several nights because she is the partner of the head of WEF security and they had a falling out. And long story short, she's planning a little revenge on him," Ma said, laughing. "She wanted to come back to the hotel with me, but I resisted, but I think she will be helpful to us on the digital raid."

Avis chuckled.

"Just like you, Ma, to have that kind of encounter. Be careful, she could be a setup. We have no idea who may be lurking about, but you know, if you have to keep her happy, mums the word on this end." Ma laughed and Avis laughed. "Pants on."

CHAPTER FORTY

Ryan Snyder returned to San Francisco to again work on the murders that were beginning to haunt him. Eddie Davis in Salt Lake received a mental evaluation and was deemed unfit to stand trial for attempted murder or any other crime for that matter.

What bothered Snyder about the other cases which all had similar MO's, methods and outcomes was what type of person had the personality to carry out such heinous crimes with such precision and without warning. Such a person understood the justice system, killing methods, the importance of timing and a precise, although chilling, personality. That person was involved on some sort of police work, most likely undercover, or was a war veteran, spy or worked daily in such an environment. So, the pool to work from was every police officer in the country, CIA agent, NSA type and even the FBI. He needed some input to go forward.

The news on Wednesday, April 7, involved a massive apartment fire that destroyed a block of exclusive apartments in the old part of Davos that was going through extensive restoration as more and more young people clamored for a spot in Davos' booming economy. Many of the apartments were undergoing renovation, some were occupied and some were held as lucrative investments by well-heeled real estate types from across the globe. One such destroyed property was the apartment Beverly was supposed to occupy during her visit to Davos. Had she arrived as originally scheduled, she would no longer have to worry about concerts, the Treasury department, Harris, Haley, Denise or Reese. Luckily, the unit was empty, but the neighbors had to scramble in the middle of the night to escape the voluminous blaze. The mayor of Davos hinted in his press conference that arson could not be ruled out.

The fire had been on the digital theft agenda for a long time, intended to be a diversion from the task at hand and buy some time for the break-in. With the situation in England now front and center around the world it became an unexpected insurance benefit to the building owners. Lionel and Xing Ma smiled at each other as Beverly handed the keys over to Tomas. Beverly was concentrating on preparations for the concert, something she'd done hundreds of times.

The WSG was winding down and a large crowd persisted as they looked forward to what amounted to a reunion between the Blaze and Beverly, especially after the disastrous start to their ill-fated world tour earlier. The WSG was abuzz with anticipation that one of the world's greatest female rock stars was going to perform for them.

Beverly was upbeat and smiling when she got to the meeting. She thanked everyone for coming, thanked Lionel for his leadership and introduced Tomas and Charlene to the others. Everyone left pumped up for the concert and their forthcoming tasks as they said good night and went their separate ways.

Beverly was leaving the conference room when she saw a call from Darden.

"What's up?"

"Hi, Beverly. Time has a way of slipping away between midnight feedings, diapers and trying to run a household," he said, laughing nervously into the phone.

"I get it," she said. "I have decided to dedicate this concert to Q. Under other circumstances, he would've been here. What do you think?"

"I think it's fitting and a wonderful way to honor that great man," Darden said. "Go for it! You think it will make Hans Richter mad?"

"There will be so much going on by the time we get to the concert, he won't care one way or the other."

"Got it. How are the last minute preparations shaping up?"

"Couldn't be better. Wish you and Cynthia were here . . . And your daughter, too."

"Next year."

"That's the spirit. Later."

CHAPTER FORTY-ONE

Ma gave Jeffrey and Mica a tour of the WSG facilities courtesy of Giselle, Xing Ma's new security friend, dinner and lunch date, soulmate and soon to be lover. While she chattered away with Jeffrey and Mica, Ma was silently measuring footsteps between doors, checking, photographing and counting surveillance cameras, unlocking doors with his phone, remembering air vent locations and paying attention to all the external entrances. When Giselle questioned him, Ma told her that he was recording existing conditions to propose a new security system.

When they finished, Ma promised to take Giselle to lunch after her shift ended and said he thought it would be nicer and quieter in his hotel room. She agreed and told Ma that she couldn't entertain him at her house because she had no idea if or when her estranged partner might return even though he had moved out. She wouldn't change the locks because that would make matters worse. She wanted to spend time alone with Ma and agreed to lunch in his hotel room.

"Nice meeting you, Jeffrey and Mica. Enjoy your vacation," Giselle said. "Ma, I will text you when I'm leaving my shift."

Ryan consulted with other members of the FBI team on how to proceed. The best suggestion was to sort of work in reverse and talk to the directors of the CIA, FBI and NSA to develop profiles of potential persons that fit Snyder's proposed personality profiles. Time was of the essence because no one had any idea when the killer might strike again. The team started calling, emailing and texting each agency for a more detailed discussion. Snyder assigned himself the task of contacting Richard Dexter.

Ma was very organized and had a checklist of things that had to happen in order for the digital theft to be successful. He and his two hackers went to the offices Lionel had rented. It had been swept for electronic bugs and re-wired so Mica could work from there. Ma went through his list:

Get IP address on all the WEF members - Done
    Get all the IP addresses for the FAANG companies - Done
    Test fire the Malware - Done
Prepare Note and Unlock Protocol - In process
    Review digital strategy with Mica and Jeffrey - TBD
    Emergency exit strategy*- Done

*Guns had been properly obtained and permitted and getting a gun permit in Switzerland was like applying for citizenship in the United States . . . Lengthy, difficult and time consuming. Somehow it happened.

Mica's malware protocol daisy-chained to other computers as they were opened. The machines would still function for any user regardless of what was happening behind the scenes. Monitoring the malware operation would be done in Switzerland and at points in the United States once the operation began. If the digital theft yielded no consequential results, the malware operation would be halted and no one outside the operation would be the wiser.

Ma reiterated that all of the malware operations were contingent on what the digital theft uncovered. Jeffrey and Mica were to use the time during the theft to set up their computers in order to proceed with the malware attack, check and double check their wifi connections and protocols to make sure they could disconnect from any and all technical sites they captured at will.

"OK, good. Now get a good night's sleep and be ready to roll tomorrow at 8:00 pm," Ma said. "Mica, you will go with me and Jeffrey you will stay behind and receive the technical input from Mica. Try to do something fun during the day and if you can, take a nap. I know that sounds corny, but you'd be amazed how refreshing a 20 minute power nap can be. It will be a long night and you don't want to miss Beverly Swift's concert with the Blaze. She is amazing on-stage and you won't believe it's the same woman."

CHAPTER FORTY-TWO

Tomas and Charlene stopped at the Summit bar on their way back to the hotel. Charlene always seemed happy and interested in the here and now. Tomas had decided that she wasn't so bad after all, especially when he found out that she had a younger gay brother who almost died from AIDS that she nursed back to health the summer between Vassar and Harvard.

"How do you like Switzerland? Have you ever been here before?" Tomas asked her at the little standup table where they waited for their drinks.

"It's fine and really beautiful and I hope I can convince Beverly to let me come back to DC a little late in order to see some of the country besides the inside of a convention hall and my hotel room," she said. "Maybe if we both hit her up for it, she'll let us stay a longer."

Charlene was throwing that killer smile on him.

Tomas looked around the bar and then said, "Yes, that would be nice. I'll be right back."

A man at the bar was looking at Tomas and motioned him over. He returned ten minute later.

"Well?"

"Actually, he was asking about you? He thought maybe I was your boyfriend or husband or whatever!" Tomas offered.

"Did you tell him whatever?" Charlene said, giggling. And then Tomas started laughing.

"You know, I never used to like you very much, but, you're all right."

"Well, thank you very much. I like you, too. But, you know, you didn't hide your disdain very well."

Tomas raised his wine glass toward Charlene.

"Here's to Auld Lang Syne," he said. "And a new chapter in both our lives."

Bernie Dennis was an old friend of Lionel Kitting's and supplied news to him about Britain whenever he could. He'd been the one to alert Lionel of Prince Philip's rapidly deteriorating health. When the phone rang, Lionel fumbled to see the time, having been sound asleep for hours. It was 2:30 a.m. on April 9.

"Lionel, old chap, sorry to wake you, but the prince has departed this earth for a better place," Bernie snuffled to keep from crying. "I will let you know the funeral arrangements as soon as they are released."

"So sorry to hear that my friend," Lionel managed, knowing that nothing he said would be sufficient, meaningful or remembered. His earlier headache was suddenly gone.

"I have many calls to make old chap so I will not tarry. I will speak to you soon," Bernie managed to say before the tears rolled down his face. "Good night ... And sorry to wake you."

Lionel was wide awake now and decided to get some work done now that Prince Philip was gone. As hard as it was to hear of the Royal death, it would make things much easier for data collection if Hans Richter could be convinced to attend whatever service there would be for the Philip.

Lionel showered and shaved and sent an email to Hans encouraging him to attend the service for his old friend and hunting partner. At 4:30 a.m., Lionel got some of the best news he could hope for when Gerard Meister replied saying

"Hans had also been informed of Prince Philip's death and will be departing for the UK on Monday, April 12 for services. He thought about canceling the Blaze concert but decided to hold it on Sunday, the 11th, instead. Hans would like to invite you to a reception honoring Beverly Swift on the 11th at 6:00 p.m. at his home in Davos. RSVP is not required."

Lionel was so ecstatic that he wanted to dance, so he stood up and waltzed around his hotel room with an imaginary partner named Marilyn, humming an Austrian waltz he'd learned as a kid and had completely forgotten until just then. When the dance was out of his system, he sat back down and quickly replied that he would be delighted to attend the reception.

Resisting the urge to email the digital team with his good, but bittersweet, news he ordered breakfast and dressed while the order was being prepared. He called Avis at 6:00 a.m. to tell him what had transpired in Britain and that Hans Richter would be attending the services for the prince. He invited Avis to come to his room to share breakfast. In the meantime, he called Marilyn, but got her voicemail.

When Avis arrived, looking like he had just stepped off the cover of GQ magazine, they toasted the news of Hans' temporary departure with cold coffee. When breakfast arrived they enjoyed the early morning feast. As they were about to turn the World News program on the television, there was a knock on the door.

Captain Terrence Sansby, Sven Alston, the hotel general manager and another man Lionel had never seen before were standing in the doorway. Alston introduced him as Bjorn Somers, the local medical examiner. Beverly was standing in the doorway with tears rolling down her face.

"What on earth is going on, Beverly?" Avis gasped.

"Tomas found Charlene dead in her room this morning when she didn't answer her wakeup call or his texts, " she said, her eyes bloodshot from crying. "Sven was kind enough to let him in her room."

"Call Tomas right now and get him over here," Lionel demanded. "He may have been the last person to see her alive. Does anyone know what happened?"

CHAPTER FORTY-THREE

Tomas arrived three minutes after Beverly called him. He had a black and blue mouse under his right eye and a cut on his left cheek about two inches long that was open slightly along its edge. It appeared to be a fresh wound that had not been treated. "What happened to you?" Beverly said, examining Tomas' swollen eye and cheek.

"Charlene and I went to this bar called the 'Summit' to have a nightcap on the way back to the hotel. A few minutes into it, this guy at the bar called me over to ask about Charlene. A white guy," Tomas said, rolling his neck around to keep it loose. "Charlene and I were celebrating the fact that we really did like each other after all. We were just enjoying the evening and each other."

Sansby, Alston and Bjorn Somers left Lionel's room to go the crime scene as Tomas was finishing his description of what happened at the Summit Bar. They indicated they would be back to talk to Tomas. Lionel told Avis to go down to that bar and find out if there was any security camera footage available. He gave him 500 Euros.

"This might refresh their memories," he said. "Bring the tape back here if it exists."

Avis nodded. "Be back as soon as I can."

He motioned Lionel closer.

"Did you bump your head. There's a trickle of blood coming from your forehead."

Lionel felt his forehead and came away with a little blood on his finger.

"Thanks. I'll take care of it."

Avis held the door for the medical examiner and the hotel manager who returned to question Tomas.

"Excuse me, folks, but I'm Sven Alston, the hotel manager and this is Bjorn Somers, the medical examiner. So sorry for your loss," he said, looking directly at Beverly as he spoke. "We've been to the deceased's room and she is dead. We need some time to check out the crime scene, but ask that none of you leave until after we come back here for further questioning. Who saw her last?"

"That would be me," Tomas said. "I left her about two a.m. I think I may have been the last person to see her alive."

Bjorn looked at Tomas. "When I come back, I'll have a look at those wounds."

"Thank you," Tomas said.

Sven and Dr. Somer left again. Beverly plopped into a chair and started to cry, shaking her head and muttering about how unfair it all was.

"Tomas, you were saying something about a nightcap?" Lionel said. "You and Charlene were celebrating . . ."

"Oh, yeah. Well, the stranger from the bar came over and joined in our revelry. Bought another round and started talking with Charlene like I didn't exist," he said, checking his wounds in the mirror above the clothes chest. "He whispered something in her ear and she told me she was leaving with him. I mean, I've never partied with Charlene before, but she never struck me as the type who would leave a bar with a man she'd only known for maybe thirty minutes. So, I paid for our first round and left with them."

"So, what about your cheek and eye?" Beverly said. Tears rolled down her face. "How'd that happen?"

"Well, when we got to Charlene's room the other guy said this party was only for two and punched me in the eye. I hit the hotel door frame and cut my cheek," he said. "The guy apologized immediately and escorted me to my room on the fifth floor, gave me a couple aspirin and tucked me in. There must've been another pill besides aspirin because I was out like a light in like ten seconds until I woke this morning. I immediately called Charlene's room phone, cell phone and I texted her and that's when I realized something was wrong."

"Thanks, Tomas, I know that was not easy to recount," Lionel said.

Avis returned, tape in hand. He popped it into the video recorder that Lionel had ordered from the front desk and fast forwarded to a man standing at the bar as Tomas approached him. They watched the replay just the way Tomas described it and then watched it again.

"That guy looks just like Wyatt Douglas, my realtor in DC. Could that be?" Beverly screeched. "But, why on earth would he be in Davos?"

Lionel and Avis knew the answer. Don Olson sent him to keep tabs on Beverly and Avery Saxton, but they wanted to spare Beverly the details. They both shrugged and grabbed a cup of coffee from the breakfast cart.

"Whoever he is, let's just hope he's still around because someone has a lot of explaining to do and he would be a good place to start," Lionel said, rubbing his temples. "Let's ask Tomas if he ever mentioned his name and then start checking around. We can start with the hotel desk clerks here. Let's go have a look at Charlene's room. And, Avis, before I forget, do you have an old picture of Wendell Bennett? Anything more than two years old? I overheard a conversation earlier this morning down in the lobby and one of the men identified himself as Avery Saxton."

Avis rubbed his chin.

"I'll have to look in my database. There might be something from when Beverly ran for president," he said. "I'll join you down in Charlene's room in a few minutes. I want to get some stills made of the tape to ask around. There's a camera store across the street."

Beverly and Lionel went to the second floor which had been cordoned off the entire length on Charlene's side of the hotel. Tomas went in the room, did an about face, covered his mouth and bent over, bracing himself in the doorway. He didn't look too good and took deep breaths to keep from throwing up.

Charlene was lying naked on her back with her legs spread like she was making snow angels on the bedspread. There were no marks on her body, no bruises or cuts and nothing to indicate trauma of any sort. One of the bed pillows was crumpled next to her right arm. Bjorn had closed her eyes and was talking on his cell phone to the police. He was nodding and saying 'yes sir' and 'no sir' to the party on the other end. He hung up after one final nod.

"Looks like she was asphyxiated with the pillow. Notice there are no other markings on the body indicating trauma or a struggle and her body is limp like she was quite relaxed or drunk or drugged," Dr. Somers said. "Although rigor mortis is starting to set in a high blood alcohol level would slow that down."

"Any indication of intercourse or sexual mutilation?" Lionel said.

"Yes, she had sex before she died, but she was not raped," Bjorn said. "It was consensual. There's nothing to suggest trauma to the vaginal walls or her stomach or a struggle with someone."

Avis came into the room along with Tomas.

"Tomas," Bjorn Somers said, looking directly at him. "Would you characterize Charlene's mental state as being drunk when you left her and the other man?"

"Not at all. She hadn't had enough to drink while I was around, but I don't know what happened when I left. I was sidetracked with my eye and cheek."

"Pictures from the hotel security cameras look like a Walter Gibbons was registered at the hotel, but has since checked out," Sven Alston said. "His picture on the hotel security tapes match the image from the bar. We called the airport and they have pictures of him and will detain him until the local and International authorities can question him if he's there."

"Avis, why don't you and Beverly head to the airport?" Lionel said. "If it is her realtor we can kill two birds with one stone and ask some questions. Terrence Sansby can tell you who to ask for at the terminal."

Beverly nodded and turned to Lionel.
"What on earth did you do to your forehead?"

CHAPTER FORTY-FOUR

When the police arrived, Lionel went to the bathroom to inspect his head wound and apply something to it. He cleaned the wound, applied a cortisone cream and a bandage. He took the stairs two at a time to the second floor to Charlene's room.

It took two hours for the police to dust for prints, collect DNA, re-examine the body, take pictures, question guests in adjacent rooms and release the body to the medical examiner after concluding the same cause and time of death and sexual interaction as Dr. Bjorn Somer had done. Bjorn reluctantly got the task of calling the family in Connecticut to break the news to them. Beverly went with him and talked to Gail, Charlene's mother.

She had to hold the phone away from her ear when Bjorn broke the news to Gail Evans. Beverly managed to get their address and the name of a funeral home amid the screams, wailing and general confusion such news brings. The medical examiner was shaken from the call. He took Charlene's body down the freight elevator to the city morgue where it would be prepped for the return trip to the United States. Her other belongings would accompany the casket.

When Beverly arrived at the airport after arguing with Lionel about going late, she was met with roadblocks, sensitive security measures and an army of police cars blocking the entrance to the American Airlines terminal. The Davos airport wasn't that big and it quickly became clear to everyone that something extraordinary was going on. Beverly found Avis sitting in the backseat of a police cruiser.

"Has Janet left Switzerland, yet?" Avis said.

"Not yet. She's planning to leave right after the concert. I have been trying to reach her, but I think she has her phone turned off," Beverly said. "I think she may be going to London for Prince Philip's memorial service. She must know by now what happened."

"Maybe not," Avis said. "Don't you think she would have called you by now?"

The police were about the only people left in the airport. All the ticket counters were shuttered, the entrances blocked off and all concessions closed. The lead investigator told Beverly and Avis that only one passenger so far had even remotely matched the photo and description of the man in the videotape. He had been questioned and released to board his flight. Avis shook his head and Beverly shrugged.

"Could it be that Charlene had sex with that guy and then someone else actually killed her?" Avis said.

"Or, the guy she met at the bar was wearing a disguise," Beverly noted. "There is only one way to know."

"DNA." They said together.

"The police need to search his or her room, too," Avis said. "Let's get back to the hotel. Hopefully, that room hasn't been cleaned yet."

A police captain was waiting for them when they got back to the hotel.

"We checked the suspect's room and found some disguise material . . . cheek enhancers, makeup and a hairpiece and glasses. We also found some partial fingerprints on a bathroom glass, the shower controls, and door handles," the captain said. "We're running a match with the prints found in the girl's room as we speak."

"Has this person checked out of the hotel?" Beverly said.

"Yes. At the normal check out time," Sansby said. "Which leads me to think he's not the killer. We think the killer would've left before Charlene's body was found."

"And, perhaps she or he did, captain," Beverly replied.

Captain Sansby's cell phone went off. He answered, nodded his head a couple times, jotted some info on his notepad and disconnected.

"We took some saliva from the bathroom glass," Captain Sansby said after returning his phone to his pocket. "The DNA found on the glass and the DNA found on the victim match. The fingerprints do not match. The prints match a DC realtor named Wyatt Douglas, but not the DNA, so he couldn't have killed her."

"That means the killer could still be in Switzerland or even here in Davos. Has anyone checked the car rental agencies?" Avis said.

"We thought of that already," Sansby said. "There has not been a car rented in Davos in almost a week and no renter named Douglas, Gibbons, Smith or any other name has tried to rent a car," he said. "The attendees at the WSG are shuttled to and from the airport as they wish. My suspicion is that whoever did this is still in Davos."

"Any word on who the fingerprints belong to?"

"There were several sets on some items like the shower curtain, door hardware, and bed linens, so the FBI is still working on it. It is hard to extract prints from fabric after a few minutes. Has anyone questioned Tomas extensively? Why were he and Charlene here to begin with?"

"They both work for me at the Treasury Department and were investigating various aspects of the WSG related to COVID19, the Great Reset and Dr. Richter," Beverly said. "Sorry, but I'm off to rehearse for the concert tomorrow night."

"Is there any concern that Tomas is a suspect?" Captain Sansby said.

Lionel and Avis both shook their heads. "Maybe we should look at the security tape again and see if there was someone else watching Tomas, Wyatt and Charlene who could've followed them back to the hotel," Sansby said.

CHAPTER FORTY-FIVE

The tape showed two people, a man and a woman, standing next to Wyatt, talking to each other. The woman had been with the man when he joined Charlene and Tomas at the standup table. When they left thirty minutes later, the woman appears to follow them out of the bar. On a second monitor, the hotel security tape came on and it showed the three partiers going to the elevator, but does not show them getting on any elevator. A few seconds later the woman goes to the elevator lobby and darts into a stairwell.

"Any idea who the woman is?" Captain Sansby said. He enlarged her image to a profile view. "I'll get our technician to rotate the image when we're done here to see her face, but she obviously knew Ms. Evan's room number because she never followed them into the elevator or left the stairwell. Maybe she worked at conference registration or the hotel."

"Or pretended to work at either place," Avis said. "Let's get the profile turned and send the photos to Interpol."

"Excellent idea," Lionel said. "I just got a text message from Beverly. She sent me a stateside phone number for Gail Evans, Charlene's mother, and said it was urgent. I will call her back."

"Mrs. Evans, this is Lionel Kittring, in Davos, Switzerland, and let me first say how sorry I am about Charlene. I am working with the Treasury Department to find out what happened," Lionel stated. "Do you know anyone who would want to do her harm?"

Gail Evans laughed nervously.

"Charlene was a talented, beautiful, happy African American woman using her gifts to help America, so I'm sure there are many 'Any ones' out there who would want to see her fail."

"Any disgruntled boyfriends, lovers, associates or classmates that you know of?"

"Before Charlene left for Switzerland she was pretty jazzed about some things she was investigating. She sent us a copy of her findings," she said. "I'm sure it's still on her laptop."

Her laptop was the last thing on anyone's mind and to Lionel's knowledge, no one had found it or looked at its contents.

"OK. We'll take a look, but perchance if it's not there, I will be reaching out to get the copy she sent to you. Thank you for your time, Ms. Evans."

"No worries. Thank you for reaching out." The line went silent.

Lionel found Captain Sansby in the detective bullpen talking to his charges about the case.

"Did anyone find Ms. Evan's laptop? Her mother said that right before she came to Switzerland she found something disturbing in her research and sent a copy to her parents," Lionel said. "I don't remember anything about her laptop. Do any of you?"

CHAPTER FORTY-SIX

"It's possible Tomas picked it up," Sansby said. "Easily forgotten in all the turmoil."

Lionel called Tomas on his cell phone and woke him from a nap. He was groggy and a little reticent to talk until Avis took the phone from Lionel to tell him that the killer might be someone at the conference.

"By the way, have you seen Charlene's computer? It was not in her room when the police examined the body."

"Yes, I have it," Tomas said, excitedly. "She asked me to take it when I left her room last night because she had some research on it that she didn't want lost or stolen."

"Do you know how to get into her computer?"

"She texted me the password, but I haven't tried to open it," he said cautiously. "Do you want me to try?"

"No. Bring it over to the police station. A car will pick you up in ten minutes," Avis noted. "Put it in your computer bag. Stay in your room and I will call you when we get there."

Tomas packed up the computer and waited for Avis to call. The message light on his hotel phone was blinking and a female voice said,

"This is the front desk, Mr. Hogan. Your transportation to the airport is here. Please bring your luggage down or call the front desk at #400 if you need assistance."

The call was thirty minutes old. He went to the door to make sure no one was lurking in the hallway. He never requested transportation to the airport at any time. When his cell phone rang, it startled him. He asked the officer to come to his room on the fifth floor. He told the officer to knock three times. The room phone rang again, but he ignored it.

The police took the laptop case. Tomas noticed when he stepped out of the room the elevator doors opened and closed with no one getting on or off the fifth floor. When he and the police officer got to the lobby, a woman got off another elevator and walked in the opposite direction from them, holding her covered head so as to conceal her face to the security camera. She wore white gloves.

At the police station, Lionel had the picture of the woman from the bar security tape fully rendered and slightly enlarged.

"Tomas, have you ever seen this woman before?"

Tomas nodded.

"Yes, she worked the registration desk the day we arrived. She checked us all in and insisted that she show us to our rooms," he said.

"I caught a glimpse of a woman over at the hotel just now and I think this is her," the officer who escorted Tomas to the police station offered.

"OK, let's grab her for questioning," Sansby said. "And get a match on those fingerprints. Mr. Hogan, I am placing you in protective custody until I feel confident we have the right suspect and you are out of danger."

The woman from the picture cooperated fully until they started asking questions about Charlene's murder, then she clammed up and demanded to have a lawyer present. She spoke with a slight accent and was dazzlingly pretty, perfect skin with a taunt jawline and slender neck, impeccably dressed and cool under fire. She reminded everyone of Audrey Hepburn.

Lionel noticed that she wore white dress gloves that were a part of her ensemble or maybe concealed something about her hands. Avis guessed this was not her first confrontation with the authorities. Her attorney arrived within ten minutes of being called.

The woman relaxed when the attorney arrived. She started to cooperate, admitting that she worked the registration table as a temporary employee of the World Solutions Group. Her name was Sylvia Lindstrom from Quebec, Canada. Avis called her name into Interpol and within seconds they confirmed her identity. She had a tidy rap sheet primarily for embezzlement and fraud, but nothing close to assault or murder.

"So far so good, Lionel."

He nodded.

"Ms. Lindstrom, did you know Charlene Evans before you met her at the registration table in the hotel lobby?" Sansby said.

She looked at her lawyer and he nodded that it was all right to answer.

"No, but I did see her later in the evening at a local bar."

"Did you follow her back to her hotel?"

"Yes."

"Did you go into the hotel?"

"Yes." She looked at her attorney. He nodded again.

"Did you go to her room with her?"

"Don't answer that question," her attorney said.

"OK. Did you see her again after you entered the hotel?"

"No."

Sansby nodded to Avis.

"Ms. Lindstrom. Do you always wear gloves?" Avis said.

She looked to her attorney for help and he nodded again.

"Most of the time," she said. "I have severe eczema and my hands itch and flake all the time." She took off one glove. Her hand was bright red, like she washed dishes all the time or had been in a fire at some point that damaged her hands. They were swollen and the skin flaked off."

Captain Sansby leaned over to the other officer.

"Check the hotel tape again and pay attention to her hands."

"Thank you, Ms. Lindstrom, that's all the questions we have for now, but we do ask that you not leave town until we have released you," Sansby said "We may have more questions."

"No worries, captain. I'll be here."

Ms. Lindstrom and her attorney left and Captain Sansby looked at Lionel and scratched his head.

"Got any ideas?"

"First, I think Tomas Hogan needs to get into Charlene's computer to see if he can find the unidentified information she sent her parents," he said urgently. "We need to check the hotel security tapes again especially the stairwells. Something tells me someone got into Charlene's room, possibly when she was asleep and killed her. I don't rule out either Tomas or Sylvia Lindstrom. But, first where are we on the fingerprints?"

Detective Thatcher spoke up.

"I'm afraid not very encouraging, sir. The only prints they found were for Tomas on the bathroom door handle and the flush handle, very poor prints of the cleaning staff on the bed linens, doors and sink and Ms. Evan's prints everywhere else that we found prints."

"Thanks, Noah. So, let's find some other tapes and let Tomas Hogan play detective on her laptop," Sansby said. "The concert security force needs to take a rehearsal at the venue."

The meeting broke up and Avis went to see Tomas and tell him what needed to be done. Beverly caught up with him as he was going to the cell block.

"Are you done rehearsing?"

"Nothing left but the shouting and to let the fat lady sing. We sound good if I do say so myself especially since we haven't played together in a while" Beverly said, smiling. "I do need to find a piano tuner, though."

"I'd try the front desk at the hotel," Avis said. "There's a grand piano in the lobby that someone plays."

"Thanks. Made any progress on Charlene's case?"

"Not enough. I'm on my way back to Tomas' cell to ask him to check Charlene's laptop and find the email she sent her parents," Avis noted. "They're going to release him to my custody."

"Why did they arrest Tomas?" Beverly said.

"Protective custody, that's all, but he hasn't been ruled out as a suspect."

"Yes, and unfortunately, they didn't have the best relationship, professionally."

"Don't open that can of worms."

"No worries. I've got to find a piano tuner."

"Have you had a chance to look at Lionel's cell phone?" Avis said.

"Not yet. I keep waiting for him to go take a nap or leave it laying around," Beverly responded.

"I will encourage him to do the nap and see what happens," Avis said. "Do you think he suspects anything?"

"No, I don't. He's been too busy."

"Another tactic would be to ask to borrow his phone and say we don't have ours."

"Good point."

CHAPTER FORTY-SEVEN

Between calls to the directors of the CIA and NSA, Ryan found out that most everyone who could shed light on the suspects in the five murders was in Switzerland for the WSG summit. Ryan thought briefly about going abroad himself until he found out there were at least six FBI agents already there. They were backing up the Secret Service protecting Janet Yellen, and to a lesser extent, Beverly Swift.

Snyder's communication with the CIA rendered no useful information about potential murder suspects. Director Wallace continually reiterated that the CIA did not operate in the United States on an on-going basis. After that conversation, Ryan was anxious to talk to Director Dexter of the NSA. Rumors were flying about Lionel Kittring, but the last thing Ryan Snyder wanted do was contact the police chiefs of all the Western towns and cities where these murders had taken place. He didn't have that kind of time.

The Blaze concert was not only a huge success, but a welcome relief from Sars-CoV-2, the pandemic, all the fake news and angst the world was generating just then. The band played five encores and Beverly had to stop after that for fear of completely losing her voice. She received a dozen red roses from Hans Richter and a conciliatory note about not being able to meet with her since he was off to England and Prince Philip's Memorial Service.

"Normally, I would not make such a trip, but the prince was a very good friend and hunting partner and I feel I must go. Your concert was the talk of the WSG and I want you to come back next year and do it all over again. The meeting next year will be in late January. Feel free to come back any time you like."

Beverly did not have a private meeting with Hans before the performance as planned because the elder statesman was busy preparing for the memorial service, including some last minute remarks eulogizing his dear friend if he were asked to say something. There had been rumors that Hans Richter was anxious to get Beverly in his bed and was still pretty active sexually, although the thought of such a thing was disgusting and repugnant to her. She was relieved when someone told her that Klaus' sexual proclivity was nothing more than wishful thinking. That rumors about his sex life were greatly exaggerated by outsiders whose job it was to discredit him.

There was no mention of Charlene's death before, during or after the concert even though everyone in Davos knew about it, thought about it and talked about it with others they knew. Davos was not a crime-ridden city and the talk of the incident, like all incidents in a town that didn't experience such things enough to keep their doors locked at night, put citizens and guests on high alert.

Xing Ma and his henchmen went right to work after being reassured that the concert was underway. They began to capture and download the digital files while Beverly and the Blaze wowed the WSG participants . . . Twenty-five thousand strong, including guests, spouses, Davos locals (the concert was free to them) and security forces.

Jefferey Olson was back at the rented office and Mica Hrbek was joined at the hip with Ma who had memorized the order of things to be captured and their respective locations. Starting with the Group venue, general offices, web facility, mail services, order entry, Hans' private office, Gerard Meister's private office, security, all the director offices, sponsorships, events and communications.

The ten directors made for twenty-three separate locations at a rate of eight locations per hour. . . Revised to six locations per hour just to be safe, lessen the stress and insure no mistakes. There was not a moment to spare. One member of the team did nothing but circulate among the teams with coffee, water, chocolate and salted peanuts to keep everyone energized.

Ma marveled at how calm and helpful Mica was as they laid out the first eight office downloads. Most 23 year old's would be in the bathroom throwing up or cowering in the corner. Mica was actually having fun even though a couple of times she had to dodge a very heavy security patrol, the laser alarms and the occasional code that didn't register. Then, she had to open a secure location with an electronic scanner/reader which took more time and patience. But, she never wavered or gave up and Ma marveled at how calm and self-assured she was. From nine p.m to four a.m., they visited all the offices, downloaded three hundred files with eight terabytes of information and no casualties. Not one plastic bottle or candy wrapper was left behind. Over seven hours they collected data from every office and department, Richter's homes in Geneva and Provence in the South of France. When the concert ended around midnight the teams had to be especially cautious of anyone who might wander into the target offices or other locations just for kicks, to retrieve a personal item or kill time.

Jeffrey and Mica worked tirelessly into the wee hours of April tenth reading, downloading and notating the files that were then given to Beverly, Avis and Lionel to review. Lionel concentrated on Hans' personal files gathered in the distant locales while Avis and Beverly went through the Davos information. Circumstances would make for an extremely busy situation the next day.

"This is embarrassing," Avis said after finding nothing that could equivocate or compromise Hans Richter's work, companies, reputation or writings.

"I think we've got more lurid information on each other," he said sarcastically.

Even Lionel was becoming skeptical.

"This is not like anything I expected to find. But, like I've said all along, Hans Richter has done nothing wrong that would be outwardly visible to us or to the world. Since I've known him, he has always cultivated his public persona very carefully and the concept of what is the real purpose of the World Solutions Group," Lionel said. "Well, we've come this far," Beverly said, barely above a whisper. "Let's keep going. Has Tomas finished downloading the information from Charlene's computer?"

Avis stood up, stretched and yawned.

"Good point, Beverly. I'll go check."

Jeffrey and Mica were beginning to think they'd done something wrong despite repeated assurances from Ma that nothing could be further from the truth. It did appear that their cyber-attack was not going to be necessary and that frustrated Mica even more. She talked everyday about how anxious she was to see if her malware Bot worked. It was not solely her invention and she had added some features to existing programs found on the Dark Web and was looking forward to testing them for real.

There was still hope.

Xing Ma decided to make one more tour of the facilities to make sure he didn't forget anything, skip an office or, God forbid, leave something behind that could be used as evidence. He wanted to make sure he got every last strand of evidence to ease his own mind. Mica volunteered to go with him, but Ma told her he would go alone.

"If something has gone wrong, no need for both of us to go down."

He was pleased with himself until he back out of the last office and into the barrel of a gun, or something similar, only to find himself surrounded by ten security guards, guns drawn, aimed at his chest. If it were one or two guards, he could easily take them, but ten guards would be suicide. Avery Saxton was standing behind the guards.

"You're under arrest, Xing Ma," Avery said. "You will be entitled to one phone call from the police compound. Cuff him."

Xing Ma did not resist. He only hoped that Lionel was available. He let out a long sigh as the officer placed him in the Paddy wagon. Ma pressed his head against the otherwise empty vehicle and closed his eyes.

"Almost made it," he whispered.

CHAPTER FORTY-EIGHT

Tomas was still breathing when Avis got to him. He'd been shot in the back and then knocked cold in an effort to speed his death, but he was still alive. The thumb drive was missing and the computer was still on. Avis called the local emergency number for an ambulance and then Sven Alston. Alston met him in Tomas' room as the massive blood loss edged across the carpet towards the door.

"Is there such a thing as a pass key where the locks are all keyed alike on plastic cards with chips embedded in them?" Avis said, putting pressure on Tomas' wound to slow the bleeding. "Because if there is, you've got a serious security leak. Somebody is watching us very closely."

Sven swallowed hard.

"Yes, a pass key can be made for all the key cards, but we watch their distribution very carefully. The employees are fingerprinted, given a lie detector test and can only have them when they are on duty," Alston confessed. "The keycard is used sparingly and tightly controlled. I'll find out quickly if anyone is missing their keycard."

The EMS team arrived and attended to Tomas, placed him on the stretcher, oxygenated him and started down the corridor.

"Which hospital are you taking him to?" Alston said.

"Mary Catherine."

"We're right behind you."

Avis called Beverly and told her the name of the hospital. He turned to Sven.

"Better check your control process again. You've got a serious breach."

Lionel just stared at Avis.

"Tomas is still alive?" he said, haltingly. "Well, that's great news. Where is he now?"

"Xing Ma has been arrested for B&E and trespassing. About an hour ago," Avis added. "Avery Saxton arrested him. We need to go bail him out . . . diplomatic immunity and all that."

"Where did you say Tomas was now?"

"He's fine and in good hands. We need to worry about Xing Ma because I don't know how long they can hold him without charging him with something?"

Avis was increasingly suspicious of Lionel's motives and behavior. He did not want to tell Lionel where Tomas was because he was beginning to wonder about Lionel's state of mind. He'd gotten a call from a good friend in the Bethesda police department saying they found Marilyn stuffed in an old laundry chute in the Kittring home with a plastic bag wrapped around her head. The police got a tip and it turned out to be Marilyn's sister, Adele. Then, there was the matter of the wound on his forehead that oozed blood.

"It seems odd to me that Lionel didn't report it," the officer said.

"How long she been dead?" Avis said.

"At least three days. It was getting pretty stinky in there," officer Waters said. "Do you know where Lionel is?"

"How did you find out where she was?"

"We got a tip from an anonymous caller, but she and Lionel have diplomatic status and their cell phones and laptops are registered with the local police for rapid deployment," he said "After twelve hours, any device that is not functioning properly alerts us. So, we sent a patrol car over. Unfortunately, that's when we found her, at least the smell anyway. She'd been there awhile. It was not Marilyn, but her twin sister, but a mess just the same."

"I think I get the picture. Lionel was just at the house a week ago. Spent a couple nights there and he never mentioned anything unusual . . . Smells or otherwise."

"We think she's been dead longer than she's been in the laundry chute. Someone moved her there," Waters said. "We're in Switzerland at a conference. You want to talk to him?" Avis said. "I can have him call you back."

"That would be a good idea. Thanks, Avis."

"Sure thing. I will tell him when he comes back. Should he call this number?" Avis said. "It shouldn't be too long. Don't tell him it's Marilyn's sister. I will explain later."

"Got it. Yes, this number will be fine. If I haven't heard from him in three hours, I will call again. This is quite urgent."

The line went dead. Avis realized that he needed to get a look at Lionel's cell phone ASAP. He thought he might swap phones with him when he was he was distracted by something else. Lionel was careless about leaving his phone lying around.

Lionel was whistling when he came back to the temporary office. His demeanor had changed and the grumpiness he had been exhibiting was gone. He stopped whistling and his face went blank when he saw Avis' expression.

"What's wrong, Avis?"

"You better sit down. It's not good news . . . I'm afraid Marilyn is dead. Officer Waters with the Bethesda police department just hung up from talking with me," Avis Marsden said, pulling his friend and colleague close to him as they both cried on the other's shoulder. "You better call him back. The number is by the phone."

"Where? How? What happened?" Lionel said. "I just spoke to her the night before I came here. There was a miscommunication during her trip to Europe and NSA thought she'd been kidnapped. At the time, she didn't say anything about coming back early."

"I don't know all the details, Lionel. Call the officer in Bethesda. That number is his direct line. I'm going back to the hotel," he said. "I need a break. Too much going on."

"No wait, Avis," he said, plopping himself into the desk chair and looking at the phone number. "Please stay. I don't know if I can do this without some moral support."

He started bawling again. Avis locked the hotel room door. When Lionel connected with officer Waters in Bethesda, he mostly nodded and said 'yes', occasionally, almost in a whisper. When he got off the phone, he was dry eyed and angry.

"Whoever brought her body back to the house had to be watching me in order to make sure they didn't come while I was there," Lionel noted. "When they pulled her out of the laundry chute, she was already badly decomposed and they had to cremate her."

Avis thought Lionel's response was a little unusual to be going on about the circumstances and not the tragedy of her death, but he kept quiet.

"Do you think this happened right after you talked to her? That she was in Bethesda all along? Perhaps the miscommunication triggered her tragedy?" Avis said, sounding empathetic and weary. "None of it makes sense. If Marilyn was in Europe when and how did she get back to Bethesda such that she was murdered at a different location and then brought back to the house to decompose for three days."

"I'm not sure. According to officer Waters, there is no police report on her whereabouts after she and I talked while she was in Paris. She told me she was going to freshen up and then go out with her group on a tour of Paris," Lionel admitted. "Which is odd because she knows Paris as well as she knows Bethesda. Been there many times."

"Are you sure you were talking to Marilyn?"

"No, I'm not! And that *is* very disturbing to me."

"Then we need to start there! Could her sister have anything to do with this? By the way, where were you?"

"Mary Catherine hospital," Lionel said. "One of my old gunshot wounds was acting up and the hotel sent me over there. It was nothing but a little indigestion. I don't think Adele would be involved."

Avis's heart fell to his stomach, but he didn't say anything about Tomas and hoped that Lionel wouldn't either. It would be easy enough to confirm his story, but Avis wasn't going to say anything if Lionel didn't.

"By the way, what's the latest on Tomas? I haven't heard you mention him recently?"

Avis was certain Lionel already knew something and was fishing for how much Avis knew. He was playing cat and mouse, one of his favorite spy games. Lionel just needed to determine who was the cat and who was the mouse . . . And then he could figure out how to win. And wait for the next shoe to drop. Since he didn't ask what hospital Tomas was in, Avis was convinced he already knew.

"And what about the data collection. How's that going? Are Jeffrey and Mica here?"

"They went to get some lunch," Avis said. "The data collection is going fine, but not really yielding anything significant. Mica is very frustrated."

"Why is she frustrated? She's done a fine job and there weren't any constraints placed on her to find anything in particular," Lionel said.

"I think she was hoping to release her new malware bug, but it looks like it won't be necessary based on what she's finding from the data," Avis noted. "The World Solutions Group looks to be pretty clean and it would be political suicide to start disrupting the members with unsubstantiated claims."

"Have you looked at any of the data? I can't believe there isn't something that's suspicious," Lionel said. "I never expected to find piles of information, just some juicy tidbits in all that data. Look for the grains of sand and not the beach. Where is Ma now?"

"I suspect he's at the hotel. He texted me when he got out of jail and said he'd been up all night for fear of being beaten or molested for being of Asian descent," Avis noted. "I had Beverly go over and post his bail, but there will be a firestorm of negative publicity tomorrow, so be ready."

"Should we try to stop the negative press? I understand you're pretty effective at doing that."

"Let me contact Fiona. She has all the connections and if we can't stop it, we might be able soften the blow."

Avis got on his cell phone and spoke to Fiona. The story had come across the wire and she had some information on it, but nothing substantial. She said she was on it and would try to get an advanced copy of the story before it went to press, but she wasn't promising anything. Avis relayed her thoughts to Lionel.

"Well, we can't ask for much more than that, I guess," he said

When Jeffrey and Mica came back from lunch, Avis refocused their attention on the minutiae of the data collected and what to look for. That seemed to help Mica who was now refocused and excited to dig in. Jeffrey was pouting, hoping for more action and intrigue.

Lionel's phone lay on the hotel room desk next to Avis'. He walked away to speak with his two young proteges.

"He watches too many spy movies," Mica stated, roughing Jeffrey's hair.

CHAPTER FORTY-NINE

Ryan Snyder was looking at the blow up photo of the tattoo on the suspects left arm. It was an unusual design that looked like it could be a Chinese alphabet character. There were two Chinese agents in the office that day, but only one of them was at his desk. Ryan threw a paper wad at Daniel Cho to get his attention and then motioned him over.

"Do you recognize this symbol, Dan?" Ryan said.

"Yes, Ryan, it is the letter M in the Chinese alphabet," he said. "Is that a tattoo?"

"Yes. Have you seen this tattoo before?"

Daniel Cho pulled up his shirt sleeve to reveal the same symbol on his right arm.

"Now, a little lesson in Chinese folk lore," Cho said. "My middle initial is M which stands for Martin and is on my right arm. It it were on my left arm, the initial would stand for a loved one."

"Very cool. This tattoo is on the left arm, so it would be a loved one . . . Right?"

"Correct. Now the other thing, not many tattoo parlors can or will do this design. If you're trying to find out who might have bought this one, check cities that have Chinatowns."

"Thanks, Daniel."

Xing Ma showed up at the office about four o'clock, looking a bit hungover and puffy eyed, although he hadn't had a drop to drink. He apologized to Avis and Lionel for getting caught. He told them he had been napping at the hotel, but he was actually in a meeting with Hans Richter and Avery Saxton, fessing up about the digital theft and collecting a handsome reward for his efforts. He had briefed Hans in his meeting with Gerard before the theft so they could take measures to relocate the most sensitive files, programs, algorithms and member information before Ma and Mica romped through the WSG offices.

In a fit of anger over the whole theft scenario and while Lionel was in one of his headache stupors, he threatened to cut Xing Ma out of the expected booty from the theft over some petty procedural matters in an email to him. Ma felt his only option was to snitch . . . To the tune of a fifty million dollar payday from Hans and Gerard, a pittance compared to the amount of time and money Ma's confession saved the World Solutions Group. Lionel didn't mention the angry email to anyone because he didn't remember doing it.

"I wanted to make one last round of the offices to make sure we captured everything. I got a little sloppy watching for security," he said. "They were actually pretty nice about it, but threw me in jail to prove a point."

"No worries, Ma, " Lionel said, holding the side of his head. "I'm going back to the hotel to lie down for a while. I have a splitting headache. Can we talk later and assess how things went this time?"

"Sure thing, Lionel," Avis said. "Give me a call."

Lionel left without his phone and Avis grabbed it and stuck it in his jacket pocket, patting it lightly as reassurance that it was there. When the door closed, Ma locked it and looked around for Jeffrey and Mica. They had locked themselves in the small conference room, wading through the data files looking for the grains of sand in all the information they had collected. It would be a long process. Ma took a thumb drive from his pocket and handed it to Avis.

"Take a look at this. This may be the information Charlene found what cost her her life," Xing Ma said. "It's a very telling conversation between WSG, the FAANG companies and Hans from about six months ago. I need some confirmation of what this is telling me. Don't look at it on your personal computer or one issued by NSA. They will hack it for sure."

"Will do. I found out that Lionel was not fired from NSA. He quit to join forces with our old nemesis, Don Olson at R.L Thornton. I think that's why Jeffrey is working with us, to keep tabs on Lionel for his grandfather," Avis said. "Don is not doing very well health wise. That cancer has caught up with him."

"How is Tomas doing? Does Lionel know where he is?" Ma said. "I heard that the Swiss authorities were going to move him to an undisclosed location as soon as he was well enough to travel. I think they're trying to trap the suspected killer."

"Lionel was at Mary Catherine to be treated for his old gunshot wound yesterday. He told me it was just indigestion, but I think he tried to see Tomas or at least locate his room," Avis noted. "Did you hear anything?"

"I heard that someone asked about Tomas Hogan's current location, but the hospital staff had been directed to not answer any questions about Tomas under any circumstances," Ma said. "Did you hear about what happened in Connecticut?"

"No! What happened?" Avis looked shocked. Another incident was not needed right now.

"Two nights ago, a masked team of thieves broke into the Evans' home, tied up Mr. Evans, molested Mrs. Evans and demanded the file Charlene had sent them before she came to Switzerland," Ma said excitedly. "Fortunately, they had uploaded the file from the computer to a thumb drive and hid it. Mr. Evans' told the intruders it was on their computer and they downloaded it to their own thumb drive, not knowing it was already corrupted and not readable."

"Wow! What an ordeal. Is everyone all right?"

"Yes. And they caught the intruders. Two of the four were former NSA employees, which is telling."

"I'll say. I think Mr. Evans sent the files to Lionel before the intrusion. I need to check again," Avis said. "Call Mary Catherine and see if anyone has inquired about Tomas in the last thirty minutes. If so, we might be closing in on the killer."

"Will do. By the way, did Lionel ever mention explosives to you as a subsequent follow-up to the theft if things didn't work out?" Ma said, rubbing his eyes.

"He mentioned it before we left the states, but I objected loudly, convincing him, I think, that it would kill a lot of innocent people and most surely get traced back to us making for a never ending stream of lawsuits, trials and damaging press," Avis said. "Besides, how the hell would he get the explosives across the big pond. He never mentioned it to me again."

Ma saw Mica waving at him through the view window into the conference room, motioning him to join them. She seemed excited about something and was waving her hands frantically.

"Let me see what's going on with our budding digital criminals."

"Take a look at this, Ma. This is from the digital imprint in the media room and is date stamped March 21, 2020, from Hans Richter," Mica said. "It's a video clip of Hans talking to Eric Schmidt from Google about the Great Reset."

"Hans: The WSG has to be careful not to reveal the details of the Great Reset too quickly as people recovering from COVID19 or those low on money or skeptical about it will not go along with a CBDC (Central Bank Digital Currency), microchips in the next round of booster shots or continued mandatory masking. The whole social engineering experiment will go up in smoke."

Xing Ma looked up, shaking his head. He waved Avis over to the conference room door.

"You've got to see this, Avis. This video clip is very damaging."

Avis looked at the video clip and agreed with Xing Ma.

"I think we need to show this to Lionel because he knows Hans as well as anyone," Avis said. "Mr. Richter is not known for being public and we need to make sure it's not a plant or a fake. Is there another way to verify this, Mica?" Avis checked his watch. Lionel had been gone for over two hours and was surely rested by now. Avis dialed his room.

"I'll be right there," Lionel told Avis. "It does sound like an interesting find."

Lionel looked a little ragged. His eyes were puffy and he had red splotches around his nose like he was allergic to something in his room. He watched the video clip three times, each time looking closely at Hans Richter's gestures, demeanor and speech.

"I think it is Hans in the video, but I don't think he knows he's being recorded. He never looks at the camera or even acknowledges that it's there," Lionel said. "This is a great find, Mica. Lift the data and put it on a separate thumb drive for future reference. We might just casually run this by Hans."

Lionel stood up and lost his balance momentarily before leaving the room suddenly holding his head with both hands.

Avis tracked Beverly down and told her he had Lionel's cell phone and thought if she could get over his room, they could dissect the mystery phone calls together.

"OK! Give me fifteen minutes," she said. "I'll be right there."

CHAPTER FIFTY

The afternoon edition of the Guardian newspaper in Davos, screamed:

SECURITY BREACH AT WORLD SOLUTIONS GROUP

And that was the headline, or something similar, in every major newspaper around the world. The Guardian was not kind to Xing Ma since he had been captured by authorities at the headquarters. He became an overnight sensation for the wrong reasons, but took it all in stride as the price you pay for fame. Everyone laughed.

Captain Terrence Sansby cringed when he read it. Hans Richter chewed Sansby out and then summoned Lionel on the phone and asked him straight away what he knew about the break-in. Lionel played dumb, telling Hans that what he knew he'd read in the papers like everyone else. "Who is this Xing Ma and how did he get caught," Hans demanded, playing dumb. "And how do you know him?"

"I don't know him, Hans. All I know is that he is from China and was hanging around the WSG. Have you ever heard of him before?"

"Never!" Hans screamed into his phone. "Good bye."

Ryan Snyder had sent emails to every Chinese tattoo parlor in every one of the sixteen cities in the United States that had official 'Chinatowns'. Attached to the email was the image of the Chinese letter M from the elevator lobby picture taken of the suspects left arm, a return email address and a telephone number. Twenty-five hundred emails were sent. Twenty percent bounced back as undeliverable. Daniel Cho estimated that 20% were never opened and twenty percent went to the wrong email address. So, that left a thousand email gamble that Ryan and Daniel could rely on.

Additionally, an email was sent to the three hundred tattoo parlors listed as the official overseas listing for shops in in London, Madrid, Amsterdam, Calcutta and Beijing, Hong Kong and Sydney. All they could now was wait . . . happy in the fact that there had not been another recorded murder except for the discovery of Marilyn Kittring by local police.

Beverly asked Gail Evans if she had opened the urgent message from Charlene about the WSG news item that got buried by someone at Shell Oil and may have caused her death. Gail had not looked at it because Charlene told her to move the information to a different file location, like a thumb drive, floppy disc or remote storage to get it off their main computer. And then she and George were attacked.

"To be honest, Ms. Swift, if I never see that file it will be fine with me," Gail said. "George has looked at it. But, he's not here right now. I can have him call you."

"That would be fine. You take care of yourself and please let me know when the funeral or memorial service for Charlene will be held," Beverly said. "I will be back in the United States on Sunday. Have her remains arrived in Connecticut?"

"I will keep you posted. I am not looking forward to any of this," she said. "Her remains are supposed to be back Saturday. That's where George is now . . . checking on her arrival."

"I can assure you of one thing, Gail. Our government takes the death of every American citizen very seriously, especially under circumstances like Charlene's, and will go the extra mile to get her home. Peace be with you, Gail."

"Thank you, Beverly. That does help and makes me feel better."

Beverly went to see Tomas at Mary Catherine hospital more out of guilt than anything after speaking to Gail Evans. She had to check-in with the nurse's station to find out where Tomas was. The nurse told her where Tomas had been relocated and then asked if she knew Lionel Kittring.

"Yes, I do. I understand he was here the day before yesterday being treated for an old gunshot wound that was bothering him."

The nurse glared at her.

"I don't know about that, but he was treated for severe headache pain he has been having for a while," she said. "We did a MRI and a brain scan and the results are in, but he didn't leave any way for us to contact him. Do you have his phone number?"

Beverly took her phone from her purse and showed the number to the charge nurse. She jotted it down and thanked Beverly.

"Is his condition serious?"

"I can't say, but the results were less than ideal. I'm going to call him right now."

"I think he may have misplaced his cell phone, so call the hotel switchboard and ask for room 537."

The nurse turned around to use the phone and Beverly read Lionel's chart upside down. *'What the hell is Glioblastoma?'*

Tomas was not awake and had only been back from his second surgery for an hour when Beverly arrived at his bedside. He was on a ventilator and strapped to monitors for his heart and lungs. The doctor there when Beverly came in and told her that what saved him was that the bullet in the back missed his heart and lungs, but grazed one kidney and exited through his groin, missing his genitals, but tearing a good sized portion of muscle in his right hamstring.

"It's also a good thing that he's thin, in good general health and shows no sign of HIV or AIDS," the surgeon said. "But, he's not going anywhere anytime soon."

Beverly thanked the female doctor and left to return to the hotel. Avis was coming toward her across the hospital parking lot.

"Have you been to see Tomas?" he said. "I was just on my way to see how he's doing."

"There is not much to see. He just came back from another surgery and the doctor explained his condition and the wounds," Beverly said. "He was either very lucky or the shooter was not very good."

"Or the shooter did it on purpose and knew exactly what he or she was doing." Beverly shrugged and nodded. "We do know one thing, it wasn't the woman from Canada. They released her and she left an hour ago to go back to go home."

"I guess we'll never know," Beverly said. "You have to go to the main hospital reception to check-in. They move him around to reduce the chances of . . . well, you know why. If you aren't on the list of visitors, forget trying to see him. His room is heavily guarded." Beverly paused. "Do you know what glioblastoma is?"

Avis looked shocked and his jaw dropped.

"It's a rare form of untreatable brain cancer," he said. "He doesn't have that, too, does he?"

"No. But, Lionel might," Beverly said, her voice dropping off. "He did not go to the hospital the other day for his old gunshot wound. He went because of his severe headaches. They did a MRI and a brain scan. I happened to see his chart accidentally and it said glioblastoma with a question mark by it."

"That explains a lot. Well, if I'm not on the list, I'll come back to the hotel. I think Lionel has a meeting with Hans tomorrow and maybe Gerard Meister, too," Avis added. "I think he wants me to go with him. Rumor has it that Hans Richter is incensed over the break-in and threatening a lawsuit."

"Against who . . . Xing Ma? No evidence, no crime," Beverly said. "Speaking of crimes, I have a call into Jordan Quincy to check Q's cell phone for some of the numbers we found on Lionel's phone."

"Good show. All the other numbers match the people Lionel called," Avis noted. "And several calls to the White House switchboard, but none of those calls were ever connected."

"You think he was calling the president?" Beverly said.

"Possibly or any number of other henchmen."

CHAPTER FIFTY-ONE

Ahmet Troi owned the Tattoo Nation tattoo shop in Rockville, Maryland and was neighbors with Sergeant John Waters of the Bethesda Police Department. He was vaguely familiar with the Marilyn Kittring case from discussing the bizarre situation surrounding her murder. Troi opened the email attachment from the FBI and sent it immediately to Sgt. Waters with a note that said, 'I thought you might find this interesting!' Ahmet had never seen that symbol as a tattoo before.

Several tattoo parlors in DC were not on Ryan Snyder's original list, so he passed the information on to those shops, too. Five thousand dollars was a nice reward.

Avis was in Tomas' room when the heart and lung monitors flatlined and the alarm bells sounded. The nurses rushed to his side, removed Avis from the room and tried for thirty minutes to revive Tomas before calling for the medical examiner. Bjorn Somer came quickly, pronounced him dead and promptly started post mortem proceedings. Bjorn shook his head in disgust. He had examined more accidental deaths in Davos in the last two days than the previous two decades.

Avis sat in the hospital corridor with tears in his eyes as he called Beverly, Lionel, Jeffrey and Mica. It was an unfortunate day for the Hogan family because Tomas' father, Richard, the local hospital where Tomas was born. He had only been sick a short time and like Tomas, never recovered. Mrs. Hogan was overwhelmed at the thought of arranging two funerals, not to mention suddenly being alone.

The attending physician, the only doctor present, told Avis that he thought the size and severity of the wound was just too much for Tomas' body to overcome. He didn't quite understand Tomas' sudden death because although his wounds were severe, he was making good progress. There was no outward sign of his air passages being blocked or other body trauma, but an autopsy would be performed to make sure. Under the circumstances, it was the law in Switzerland and no one thought to ask about surveillance tapes.

Avis described his conversation with the doctor to Beverly.

"Maybe this isn't as clear cut as it seems," Beverly told Avis. "Ask the doctor to have a look at the security tapes to see if there has been any suspicious activity."

Beverly volunteered to contact Jenny Hogan to tell her about the required autopsy, but it went to voicemail. When she called back an hour later, she acted like nothing had happened to her son or to her husband. She did mention that she would have them both bodies cremated. Beverly called Avis explaining Jenny Hogan's bizarre behavior. Avis explained that she was more than likely in shock and responding auto-tonically as if she was in a trance.

Avis glared at Lionel when he told him about Tomas, but Lionel just hung his head and didn't respond. Avis stopped short of accusing him, but really wanted to interrogate him about his whereabouts and what he was doing. Tomas' death was unnecessary and Avis wondered again about foul play.

Beverly's phone rang. It was George Evans returning her call. She had met him once in Washington. He was a pleasant, impatient and learned man who was a successful academic in Connecticut. At the time, he kept talking about how helpful her real estate agent had been, a man named Wyatt Douglas, who assisted Charlene in getting moved in to her new condominium. Beverly had forgotten all about Wyatt's connection to Charlene.

"Hello, Ms. Swift. Gail said you called about the file Charlene sent us."

His voice cracked when he said his daughter's name.

"Yes, do you remember anything about it?"

"Sure do. Charlene discovered a connection between big oil and the World Solutions Group, specifically Hans Richter and Gerard Meister. There was a large donation from a cartel of Big Oil firms like Exxon - Mobil, Shell, BP, Standard Oil and some of the biggest banks . . . JP Morgan Chase, Citigroup, Mellon and the like. We're quite certain that whoever broke into our house was tied to one of those groups."

"Quite possibly. Did the intruders ever get the file?"

"They got a file, but not the one Charlene sent us," he said proudly. "They left in a hurry when I got loose from being tied up and grabbed my gun from the desk drawer. Wounded one of them."

Beverly smiled to herself, imagining that scene.

"Would you do me a favor?"

"Certainly."

"See if you can find out what hospital or clinic some random, wounded man was treated at for a minor gunshot wound that night," she said.

"Sorry, I was thinking about where he or she might've gone."

"Well, think about it some more, if you will."

"Thank you. No one will miss her more than me."

CHAPTER FIFTY-TWO

Hans Richter was in a wheelchair prompted by the stressful and emotional trip to his old friend's memorial and the stress of being blindsided by the break-in. "So, whoever masterminded this digital theft didn't get much in the way of information, at least not what they were expecting," Hans announced, directing his comment to Lionel who was standing in front of Xing Ma, Avis, Beverly and Jeffrey.

"Who is Xing Ma, who does he work for and why was he sneaking around our offices when he was caught?" Hans said, looking directly at Lionel.

Lionel motioned for Ma to come forward.

"This is Xing Ma and he works for me," Lionel said. "After we heard about the break-in, Ma went out to inspect the situation to make sure things were under control. He was mistaken as a burglar because he did not have his credentials with him. Avery Saxton caught him. "

Hans held up the picture from the front page of the Guardian.

"You said before that you didn't know him, Lionel. So what's the truth?" Hans said, his face turning red. "And does he always goes out dressed all in black?"

"Harder to see 'dressed in black' given the volatile nature of things. He wasn't concerned so much about his dress as the timeliness of his visit," Lionel argued. "He told Avery what he was doing when he was caught. I don't remember telling you I didn't know him, Hans."

Avis glared at Lionel. He was the best liar Avis had ever met. And he had done it again, convincingly.

Hans rubbed his chin, his eyes darting back and forth between Lionel and Xing Ma. He was generally not a vindictive or confrontational sort, but he couldn't let this one go. Hans decided he was going to let the courts handle it even though it might take a long time. He summoned Gerard to get the legal machinery cranked up.

He motioned for Beverly to come closer. He took her hand.

"I really enjoyed the concert you and your band gave," he sighed. "Will you come back next year to perform?"

Beverly didn't hesitate. "Yes, of course we will. Everyone was so nice to us and we enjoyed playing for such an important international audience."

He was trying to urge her closer, but Beverly gently withdrew her hand.

"When are you going home?"

"We leave tomorrow. I have some unfortunate and sad connections to make with the parents of Charlene Evans and Tomas Hogan. And my children must get back to school."

"Yes, I heard about Mr. Hogan. So sad. Are the police any closer to finding the perpetrators?"

"Not that we know of, Mr. Richter," Avis interjected.

"Well, the World Solutions Group will pay all funeral expenses, including transport, and we are offering a 500,000 kroner reward for any information leading to the capture and arrest of the perpetrators," Hans said in a loud and firm voice. "I think that is the least we can do," Hans said. "Meeting adjourned, but Lionel can you stay behind for a moment. I need to discuss another matter with you."

"Certainly, Hans. Let me just get some coffee."

Avis's phone was silenced during the briefing, but he could feel it vibrating. The screen announced a call from Mary Catherine hospital. He hoped it was the doctor calling about the surveillance video.

"Mr. Marsden. This is Dr. Ian Jenko, from Mary Catherine hospital. If you could, please come back to the hospital as soon as you can. There is some interesting security footage you should see. Bring Ms. Swift with you."

The video could have been taken from LA County hospital when Q died. Same scrubs, same life support sabotage, same build on the perpetrator. Beverly still had the LA footage on her phone and showed to Avis and Dr. Jenko.

Avis and Beverly looked at each other. Beverly tried calling Jodie again.

Beverly took a deep breath and answered her cell phone that had been vibrating for the last five minutes. It was Denise, who was trying to corral everyone to get finished packing.

"Sorry Denise, I was wrapping up a meeting with Mr. Richter. What's going on?"

"Are Harris and Haley with you? I have been so busy trying to get us all ready for the trip home tomorrow, I have lost track of them."

"No, they're not with me," Beverly said, reliving, suddenly, five years earlier and the botched kidnapping attempt by Don Olson. Beverly remained calm and tried to remain prescient. "You check the restaurants and the pool and I will check that little park they liked so much. I'll be back to the hotel shortly."

"Beverly, I *am* so sorry. I should've been watching closer," Denise said. "I just got so preoccupied."

"Don't fret, Denise. They are bigger now and can fend for themselves. We'll find them," she said, not as confident as her voice sounded. "I'll be back in fifteen minutes."

Beverly excused herself without saying a word about the children. Avis approached her and asked if everything was all right because Beverly Swift wore her heart on her sleeve.

She sidled up to him.

"Harris and Haley are not with Denise," Beverly said calmly. "I am going to the park they liked so much and Denise is checking the hotel pool and restaurants."

Avis nodded, but did not change expression. "I'll call Sven Alston at the hotel."

Beverly kissed Avis on the cheek and stepped out of the World Economic Forum conference room and was greeted by Captain Sansby.

"Come with me."

Hans stood up and walked over to two lounge chairs that were sitting in the corner of the conference room. He motioned to an aide to turn off the sound system and cameras for his chat with Lionel, who had returned with a coffee and a black tea for his host. Hans had already seated himself.

"Lionel, I heard about Marilyn and I am so sorry about what happened. My condolences to you. Seems like this week had been all about death for many of us."

"Thank you, Hans, that means a lot coming from you, dear friend," Lionel said. "Unfortunately, we did not have much time together as marrieds."

Hans nodded.

"I have something I need to have you do for me, dear friend," Hans said, mimicking Lionel's words and patting his hand. "Charlene Evans or Tomas Hogan came upon a document about me and the WSG related to Big Oil from a good while ago. It was a plant or it was edited to make it appear that the WEF took money from Big Oil in exchange for certain, shall we say, favors? I need you to make sure it goes away. Two people have already died over it and we don't need any more situations like that, lest I have a lot of explaining to do."

Lionel nodded. Hans Richter was a master manipulator and could turn almost any phrase or event in his favor. Lionel recalled the document and how Hans manipulated it to the WSG's favor. It was accurate as written, thoroughly researched by one of journalism's best minds. Hans needed money to grow the WEF and Big Oil reached out, willing to help in exchange for Klaus reducing his rhetoric about how the oil companies were going out of their way to damage the environment, keep profits up and appease shareholders. That document and a few others is what caused the rift between Lionel and Klaus and partially why Lionel left the WSG. Right or wrong, Hans always got his way and worried about the mistakes until it was often too late to correct them.

The big eight oil companies each pitched in ten million dollars which the WEF promptly accepted and turned their attention elsewhere. Then Charlene dug up the agreement. Not from World Solutions Group files but from Shell Oil shareholder meeting notes from 2015. The WSG did not have to allow public access to their files because it was still, and always would be, a private organization as long as Hans was alive.

"I'll see what I can do," Lionel assured his friend and mentor. "It's a bit of a hot topic right now, so I may have to let it simmer down first."

CHAPTER FIFTY-THREE

Captain Sansby smiled when Beverly asked if her children were all right.

"They're fine," is all he said.

Beverly called Denise's cell phone and got voicemail and said simply that the children are all right and hung up. When they got to the police precinct, Denise was waiting in the lobby. Tears streamed down her face. She grabbed Beverly and squeezed her tightly.

"Wait here, Ms. Swift," the captain said.

He brought Harris and Haley to the front desk. Harris wore a smirk and Haley was crying. Beverly didn't care either way and hugged them like it had been a month since she'd seen either of them.

"What happened, Harris and Haley?" Beverly scolded.

Haley volunteered.

"Harris wanted to see the inside of the jail, but rather than asking one of the officers on duty, he decided to shoplift at the pharmacy across from the hotel," she said, crying again suddenly. "And he got us both arrested."

Sansby was shaking his head standing behind Harris, trying not to laugh.

"OK, Harris, let's hear your version of the story," Beverly said.

Harris crossed his arms and looked askance at the ceiling.

"I have nothing to add, so there?"

"So, why didn't you come to the police station and ask the desk clerk for a tour," his mother said.

He turned back to his mother and pointed at the sign behind the desk.

NO ONE UNDER 18 YEARS of AGE ALLOWED

"I see," Beverly said, doing all she could to keep from laughing. A smile leaked out. Denise had to step outside as she couldn't hold back her laughter any longer..

"So, I figure the next best thing was to get arrested," Harris said in his twelve year old wisdom. "Haley's such a baby. She cried the whole time."

Beverly covered her mouth to keep from laughing in her son's face.

"OK. I got it," she said. "But next time, just ask."

Harris crossed his arms again.

Beverly's cell rang as they were leaving the precinct. It was Jordan Quincy.

"Jordan, let me call you right back. I'll explain," she said and disconnected before Jordan could answer. When Beverly called back her first statement was whether or not Q's cell phone was intact.

"Look for this number . . . 975 770 2100," she said.

It took a minute for Jordan to open the phone, but she found the number quickly, several times.

"I found the number on the screen and in voicemail at least half a dozen times," Jordan replied.

"Great! Do any of the calls coincide with when Q was in the hospital . . . Within a few days?"

There was silence on the other end while Jordan perused the phone call list.

"Yes, about a week before dad went into the hospital there were several calls from this number, " she said. "The first call was lengthy, over ten minutes, but the other calls were less than a minute each."

"Thanks, Jordan. I think we may have found our killer." Beverly said. "I'll be in touch."

CHAPTER FIFTY-FOUR

Three hours before they were supposed to board the plane home, Captain William Sansby dropped all charges against Xing Ma for lack of evidence and a generous donation to the Police Benevolence Fund on behalf of Lionel Kittring. At the airport, Lionel gathered everyone into a private meeting room. He explained what he told Hans Richter about the break-in and the instructions he gave to Mica Hrbek concerning the malware attacks.

"Suffice it to say there is going to be a firestorm of publicity about how certain company's websites have been attacked for ransom payments on behalf of the IMF, the World Bank, International Bank of Settlements and the World Solutions Group," Lionel said. "This was done to create even more confusion over the digital theft that we pulled off last week. Since the powers that be in Davos saw fit to drop all charges against Ma, it clears us all in a manner of speaking."

"How does that affect us?" Jeffrey said.

"Well, technically, it doesn't. Some reporter out to make a name for him or herself may ask questions, but we should be fine, collectively. Just answer their question to the best of your knowledge."

Lionel massaged his temples some more and took two pills from an orange pharmacy bottle.

As Beverly finished packing for the trip home, Reese called her cell phone.

"Hi. Just wanted to check that you are still coming home tomorrow? You're quite the star again back here in a couple different ways . . . One good and one not so good," he said. "Your concert got rave reviews from Rolling Stone, the Guardian and the New York Times, but the news about Tomas and Charlene and the WEF break-in trumped them all, no pun intended."

"Hello, Reese, it's nice to hear your voice," she said stiffly. "I feel like I've been away for a year, so much has happened. Thanks for the heads up," she said, tossing the last of the dirty clothes into her suitcase. "Did you hear about Lionel Kittring's wife?"

"Yes, I did," he said. "Is it true they found her in the laundry chute where she'd been for three days?"

"That's true."

"Just wanted to tell you two things. I will be out of town starting tomorrow until Wednesday and I've checked on your new house a couple time and nothing much seems to be happening. Better call Wyatt."

"Yes, I will, thanks for telling me. We did raise about twenty million total for the Leukemia Foundation, No Kid Hungry and Children's Cancer Foundation. Hans Richter invited us back next year, too."

She decided to leave the Harris and Haley jail story for later.

"OK. Safe travels and I miss you and will see you on Wednesday. I presume you're headed to New York for the weekend after having been gone so long."

"Yes, after I go to New Haven for Charlene's memorial service. Has anyone phoned about the New York apartment?"

"Yes, mostly real estate agents. I left the messages on the machine."

"Great! I'll have a look when I get back to DC, on Tuesday.

"Have a safe trip."

"Thanks. Kamala Harris and I are going back to the border to try to get that straightened out. Should be interesting. I have never traveled with the Vice President."

"Good luck. If anyone can get something done, the two of you can. Ciao!"

"So long."

Beverly picked up the call on first ring. It was Jordan Quincy.

"Hi, Jordan. That was quick."

"Forgot to tell you a couple things. Congratulations on the concert in Switzerland," she said. "It got rave reviews out here. Some of the other news from over there not so much."

"I presume you are talking about the two murders and the break-in? They were indeed low spots for the trip," Beverly said. "I'm going to New Haven, Connecticut tomorrow for one of the funerals. I'm not looking forward to that trip. What's up?"

"I have been going through Q's papers and keep running across the name Lionel Kittring, the same guy I met with shortly after the funeral. Who is he?"

CHAPTER FIFTY-FIVE

Lionel was nearly incapacitated when they got to the airport. Beverly and Xing Ma got him in a wheelchair and when they got to the gate, Beverly asked the attendant to reissue Lionel Kittring's seat assignment to the very back row in coach so he could stretch out and sleep for the nine hour flight home. Ma wheeled his friend and mentor to a row of empty seats, row 37, got him strapped in so he could maneuver himself enough to lie down and then pulled blankets from the overhead bin. The flight attendant fussed over Lionel long enough to wrangle a smile from the old spy.

"Ma, will you sit with me until we takeoff?" Lionel urged, deferring his nap until the Melatonin kicked in. Ma sat on the aisle and gently stroked Lionel's hand.

"I was so sad to hear about Marilyn. Have you heard anything more from the authorities about a motive?" Ma said sincerely. "I wanted to say something earlier, but we had other issues."

Lionel shook his head and told Ma it would be the first thing he would address when he got home, although he wasn't sure he could stay in the Bethesda house. Ma offered his Georgetown apartment because he was going back to China for a few weeks. Lionel thanked him and said he would let him know. Ma started to say something more and looked over at Lionel, who was now fast asleep.

Lionel's dreams were varied and numerous and the last of them was the consequence of a chance meeting he had with two former colleagues from NSA who now worked for member firms at the World Solutions Group. They were having a heated discussion about *Kabbalistic* studies and Jewish mysticism. They asked Lionel to join them at the hotel bar.

In Kabbalistic studies, the soul (neshama in Hebrew) is the source of all wisdom and goodness and is always trying to communicate with us. On the other hand, the yetzer hara, is always trying to block that communication. The yetzer hara is a cunning and self-sustaining intelligence that works to block that communication. Over time, the yetzer hara can win out when the soul is blackened by our evil thoughts and deeds even if you're not Jewish!

Which are you Lionel Kittring?

Lionel woke with a start and nearly tumbled off the narrow makeshift bed. He rubbed his eyes, undid the seatbelt and sat up. He was surprisingly alert and felt better than he had in days. He got up from his seat and eased into the aisle. The attractive flight attendant stopped him as he started to walk up the aisle.

"Mr. Kittring, can I help you? We'll be turning on the seatbelt sign in about three minutes indicating our initial approach into JFK. Do you need something?"

Lionel nodded. "Can you go forward and ask the man who was sitting with me earlier to come back before we land? His name is Xing Ma."

The attendant smiled. "Yes, I can. We'll be right back."

Sergeant Waters rarely got an email from Ahmet, so he opened it and discovered the tattoo symbol. Sergeant Waters made several copies of it and posted it strategically around the office, as well as sending it via email to other sergeants, detectives and senior officers. No one seemed to notice, but Waters knew that it might mean something to someone in the near future. He was wracking his own mind, reviewing his caseload in his head to see if the tattoo had any meaning for him.

Beverly and Avis had not had a serious conversation about anything for a long time and it was good to catch up. Avis told Beverly how concerned he was for Lionel especially since the discovery of the Glioblastoma and the bleeding head wound. Beverly eyes widened.

"Remember James Quincy? I didn't tell you this, but he didn't die from COVID19. He was murdered," Beverly said. "So when his daughter and I found out, we were able to get a security tape from the hospital and sure enough, about five days before he died, the tape showed someone in scrubs *adjusting* Q's medication. At the elevator, the suspect removed their skull cap to reveal what looked like a birthmark on their forehead."

Avis didn't say anything.

"Go to the restroom at the back of the plane and checkout Lionel's forehead when you walk past and tell me what you see. He's out like a light, so take a couple pictures."

When Beverly returned, she showed Avis the original picture taken at the hospital elevator and the picture she had just taken of Lionel's head. The location of the wound were approximately the same.

"Unfortunately, it's all circumstantial unless you can prove that Lionel was there and had motive," Avis said.

"Would the fact that Jordan met with Lionel two days after Q died in Los Angeles count?"

CHAPTER FIFTY-SIX

Lionel lay down again and closed his eyes briefly. He asked the flight attendant to turn on the news on his personal flight screen. The major networks opened their morning news programs with an inaccurate analysis of events, blaming Iran and then continuing their sloppy reporting by interviewing a malware expert who was still hung over from the night before. Lionel followed along and smiled egregiously after each misstep the news agencies made. His head was starting to pound again and he took two more pills, something he was doing every three hours, now.

Xing Ma sat down next to him.

"Are you feeling better, Lionel? You look much better."

"Thank you. I feel better, strange dreams and all."

The fasten seatbelt light came on.

Lionel Kittring managed to walk slowly to baggage claim. The carousel was packed with reporters waiting for anyone who could shed light on the circumstances in Davos, but not one reporter mentioned the break-in, Ma's arrest or the WSG summit. It was old news. They asked Beverly about the special charity concert, they asked Avis about the two unfortunate deaths of the Treasury staff and they asked Lionel about Marilyn. He was flummoxed about that and a little unnerved since it had been in the media for three days.

Xing Ma and the two malware thieves slipped out of baggage claim almost unnoticed. Mica was monitoring Russell to the tune of $750 million dollars in ransom paid. The next step was to figure where all that money would go.

Ma reminded Jeffrey and Mica of their obligation to a team for a meeting in six weeks.

"Don't spend large sums of money until we have our rendezvous, lay low, and if anyone approaches you about your trip, interviews or sex, male or female, the theme is no comment," Ma instructed. "Someone, somewhere has been photographing you and will want to collect from a social media site, network, tabloid or magazine for their efforts," Ma warned, "If they insist, buy the media back from them."

Just a Lionel was leaving baggage claim under his own power, a man in a black suit approached. He was clean cut like a Mormon missionary, square-jawed and very intense.

"Are you Lionel Kittring?" he said in a low voice, holding a picture of Lionel.

"Yes, I am."

The man produced a white business envelope and handed it to Lionel. "Consider yourself served, Mr. Kittring."

CHAPTER FIFTY-SEVEN

NSA did a great job cleaning up the mess left by investigators, forensics, the coroner, the police and the FBI at Lionel's Bethesda home. There were no lingering smells, cleaning solvents or other evidence that anything as nasty as a person stuffed into the laundry shoot had happened when Lionel arrived. He considered it a going away gift from the agency. Now, there were just the memories, but he decided he would try to live there. He threw the white envelope on the kitchen table and went to the library. There was only one man in the whole world who would serve him with a court summons . . . Hans Richter.

Lionel had bought a gun safe after his 2020 shooting in DC and taught Marilyn how to shoot for her own protection. He went to the first floor library to check the contents of the gun safe, which looked more like a wooden wardrobe or finely crafted cupboard. It remained as he had left it when he went to Switzerland. He unlocked the door on the first try, mentally patting himself on the back for remembering the combination after a long absence even though his head was pounding with the onset of another headache.

He opened the vault door cautiously like he expected something to jump out at him. There were three shotguns from Lionel's hunting days, his old assault rifle from MI-6 in the UK, two ceremonial swords supposedly from the Japanese surrender at Pearl Harbor, which had never been documented or verified, and an array of handguns, including two Lugers, a .38 revolver, commonly referred to as a Saturday night special, a Colt .45, two police style Glocks and a Beretta.

Marilyn's handgun with the stainless steel finish and pearl handle was missing. Lionel closed and locked the gun vault door and backtracked to the kitchen trying to remember if Marilyn knew the combination to the gun safe. He did recall giving the combination to her when he was about to go out of town so that if she felt unsafe or needed some protection, she could retrieve her gun.

He called the Bethesda police department to talk to Sergeant Waters, the officer he'd been talking to all along about the original suspect, Marilyn's demise and the sordid details of her discovery in the laundry chute. Waters was at lunch, so Lionel took the coroner's report from the stack of mail on the kitchen table and read it through twice. Marilyn had died from a small caliber gunshot wound to the chest at close range, but the coroner's report didn't say anything about it being self-inflicted.

Now, Lionel had more questions than ever . . . Where did this happen? Who shot her and why? When did she get back from Europe and did she come home early or was she in Bethesda all along?

Did I do it and don't remember? That thought was the scariest.

The phone rang. It was Sergeant Waters.

"I was just going to call you when I got back from lunch anyway. What's up?"

"I was just looking at the coroner's report and wondering if Marilyn's fatal gunshot wound was self-inflicted?"

Sergeant Waters cleared his throat.

"No, to answer your question. Did she own a gun?" Waters said. "The bullet that killed her came from a .38 caliber pistol and the perp we picked up did not have a gun on him, but he reeked of powder burns, which leads us to believe he left a gun somewhere else, threw it away or used a different gun, perhaps your wife's."

"She owned a .38 caliber handgun, stainless steel with a pearl handle," Lionel confessed. "And she knew how to use it. How did you find the perpetrator?"

"Well, Marilyn did not die instantly, and she called the police. In your neighborhood, we're there in an instant and the killer must've doubled back when he heard sirens, tied Marilyn up, put the plastic bag over her head and stuffed her in the laundry chute. There was still a lot of blood around," Sergeant Waters said, "At least that's a plausible speculation. We don't think she actually died from the gunshot wound, but was asphyxiated by the plastic bag."

"I see. Did you find her gun?"

"It was taped to her body when we pulled her from the chute, "Waters noted. "We found this guy about two blocks from the house, based on your security camera's image of him."

"Can you tell me who he is?"

"Not over the phone, but I have mug shots of several perps and if you can come down to the station, you can tell me if you recognize one of them," he said. "Deal?"

"Deal! I'll be there by 3:00."

"See you then. I am at the downtown precinct on Woodruff Street."

Lionel liked to play a game with himself about people he'd never met, trying to guess what they looked like, especially after talking to them on the phone. He didn't have a very good track record, having only guessed one person somewhat accurately . . . Avis Marsden years ago. He imagined Sergeant John Waters to be tall, maybe 6'-3", thin and lanky, with a quick wit and a generally good demeanor suitable for police work.

He turned out Waters was not that tall, only 5'10", but he was thin and lanky with a muscular build, blue eyes and red hair. When he met Lionel, Waters asked him what he was smiling about and when Lionel told him, they both laughed.

"Don't feel too bad. I do that too and I've never been right," Waters said. "Although I did figure out that you must be British."

"Well, that's a start," Lionel dead-panned.

After getting coffee and talking more about things in general, the sergeant asked Lionel to take a walk with him to the other side of the building.

"We've prepared a line up for you to look at because it's more successful that looking at pictures," he said. "I hope it's helpful to you."

Lionel saw five men of varying heights, builds, apparel and apparent sobriety standing behind a one way glass window, turning left and right as commanded by another officer. Lionel thought he recognized one man who Marilyn had hired as a gardener who had not been 'round for some time'. He knew this kind of review was tricky, but he told Waters that the only man he recognized was fourth from the left.

"Everyone can move out except number four," the officer said. "You stay put."

The other four men were led out and Lionel observed the suspect more closely.

"Do you think you know this man, Mr. Kittring?"

"I only met him once and recognized him by the small scar on his left cheekbone," Lionel said. "Is he the one you arrested?"

"He is. Of course, he denies everything, but he will have his day in court. I have to write up the formal charges and will talk to him more when I have finished the arrest report," Waters said. "He may confess when I explain his options to him. Can you come back tomorrow to sign the charges?"

"Yes, what time?"

"I'll be at my desk at eight o'clock."

"I'll see you shortly thereafter."

CHAPTER FIFTY-EIGHT

Sergeant John Waters called Agent Snyder after discovering the bizarre death of Marilyn Kittring. He wanted to know if any of the other deaths had been so strange. Agent Snyder was more forthcoming than Waters thought since most FBI investigators were tight-lipped about their cases. Ryan Snyder told Waters that the strangest case was where the killer had strangled the victim with the medical tubes attached to the monitors.

"I think the victim must've woken while the killer was rearranging things, if you get my drift," Snyder offered, sniggering a bit. "Have you got a suspect in the Kittring killing?"

"We do. The husband will be by tomorrow morning to sign the charges."

"Would that be Lionel Kittring?"

"Yes. Do you know him?" John Waters said.

Not wanting to expose his identity, an honor among thieves, he said, "Yes, he interviewed me for a government position several years ago. Tell him I said hello."

"Will do. Thanks for your time, Agent Snyder."

"The pleasure was all mine. Thank you, Sergeant Waters."

Satisfied that the police had his wife's killer, Lionel opened the envelope the process server had presented him at the airport. As expected, it was a lawsuit about the World Solutions Group break-in naming Lionel Kittring as the prime defendant and Xing Ma, Jeffrey Olson, Mica Hrbek and Avis Marsden as co-defendants. A preliminary hearing was scheduled for June 30, 2021, via satellite to review the merits of the case.

Lionel noted the date in his Google calendar and another notation to contact Richard Dexter, the director at NSA no later than Tuesday. He took the documents to the library and placed them prominently on his desk. Surprisingly, he was not angry or bitter, more concerned at the moment with solving Marilyn's murder. He took a favored gun from the gun safe, went to his upstairs bedroom and put the fully loaded weapon in the drawer of his bedside table. He took out his cell phone and noticed a text message reminder.

'Call me.' Don Olson.

It was 4:45 p.m. He rang the phone number associated with the text message. A voice answered that was not Don Olson and it didn't sound like Jeffrey, either. It was a higher pitch, more like a woman's voice.

"Hello, this is Don Olson's private line. May I ask who's calling?"

"This is Lionel Kittring returning Don's call. Is he there?"

"Yes, Mr. Kittring, thank you for calling back," the sultry female voice said matter-of-factly. "I'm Mr. Olson's private nurse, Marie. He's been quite sick, so please keep your call brief."

"Thank you, Marie. Is Jeffrey about, too, by any chance?"

"Yes. You can talk to Jeffrey after you speak with Don," she said. "Here's Mr. Olson."

Lionel barely recognized Don's voice. It was soft, low and guttural and he slurred certain words between his lucid and garbled pronunciations. He sounded tired and not at all like the firebrand Don always thought himself to be.

"Don, what's going on? I hate to say it, but you sound awful."

"I am awful and I don't have much time left to be not awful. I need to see you tomorrow morning at eight o'clock sharp," he said, his voice dropping off. "I am naming you the new CEO and President of R.L Thornton. I already have the board's approval. Come to the house. Jeffrey will give you the address. Good day, Lionel."

Lionel held the phone away from his ear while Don Olson launched into a coughing spell until he heard Jeffrey on the line.

"Jeffrey, are you all right? I'm so sorry to hear about your grandfather, but I think it has been coming on for a while. I will be there in the morning," he said. "Do you need anything?"

"I am as well as can be expected under the circumstances and yes, it has been coming on for a while. But, these matters are always unwelcome and surprising," Jeffrey said. "Let's talk tomorrow after you meet with grandfather. The address is 12 Cherrystone Lane, Westchester, New York. 10046. About an hour from the city," he said. "If you're still in Bethesda, I would take the train straight to Westchester. It takes about 3 hours from Baltimore. I can get you a hotel room if you prefer."

Lionel was looking up hotels on his iPad as they talked.

"The Olympic Hotel is close to Grand Central, so see if you can get me a room there for the night and text me with the details," Lionel said. "I will see you both in the morning."

"Great . . . and thank you. Either I will text you or the hotel will. Gotta go."

CHAPTER FIFTY-NINE

Lionel decided to drive to New York since it would give him time to think and ponder what Don Olson had basically decided for him. Don was that way and it's what made him unique, powerful and successful regardless of the methodology, which many times was questionable. He wasn't quite sure why Don chose him except that he had knowledge of world events and connections others didn't have . . . a pulse on urgent matters that needed attention. Lionel ran contrarian in several ways to the philosophy of the Posse, but they would pay him so much money that it wouldn't matter and they knew Lionel could conform to their wishes. Some members of the group had better connections than he, but few knew how to really use them the way he did.

Alex Harrington, Beverly's running mate when she ran for president, was a good example. He crossed the powers that be in the Guardians of the Gate. Although they didn't get rid of him they made sure he would never again hold high public office. He lost his wife and his family and was fortunate to get a lowly desk job with a local government.

He blew his brains out in 2018. Alex had a smile that could dazzle the most jaded individual and the gift of gab to go with it but when the cold, harsh reality of what was to come for him showed its ugly head, Alex did himself in rather than face the inevitability of his future self. Lionel, at least, knew the rules and how to abide by them without crossing the line.

Donald Trump was also fortunate to be alive and the only reason he was still alive was because he had dirt on people everywhere who typically didn't get dirty. That's the way the Donald played and almost no one caught on until it was too late. He would get his, too. Not from an assassin's bullet, but from the weight of his own insolence, treachery and debauchery. Only truly powerful men retain their power, not wannabe hanger's on like Donald Trump who was pompous, arrogant and braggadocios. He was useful for one thing . . . To make sure no one like him ever occupied the Oval Office again no matter who was calling the shots.

As Lionel backed down the driveway, his phone rang. It was Sergeant Waters.

"Have you got a few minutes to talk? It's about Marilyn."

CHAPTER SIXTY

"I do. I'm off to New York for an emergency meeting tomorrow morning," Lionel said. "Will the phone due?"

"Yes. I have bad news about our suspect. He has an airtight alibi and three witnesses as to his whereabouts that night."

"I see. So what happens now?"

"When you get home, let's have another look at the lineup you reviewed earlier today and see if you see someone else in a new light," Waters suggested. "When will you be home?"

"I should be home tomorrow afternoon. Not quite sure," Lionel said. "I will call you."

"Good thing. See if you might find an old photograph of your wife with another man like the gardener, a delivery man, a handyman, etc," Sergeant Waters suggested. "Someone you might not be familiar with. One more thing . . . would you be willing to take a lie detector test just to make sure? It's just a formality, Mr. Kittring."

"Make sure of what," Lionel said angrily, bristling at the inference. "Am I suspect?"

"Unfortunately, Mr. Kittridge, at this stage, everyone's a suspect," the sergeant said. "Until tomorrow. Thank you for taking my call. Goodnight. "

Lionel hung up the phone without answering one way or the other to the lie detector.

Funny thing is, a lie detector test would be the perfect thing to clear his name. Lie detector tests have such a negative connotation, even though Lionel had used them many times to clear NSA agents of wrongdoing.

He smiled at the thought of taking one.

Lionel arrived at the Olympic Hotel shortly after 8:30 p.m. The drive was uneventful, even enjoyable, his discussion with Sergeant Waters notwithstanding. He was thinking more about his meeting with the ailing Don Olson the next morning because the way he sounded on the phone, he might not make it until then. He texted Jeffrey to tell him he was in New York City and that he would see them in the morning at eight o'clock sharp in Westchester. Jeffrey responded.

Everything was legally in order. The board had endorsed Olson's successor whether Lionel realized it or not, and the only thing that could dampen things was if

Lionel Kittring refused to sign the documents, somewhat of a tantalizing and wicked thought. That was highly unlikely since he sought out Don Olson about leaving the NSA and joining R. L Thornton, the wealthiest private company in the world. They made Blackrock look like a startup.

Lionel knew many people in R.L Thornton and they would guide him. Lionel was already good at keeping his mouth shut and the Posse knew it. That knowledge always comes at a price and in Lionel's case it was a princely sum. He went to bed smiling.

At five the following morning, Lionel got a call on his room phone. He was sleeping fitfully and he answered on the second ring. It was Jeffrey and Lionel could tell he was upset.

"Get here as fast as you can. Grandfather is fading and you need to get here as quickly as possible."

"Will do."

Lionel shaved, but didn't shower and was out of the hotel parking garage at 5:20. His GPS told him it would take 45 minutes to get to the address, but Lionel drove fast and was there at 5:55 a.m. amid little or no traffic. Jeffrey took him directly to Don's bedroom where he was sleeping fitfully. His breathing was shallow. Jeffrey woke him gently and Don sat straight up in bed, looked straight at Lionel then lay back down.

His private nurse took over.

"I will call you, Jeffrey, when Mr. Olson can finish his work with Mr. Kittring."

Jeffrey nodded and he and Lionel went to an adjacent room set up for Don to dine, read the paper and do other day to day activities. An urn of coffee and assorted pastries awaited them.

"How its Jeffrey doing through all this?" Lionel said.

"Well, Mr. Kittring, I knew it was coming, just not so fast, especially after the trip to Switzerland and everything that happened there," he said. "I am a little overwhelmed, but I'm happy you're taking over."

"Thank you, Jeffrey. I'm honored and flattered," Lionel said. "I'm just sad that my late wife isn't here to share it with me."

"What happened, if you don't mind me asking?"

Lionel explained what he knew, that he was facing a lie detector test that he thought was a waste of time, but didn't know another way to prove his innocence. Jeffrey told him that Thornton used to own a company that made tiny cameras that could be hidden in everyday appliances to make impromptu videos. The CIA and then the FBI grabbed the technology and may have installed it in Lionel's Bethesda house as an experiment. He suggested that Lionel check the appliances and light fixtures in his home and call him if he found something.

"Fair warning, these cameras look like black lint and can reattached toamlost any surface. We still have some of the technology that can interpret the film."

Marie stuck her head out the bedroom door and smiled at Lionel.

"Don will see you now, Mr. Kittring."

CHAPTER SIXTY-ONE

Lionel quickly read the transfer documents including his management agreement that spelled out a salary of ten million dollars a year, a signing bonus of one million, a fleet of cars at his disposal and three homes . . . One in New York City, another in Paris, France and the third in Vail, Colorado. Don was beaming when Lionel signed. There was a lightness to his bearing and his mind became engaged again.

"Looks like I'll be moving again, Don," he said.

Don nodded toward Lionel.

"I hate to rush off, Don, as I'm still dealing with Marilyn's death and have things to do in Bethesda. You get well so we can celebrate, hear," he said. Olson nodded again and reclined his head to his pillow.

"Thank you for your help, Jeffrey."

Lionel had his hand on the door knob, when Marie said, "Stop. You forget your paperwork."

She brought the papers to him, including a check for the signing bonus. She stood a little too close and handed him her business card and whispered in his ear.

"Call me if I can help in any way, any way at all."

She winked, turned and brushed her bosom against Lionel's shoulder, returning to Don's bedside to make him more comfortable. She looked back at Lionel and winked again, passing her hand lightly across her thigh.

"That would be all I need right now," Lionel said under his breath. *"Although it is tempting."*

Lionel was pleased with his new position at R.L. Thornton, although he had forgotten most of the conversation with Don and Jeffrey, something that was happening regularly in recent weeks. He grabbed the pill bottle and took two more tiny pink pills chasing them with cold coffee from the day before. He shrugged and glanced quickly at his phone, expecting a message from Jeffrey that Don had passed.

Don Olson was instead still very much alive. His family, mostly grandchildren and his own children, his longtime assistant Mary and other employees came and went expecting the worst any minute. They were surprised to see him so lucid, but a few recognized the pattern . . . Gravely ill, a rebound and then the final curtain. It was the classic ending to many stories.

Jeffrey asked Don about the recording system he had described to Lionel wanting to know if it recorded automatically. Don told him it did, but did not elaborate except to say some of the equipment was in Don's home office on the first floor.

Mica showed up unannounced, beaming from ear to ear when she told Jeffrey she had just ordered a new Ferrari. Jeffrey glared at her, but Mica told him it wouldn't be in the states for six months.

"We should all be cleared by then," she said, alluding to the lawsuit from WSG. "The most recent tally is in, but let's discuss that privately."

"I know just the place . . . grandfather's office. I need your help with something down there, anyway."

"Remember that micro-movie recording system we were discussing yesterday?" Jeffrey said. "For a while, actually quite a while, the company owned another company that made microscopic surveillance equipment, so small it looks like a speck of dust to the human eye. We have some equipment downstairs that translates the surveillance video. I'm not sure how to make it work."

"Let's go have a look."

"Appears to work like a television transmission. You channel it in, depending on the radio frequency of the transmission, choose the location you want to see and then back it up or fast forward or view from the screen using the remote control," Mica said after studying the system a few minutes. They practiced on some old files when they came across 1825 Mercer Street, Bethesda, Maryland, dated November 18th, 2020.

"This is Lionel Kittring's address . . ."

"Jeffrey, are you downstairs? Come up please," Marie said. "Time for lunch. Mica is welcome to stay, too."

They left the system on, ready to review Lionel's file when they finished lunch.

CHAPTER SIXTY-TWO

The family arranged Don's birthday celebration at the lunch hour including a big cake. Don smiled the whole time especially during Marie's dance. After two hours, Don was exhausted and Marie took him back to his bedroom where she stripped naked so Don could have one last feel like so many times before. Don fell back on his pillows, rubbing her nipples and had one last gasp of air before he passed. He was smiling. Marie quickly got dressed and closed his eyes, then made the announcement that Donald Herman Olson had passed on to a better place.

Family and friends gathered around the bed, prayed for his soul (and their portion of his estate) and sang '*We Shall Overcome', Til We Meet Again' and "Ave Maria'*, the three songs requested in Don's will. Oddly, Jeffrey did not cry. He knew this was coming for days. He was now rich in his own right and tried to be the strength the family needed in their hour of grief and greed. After that, he would become Marie's lover, replacing his grandfather.

Inheritance has it's reward.

He and Mica went back downstairs to the office and punched play on the outdated recording device. A good slap on the side of the machine prompted it to start. Mica fainted when she saw the first segment of film. There was Lionel slapping his 'devoted' wife around in their kitchen, screaming about NSA secrets being leaked and waving a gun in his free hand. Jeffrey stopped the tape to revive Mica and together they figured out how to transfer the film to an iPad.

Jeffrey called Sergeant Waters. "We'll be there by four o'clock."

CHAPTER SIXTY-THREE

Ryan had a voicemail from John Waters filling him in on his first meeting with Lionel and that the suspect they had caught had an airtight alibi concerning Marilyn Kittring's murder. Sergeant Waters told Snyder that he had another meeting with Lionel later in the morning and was reviewing some other evidence just presented to him about Lionel. Waters told Snyder that he would call back, but Snyder called first to see if he could connect with Waters. It went to Sgt. Waters voicemail and Snyder suggested plugging him in remotely when he and Kittring met again.

Jeffrey, Mica and Sergeant Waters looked at the entire tape on the iPad. It became clear who killed Marilyn from the tapes because Lionel shot her in the chest in the third segment after going to the trouble of holding a gun to her head while she recorded messages into Lionel's phone pretending to be in Europe. Despite the physical abuse, Marilyn apparently still believed he wouldn't kill her if she did exactly as he asked. Lionel was angry, cruel and vindictive, treating his wife like some cheap hooker in a flop house hotel, beating her because he didn't get his money's worth. Marilyn was unusually calm like it was an audition of some sort and had been rehearsed.

"Where is Lionel Kittring now?" Waters said.

"I think he's at his house here in Bethesda," Jeffrey replied. "I saw him earlier today and he said he was coming back here. You know, it's interesting that there is no footage of her being wrapped in plastic and stuffed in the laundry chute."

"My guess he got someone else to do that at a remote location. He probably drove to the airport to record the miles on his odometer, dropped off Marilyn's body and returned to the house and then came to me about the guy in the lineup," the sergeant noted. "He's supposed to see me about a lie detector test later today. All suspects are at-large."

"He's the new CEO of R.L. Thornton Industries and will, I think, fight this evidence with everything he can muster, which is considerable now," Jeffrey said. "Will you arrest him when he comes in?"

"Unfortunately, this is all circumstantial evidence and the defense would say that anyone can make a fake tape to frame another person. We'd have to have the gun, the bloody dress or other solid evidence. Unfortunately, Marilyn has already been cremated and I think the gun was accidentally cremated, too," Waters said. "So, there's no evidence usable for an indictment or subsequent trial."

"Even so, I'm very surprised by his behavior," Jeffrey said. "Some strange things went on in Switzerland that point to this kind of behavior, too, and there were no answers and no conclusion to those incident's either."

"What happened?"

Mica explained the assaults on Tomas and Charlene. How Charlene was murdered outright in her hotel room, apparently by two different people, and Tomas died in the hospital from his gunshot wounds after he tried to download information from Charlene's computer that was potentially damaging to the WSG.

Jeffrey added that no one was charged in either case, although Lionel was the last person to see either of them alive. He told Waters that Lionel was in the hospital trying to find Tomas' room when Tomas passed, but he did not kill him outright.

"Someone really didn't want that information from Charlene's laptop to get out," sergeant Waters noted. "Anyway, my suspicion was that it was Lionel Kittring based on what you've told me."

"So what are you going to do?" Mica said. "Are you going show him the tape? He knows the system is in place at his home, but he doesn't know it actually works."

Sergeant Waters drummed the table.

"He doesn't seem like the type to go around murdering people just to kill them. Has he had any changes in his health lately or taken any new medications that might affect his behavior?" Waters said, "Because, otherwise, it doesn't add up."

"Lionel was shot last year in DC by someone who worked in the Trump White House. He lost a good deal of blood and was laid up well into this year. I think he was unconscious, too, and barely survived his emergency surgery."

"Have to find out more about that," Sergeant Waters said, almost to himself. "If there is nothing else, gentlemen. Thank you for coming in. I need to contact Lionel and get him down here. Can I keep the iPad for the time being?"

"No worries, sergeant," Jeffrey said. "We're heading back to New York. Got to make funeral arrangements in the morning."

"So sorry about your grandfather, Jeffrey. I have been so preoccupied with this case, I almost forgot to extent my condolences."

"Thank you. Understood and not to worry."

John checked his voicemail messages and called Ryan Snyder.

"You've been busy, John," Snyder said, chuckling to himself. "What's up?"

"That's an understatement, Ryan, but very accurate. Long story short, I just reviewed a tape that points to Lionel Kittring murdering his wife and as soon as I know when he will be coming in, I'll get you plugged in via Skype. Just yesterday, he was named CEO and President of the R.L. Thornton Companies, the largest private company in the world."

"Sounds like he has some legal firepower now. How confident are you in making the charges stick?"

"It's not open and shut, but it's close. Just have to see how he reacts to the tapes," Waters said. "His lawyer would eat the tapes for lunch and spit them out. How's it going in California?"

"Actually got a pretty decent response to the email campaign, but when you called about Lionel, I put everything else on hold. The emails yielded a lot of response, but only two other suspects."

"Believe it or not, three suspects is quite good."

CHAPTER SIXTY-FOUR

Lionel was having trouble sleeping because a recurring dream woke him every time he had it. Until now that was only about once every two weeks, but now he was having it nightly.

Marilyn came home with a new, floral patterned dress that cost five thousand dollars. Lionel demanded that she return it and when she refused, she pulled a pearl handled .38 revolver on him, pointing it at his head. They screamed, they argued and Lionel wrestled the gun away from her, tied her to a kitchen chair, made her perform lewd sex acts, and cut her long, beautiful red hair short like a man's. She cried the whole time and squirted tomato ketchup on her new dress so she couldn't return it. After making recordings into a tape recorder . . . some nonsense about being in Paris, Lionel grabbed her between the legs, his grip was so tight it made her cry. Then he put the revolver in her mouth . . .

He woke up with a headache that seemed to split his brain in two, the pain so severe Lionel couldn't function.

That morning, Lionel called Sergeant Waters to make an appointment to come to the precinct.

"Great. I have something to show you, but you may want to have your lawyer present," Waters said. "It's video from a few weeks ago taken in your house."

Lionel was sure he would need a lawyer, but didn't remember having one, until he remembered his new job. R.L. Thornton had a battery of lawyers as long as his arm for just about anything necessary to get a man in Lionel's position out of trouble. Perhaps he needed to see what he was up against before contacting any of them.

"That doesn't sound good, but let's have a look first or will you be arresting me?"

"I have no reason to arrest you, Mr. Kittring, but this video I have in my possession is pretty explicit. I want you to see it and then we'll decide how to proceed."

"Can we meet at 11:00? I'll have my lawyer on standby."

"Works for me. See you then."

Lionel called Jeffrey to find out about the funeral and to ask about a R. L. Thornton attorney close by who could help him on short notice should he need it.

"No worries. Grandfather asked to be cremated in his will so there will only be a memorial service on Thursday in Washington where most of his family is interred," Jeffrey said. "As for an attorney, I presume you want a criminal attorney.

Full disclosure, Mica and I gave Sergeant Waters a video yesterday involving Marilyn that I'm pretty sure he will show you today. At first I was convinced it was you, but now I'm not so sure."

"Thanks for telling me. I loved Marilyn very much and I don't think I could hurt her under any circumstances. Unfortunately, in my business, you deal with a lot of falsehoods, inaccurate accusations and people who want to ruin you," Lionel said. "So, unfortunately, I may need a lawyer sooner rather than later. I'm going to see Waters at eleven."

"I'm right here if you need me. I will contact John Carlyle right now. He's in Washington and the best criminal lawyer we have," Jeffrey said, chuckling. "Nothing but the best for the boss."

Lionel laughed. "Hell of a way to start my new job, eh? Thank you."

"No worries."

Waters reviewed the medical reports concerning Lionel's gunshot wound. It said that after several weeks of recuperating, Lionel was still experiencing sharp pain in his right side where one bullet entered and did the most damage to his internal organs.

After receiving Oxycodone for several weeks, his doctor switched him to OxyContin oral for a few weeks and then to super strength Tylenol to keep Lionel from becoming addicted. The OxyContin regimen was not included in the report Waters had obtained.

'If Lionel was also drinking heavily during this time, he might have experienced blackouts, hallucinations or fainting spells,' Waters gathered from the contents of the report. *'OxyContin can do very strange things to people.'*

CHAPTER SIXTY-FIVE

Lionel showed up on time, whistling as if he didn't have a care in the world and right at that moment, he didn't. He was suddenly extremely rich, respected and needed by others to guide the R.L Thornton Company to maintain their number one position as a worldwide private company. He'd spoken to John Carlyle who told him to not confess anything or answer questions that seemed destined to trap him.

'Plead the fifth and call me.'

Sergeant Waters was a bit stiff, but cordial, as he and Lionel chatted for a few minutes. Another officer stuck his head in Waters' office and said they were ready in the conference room. Three other officers were there, ostensibly to bear witness to the proceeding, a stenographer that looked familiar to Kittring, to record the meeting and a projectionist to start and stop the video on demand. In order to keep things legal, Sgt. Waters informed Kittring of his rights and told him an FBI agent would be joining remotely to add more analysis at the end of the meeting. Ryan Snyder was positioned like he was looking over Lionel's shoulder.

It all seemed like overkill to Lionel, but he was not there to judge.

Sergeant Waters suggested that they look through the entire tape and then go back and review it basically frame by frame for Lionel to offer comments, objections or clarifications. Everyone agreed. The overall tape was old and grainy, but also gruesome, showing Marilyn Benson Kittridge arguing with her husband, throwing things at him, performing oral sex against her will, being forced to make false audio tapes with separate short messages about being in Europe. Then she was shot and taken out to the garage, bleeding profusely but still alive.

The officers coughed, guffawed, winced and one policemen excused himself to the bathroom to throw up, but only made it as far as the trash can next to the conference room door. Lionel sat quietly at the end of the conference table, drinking water and taking notes. At the end of the presentation, Waters turned up the lights and asked for questions or comments as he motioned for the projectionist to reset the tape. Lionel crossed himself, then stood up, looked behind him and smiled at Ryan Snyder.

Much of the tape was exactly as Lionel had dreamed night after night after night after night.

"Thanks for letting me see this, Sergeant Waters, and thanks to all of you for being here to witness it," Lionel began. "First, the man in the tape is constantly using his left hand and I am right handed. There is no wallpaper in our kitchen as depicted in the tape, the dining chairs are different and our dining table has a butcher block top, not Formica," Lionel said calmly without hesitation. "Anyone is welcome to see it for themselves. What this Marilyn said into the tape recorder under duress is not what Marilyn, my wife, said to me over the phone from Paris and I have never seen Marilyn wear a flower print shirtwaist dress in all our years together."

There was total silence. Even Snyder had nothing to say. All valid responses and impossible to dispute from the evidence presented. What Waters and the other officers saw most certainly could have been staged, possibly by Kittring, but that would take further investigation and nothing would be settled by simply seeing the tape again. Still, something didn't seem quite right about all of it.

CHAPTER SIXTY-SIX

Before he went to the precinct, Lionel loaded a suitcase and a box of miscellaneous items, into his car that had DC plates registered under an assumed name, parked it on the street and took Marilyn's car to the precinct. The miscellaneous items included his wife's passport, birth certificate, cheap costume jewelry and their wedding picture from nine months before. To his attaché case, he had added an executed ten million dollar life insurance policy on Marilyn, naming him the sole beneficiary, her expensive diamond jewelry and the keys to her modest home in Morocco.

When he was ready to go, he called John Carlyle from the car. He skimmed over the meeting at the precinct and then told John about the lawsuit in Switzerland.

"Do you know anyone at the White House?' Carlyle said. "The higher up the chain of command, the better."

"I know the Attorney General, but he's not at the White House."

"For all the legal situations the president gets' himself into, he might as well be." John Carlyle laughed. "Call Mr. Patton's office and ask to speak to him," Carlyle said. "He will have more insight into an international lawsuit. Tell him I told you to called. We went to Yale together."

"Will do."

" . . . And let me know what he tells you. We can get the right attorney on it, so don't worry."

Waters requested the presence of the officers from the morning session and told them what happened. He plugged Ryan Snyder via speaker phone.

"For those of you who don't know, Lionel Kittring has just been named the CEO of R.L. Thornton, a huge conglomerate with worldwide connections and influence," Waters said. "The largest privately held company in the world."

"Still, they won't condone this type of behavior from their own," a young, fair-haired officer named Bronson said to everyone.

"That's true," Waters replied. "But, they might go to great lengths to cover it up."

"What did Kittring do before?" another officer asked.

"Based on his profile, either CIA or NSA, he has an office in the District that is owned by an entity of national security registered in Maryland. That leads me to believe he's NSA," the sergeant said.

"I guess we need to get some help from DC? Send someone to intercept him before he can leave the country."

"Great idea," Snyder said. "I can send some reinforcements from DC if you want."

"Thanks, Ryan. Let me see how this plays out."

"Will do."

Lionel had put Marilyn's 450 SL in the garage, closed and locked the garage door and drove off in the Mercedes sedan parked on the street. On the way to DC, he stopped at the Maryland incinerator and deposited the box of items he had with him, watching the box burn to ashes before his eyes.

'Good bye, Marilyn. You made me very happy while you were here,' he said under his breath, looking around for any telltale passersby. While he waited for the box to burn, he checked emails. There was one from Mica Hrbek regarding the malware distribution.

'We have netted $650 million dollars in ransom money and I have shut down the malware program,' Mica said. 'The money is in the Swiss account known to all and distribution, with interest, will happen sixty days from today.'

"Good show, Mica," was Lionel's reply.

There was a bank account, but no real money was ever deposited into it. Russell the bot was a fake just like the emails, deposits, threats and the computer program's counting function. When Ma spilled the beans to the World Solutions Group, he agreed to run a fake money gathering scheme. He altered Mica's software, authored an email to the WSG members, altered Mica's Bots, fake replies, deposit counters and made sure chats to and from Mica were routed to him first.

It was five-thirty when Lionel safely reached his office. He had forgotten the miserable traffic conditions generated in DC most every afternoon. Today was no exception and by the time he parked the car, his head was splitting in pain. He took four Tylenol to stop it.

He pulled a cell phone from his desk drawer, transferring all the identification, emails, passwords and apps. He smashed the old phone with a hammer and wrapped the remains in a paper bag. He called Jeffrey and told his voicemail to make plane reservations to Geneva, Switzerland in the name of Russell Hancock, for the following day. He told Jeffrey to call back at his new number. Lionel texted Xing Ma and told him to meet him in Morocco in three days and gave him the new cell number.

Lionel changed his clear contact lenses for blue ones, highlighted his hair with more gray, changed his reading glasses and added a different back-up pair, searched his cache of fake documents for miscellaneous passports to match his physical description and faked name. He packed what he thought would be useful to have traveling for several weeks. He decided to take a new headshot and processed a new passport on the spot, one of the advantages of being in the spy business. Just then, the phone rang and Lionel flinched. It was Jeffrey.

"Reservations made and tickets are waiting at Dulles for you. The flight leaves at nine tomorrow evening," Jeffrey said. "Hotel with open ended reservation at the Dutch Royal Hotel, which is a strange name for a hotel in Geneva, but I didn't quibble." Lionel laughed. "And remember, your first board meeting is two weeks from today. We will need to talk about any agenda items next week. You think you'll be back by then?"

"I will make it a point to be back. Thank you, Jeffrey. Buy yourself a nice gift, like a Ferrari or Lamborghini!"

"What color would you suggest?" They both started laughing. "Talk to you next week!"

"Until then."

Lionel made reservations at the Hilton at Dulles International Airport, packed the car and was ready to leave when Avis called. He told Lionel that he and Fiona and Beverly had dinner the night before and were wondering about how he was holding up.

"What prompted it was we heard something on the news about Marilyn's twin sister. None of us knew she even had a twin sister," Avis said. "Or any sister at all."

Lionel didn't care much for Adele and tried to forget about her. She lived in Towson, Maryland, but for the amount of time she spent with Marilyn, she might as well have lived in Tahiti. They were identical twins and even Lionel couldn't tell them apart when they were together. Adele was a college professor at Towson University and chair of her department, but she was very jealous of Marilyn to the point of having threatened her on more than one occasion over petty things like clothes, shoes and lipstick. Some of her jealous rages were worthy of film and Lionel thought he might have some footage that could come in handy with Sergeant Waters, but he would have to look for it and then have it cleaned up, to use NSA speak.

"Yes, she's a professor at Towson University, but unfortunately Marilyn didn't see her often. They fought a good deal as Adele was jealous of Marilyn for no good reason that I could ever discern," Lionel said, almost forgetting Avis was on the phone with him. "Listen, I have to go, I'm headed out of town on business, but I appreciate the call and we'll catch up properly when I return."

"Just one more thing, Lionel, tell me when you will be back in Davos. You and I need to talk as soon as you arrive at the hotel there," Avis said.

"No worries. I will be there day after tomorrow in the morning, Davos time," he said, lying.

The line went dead.

CHAPTER SIXTY-SEVEN

Lionel started looking for any footage of Adele and Marilyn fighting. Adele would get so mad she would turn red and turn away from the camera. He also remembered that for the longest time Adele wore her hair short like a man. She often dressed like a man, too. He checked the photos in his phone, but there was no video there. He found some older phones and the video he remembered.

Lionel recalled Marilyn talking about Adele's struggle with alcohol and pills and depression. She had been treated several times for depression, but didn't stay on the medication long enough for it to do any good. Without the medication, she angered easily and blamed her ups and downs on others, especially her colleagues at Towson University and Marilyn. That's when she would show up to confront Marilyn over petty matters and get violent.

The battery in that old phone was good enough to replay the footage. A left-handed person with short hair, dressed like a man holding a gun to Marilyn's head, without sound, in a room with a Formica table top. Marilyn was wearing a floral print shirtwaist dress. Lionel almost dropped to his knees to pray. It was a replay of what was presented at the Bethesda police station. A little tampering to add audio and Lionel had his alibi. He dropped the phone in his briefcase and went to his car. He would drop it in the mail before he left on his trip or get Jeffrey to take it by the station.

The DC police arrived two minutes later.

Traffic had not improved during the two hours he'd been at his secret office, but he was in no particular hurry to get to the hotel. As he drove, Lionel was thinking about any loose ends he might have that would delay him. At a stop light, he looked quickly at his cell phone to check messages, especially from Mica or Jeffrey. There was one from Mica with nothing in the subject line indicating that it had to do with malware, probably the final total on the monies paid to get the affected WSG entities their computers back. It was an astronomical sum of money, even if it didn't exist.

Jeffrey had gathered all the essential players . . .Mica, Marilyn, Avis, Darden, Sergeant Waters in person and Xing Ma, Bjorn Somer, Sven Alston, Beverly and Gerard Meister on Skype. There was a new face among them, Ryan Snyder, but he did not identify himself and was visible only to Jeffrey. Meister spoke first.

"We need to decide how we're going to wrap up this case and move on. Hans wants to finish things within the next two weeks, the lawsuit notwithstanding," he said. “If not sooner. What’s missing?”

“Gerard, this is Jeffrey Olson. We thought we would wait until Lionel tried to collect the malware ransom money, but as of right now, that is scheduled for six weeks from now,” he said. “We could move that up. That is the sure way to catch him with his hand in the cookie jar, so to speak.”

“Beverly Swift here, Gerard,” she said. “Have the other tapes from the hotel that capture Lionel sneaking around ever been found? If we can charge him with Charlene’s murder, game over. We have good evidence of other crimes, but nailing him with just one murder would make the other charges stick better.”

Beverly’s cellphone message sounded. It was Darden.

“Sorry, I have to go.”

“Terrence, Gerard, here. What’s the latest on those security tapes. Can you be finished by tomorrow?”

“Yes, I think so. The lab has been looking at the tapes religiously and I will make sure they are done before tomorrow,” Sansby said. “I presume Lionel won’t be here until day after tomorrow.”

“Correct. But let’s be ready. And under no circumstances is he to be arrested!”

The crime lab in Davos had been scrutinizing security tapes of the stairwell one frame at a time, but no shadowy or suspicious persons appeared on any of the tapes. It also appears that none of the tapes have been tampered with. The technician dusting the bathroom in Charlene’s hotel room lifted a partial print from the toilet flush valve on top of the water tank. Another print was found at the same location in Lionel’s room and they were attempting to make a match. When they went side by side under the microscope, they did match. If nothing else, that was enough to bring a suspect in for questioning.

Avis had been working on what he called a ‘succession plan’ . . . A fairly long, itemized list going back to better times at NSA. Lionel had been doing things there that were borderline unlawful for quite some time but Avis had never encountered a problem and the agency wouldn’t make it public without a lot of red tape allowing them time to fix the message and expunge the messenger. It was an old gambit . . . the rule of law theoretically applied, but only to everyone else.

When Lionel was shot and nearly died, something changed in him as much as if he had died and come back to life. The things that mattered before didn’t matter anymore or not as much as they once did. That attempted murder perpetrated on him changed not only Lionel’s life, but his moral compass and his code of conduct because he found that he was as vulnerable as the next guy.

The law of the jungle kicked in with a vengeance. Meeting death head-on was admittedly a scary scenario. All of Lionel's old enemies came to mind and Hans Richter rose to the top and not entirely by accident or process of elimination. Hans wanted to be perfect in the eyes of the world, a savior in his own right for the wrongs of climate change, poverty, healthcare and homelessness. And, as Lionel found out, a lot of larceny goes a long way when you're in that position.

CHAPTER SIXTY-EIGHT

Beverly was late for Charlene Evan's memorial service and arrived to a packed Yale chapel and a standing room only crowd. Many more friends came to pay their respects than even Gail and George Evans realized. Afterward, Beverly made her way to Charlene's parents who were still standing at the alter talking with the bishop who presided over the service.

"You must be Beverly Swift?" Gail said. "You still look like your last album cover. Thank you for coming."

"Thank you for having me, Gail," she said. "That's the nicest thing anyone has said to me, in well, since that last album came out."

Everyone laughed.

Gail introduced her husband and the bishop. The bishop was gathering his bible and book of Common Prayer to make his departure. He smiled, but did not say anything, hugged Gail, shook hands with George and Beverly and made his way toward the front of the chapel.

As the Episcopal bishop walked away, George whispered, "He's quite upset over Charlene's death. He has been the bishop in this Diocese since the day Charlene was born, literally, and she was the first baby he christened."

"Wow. No wonder he's so sullen," Beverly said. "Is there someplace we can talk, maybe get a cup of coffee. It won't take long."

George looked at Gail.

"Everyone's coming back to the house. Why don't you come and we can talk after they leave. They won't be there long. Bring your appetite because there's enough food for an army."

"Tell you what, let me go check into my hotel, freshen up and come right over, say in an hour," Beverly said. "What's the address?"

Gail gave her an announcement, which included their home address, and Beverly tucked it in her purse.

"Did you ever find Charlene's email to you about her WSG discovery?"

George looked at his feet and then looked up.

"We found it in our spam file, but just didn't have the heart to open it. But, we *have* seen it."

"No worries. I do have a printed copy and I want to show you what she found," Beverly said. "I think you deserve to know. You get going and I'll see you in an hour."

"Do you know how to get to the hotel?"

"Yep. I have the address and GPS. All set," Beverly said, smiling. "I'm just so sorry to be meeting you both under these circumstances."

Gail started to tear up.

"So are we and we really appreciate you coming. Charlene really liked you."

Beverly nodded, starting to tear up, too. She made it to her rental car before she broke down.

"Why does this always happen to nice people like this?"

It didn't hit her until she was in her hotel room and freshening up that if the Evans' did not have the heart to open the attachment, how did they see email? Someone must've shown it to them, maybe their intruders.

When she got to the Evans' house, the last mourner, ironically, the bishop and his wife, were leaving. He greeted Beverly warmly and introduced his wife. He seemed more relaxed and in a better mood, having accepted that Charlene was in God's hands now. Beverly grabbed food as the dining table was being cleared and sat down next to George who was finally eating, too. Gail came in from the kitchen and joined them.

Beverly took her typed Internet message from her purse and showed it to them together.

"Is this the message you saw from Charlene?"

"I have discovered a connection between big oil, the World Solutions Group and the IMF, specifically Hans Richter, Gerard Meister and Yvonne LeStatt. It was a large donation from a cartel of Big Oil firms like Exxon - Mobil, Shell, BP, Standard Oil and some of the biggest banks . . . JP Morgan Chase, Citigroup, Mellon and the like. Run through the IMF as if it was being laundered."

"Yes, that's it," George said. Gail nodded her head.

"How did you see it, if you didn't open her email?"

Gail laughed.

"Two days after we were attacked in our home, we got an email with that quote attached. We thought it was a joke."

"Who was it from?"

"Some fellow named Lionel Kittring."

CHAPTER SIXTY-NINE

That Lionel would send such an email seemed odd to Beverly. Lionel would be showing his hand too much. She tried to call Avis, but got his voicemail. She called Reese and left a voicemail to see if he could pick her up at National Airport at 7:00 p.m. He called back immediately to tell he would be there and afterward they should go over to the new house.

"There are changes I think you'll want to make," he said. "Have you heard from Wyatt?"

"No, Have you seen him?"

"Not at all. I was at the house yesterday."

"I've got one more meeting before I head out to pick you up, so I'll see you at the airport," Reese said. "Seems like you've been gone a month."

"I know. I'm going to cook dinner tonight, so if you have time, pick something up," Beverly said. "I've had so much variety I can't think of anything I really want to eat."

"I'll surprise you. See you soon!" he said. "Safe travels."

The call waiting was Avis. He sounded tired and a little out of it.

"Sorry. Two martinis at lunch and they went right to my tongue," he said. "And, I haven't slept very well since getting back from Switzerland. Despite all the rumors and innuendo, Lionel is a good friend of mine, but nearly getting killed last year changed him. And not for the better. It's like he's on some kind of mission to save the world."

"Interesting way to put it. He's not doing a very good job, Avis. Do you know where he is?"

"The tracking system said he's at the Hilton at Dulles airport. He told me he will fly to Davos, Switzerland tomorrow night. He won't be gone long as there is a memorial service for Marilyn Thursday."

"Does he know the truth about Marilyn?"

"I don't think so," Avis said. "That happened when he was still pretty loaded up on painkillers from being shot. I'm not sure he knew his name back then. It was the beginning of the end of him."

"Where is she now?"

"She's still in Paris and will be in Davos tomorrow. She told me she's met someone new . . . Much younger and they're having a ball, literally and figuratively."

Avis laughed and so did Beverly.

"You're so bad, Avis," Beverly said.

"I'm going to Davos tonight to meet with Hans and Gerard about the Great Reset. I should be back Friday."

"I'm at the airport in New Haven. I am on my way home to cook dinner, put my feet up and snuggle with Reese. End of story."

"I'm jealous . . . Not that you're snuggling with Reese, just overall jealous."

"Phew! Had me worried for a minute."

"Not me. Fiona is way more than I can handle . . . And I don't do that well enough!"

"Safe travels, Avis. We're boarding," she said. "See you when you get back. My best to Fiona."

CHAPTER SEVENTY

After eavesdropping on Jeffrey Olson's meeting, Ryan Snyder decided the best course of action was to board a plane to Davos and catch up with, meet and confront Lionel Kittring personally. Ryan had no idea when Lionel might be back to the States so he could do that sort of thing in Maryland. Snyder never got confirmation about the tattoo on anyone's arm, but a lengthy survey produced a list of patrons who had put the tattoo on their bodies including Xing Ma, several movie and rock stars, the class of 2020 from Wellesley College and Lionel Kittring.

The last piece of damaging evidence was the forehead birthmark or lesion or whatever it was and although it technically was not evidence, it could corroborate the other solid evidence.

Hans wheeled himself into the meeting room amid the gasps of everyone assembled. That included Bjorn Somer, medical examiner, Sven Alston, the hotel manager, Captain Terrence Sansby from the police investigation unit and Ander Vogel, the chief lab official working on the fingerprints found in the bathrooms of Charlene Evans' and Lionel Kittring's hotel rooms. It was the only evidence left.

Hans held up his hand.

"I'm fine. Just a precautionary measure since returning from London," he said. "A lot of physical and emotional stress over the memorial service for Prince Philip. Thank you for your concern."

It was hard not to like the old man, as Gerard Meister called him. If he liked you, he would do anything to help you succeed and if he didn't there was no place on earth where you were beyond his reach. He was strict and brilliant, admired and scorned and expected results quickly, paying dearly for your opportunity to find them. Like most extremely successful men, Hans had his fair share of failed ideas, bad businesses, broken relationships and ruthless competitors.

That's what Lionel Kittring turned out to be. Everyone saw it coming but Hans. Gerard was certain that Lionel masterminded the WSG data breach and instead of trying to catch him red handed, he just made sure the information wasn't there. They removed everything of value and importance, some fifty eight terabytes, enough to completely fill an eight x ten office to the ceiling with paper. What Xing Ma and his associates found and downloaded was largely useless and prescriptive.

Ma's team placed Bots on all the data so they could track where it went, a precautionary measure in case the stolen data could not be returned to it's original location. Then the bogus ransom emails were sent. It was all very costly, but nothing compared to the cost of retrieving actual data and paying real ransoms.

The piece d'resistance would be if the fingerprints in the hotel bathrooms matched Lionel's.

"So, gentlemen, do we have an answer to the fingerprint question?" Hans said.

Ander Vogel stood up. An erect and slender man with hair balding to infinity and a pale, long face without a hint of facial hair. He seemed slightly nervous.

"I am Ander Vogel, the chief lab official working on the fingerprints, the only fingerprints, found in the Charlene Evans murder case," he said in a loud voice that was too much for the room. "They do not belong to Lionel Kittring."

There was a collective sigh.

"They belong to the Asian fellow, Xing Ma."

The room went silent. Captain Sansby stood up.

"I just want to add that the hotel surveillance tape from the stairwell rendered nothing useful. The prime suspect in the rape of Charlene Evans slipped through security at the airport, but since Ms. Evans was murdered and the two people are not the same, we decided not to pursue extradition unless you, Mr. Richter, want us to do so."

Hans shook his head. "We have plenty to deal with."

Bjorn Somer stood up. "I understand Lionel Kittring is on his way here?"

"He will be here in the morning along with Jeffrey Olson, Mica Hrbek, Avis Marsden and the FBI, who remain undercover," Gerard said. "Xing Ma will be back day after tomorrow. Again, no one is to be arrested. We want confessions first."

Ryan Snyder had arrived in time to hear this exchange. He smiled and looked forward to meeting the elusive and mysterious Lionel Kittring.

CHAPTER SEVENTY-ONE

Jeffrey, Mica and Lionel were on the same flight to Davos and managed to sit next to each other on the plane. Mica never said much and chose the aisle seat to read comic books while Jeffrey and Lionel talked, sitting across the aisle from her. Mica Hrbek had turned twenty-four and wasn't filthy rich, yet, but much better off than before she met Lionel.

"What are you going back to Davos for, Jeffrey?" Lionel said.

"I think like all of us, I'm going back to tie up the loose ends about the digital thefts, the murders, WSG and get some closure," he said. "I did receive a big bouquet of flowers from Hans as condolence for my grandfather and he said he wanted to get the whole affair wrapped up before it brought more worldwide attention."

"I agree. There are a lot of misconceptions floating around and I intend to get them straightened out while I'm there," Lionel said, cradling his aching head with both hands. "We have a lot of work to do at R.L. Thornton and we don't need this matter distracting us. Since I took over, I must get a dozen calls a day from the press."

Lionel, in Jeffrey's opinion, was confident about the future, perhaps more than he should be. Lionel had always been highly regarded as a spy because appointments to NSA don't come easily or lightly. He was a naturalized American, but faced harsh criticism from some members of Congress who complained about everything not originally American whether it was tennis balls, Raman soup or spies. It took Lionel a longtime to not feel like an underdog and an outsider. He wasn't about to let the theft and subsequent trial derail him now.

Gerard Meister met them at the airport like they were VIP consultants for the World Solutions Group. There were three separate cars awaiting them . . . Gerard and Lionel in the last car, Avis and Jefferey in the second car and Mica and the head of security for the WSG in the first car. Mica Hrbek had never met Jonathan Simmons before. A stern looking man, thick around the middle such that he seemed to like to eat and drink, but little else. He had a round face and a bulbous nose, thinning hair and the poorest excuse for a mustache Mica had ever seen. But as it turned out, knowledgeable and friendly. He stuck his hand out to shake Mica's when she settled in the seat across from him.

"I understand you designed the software to download the data breach last week . . . Or maybe the week before. I forget dates and times right after the WSG meetings," Simmons admitted. "I just wanted to say it was a job well done and that it worked well. If you're interested, there may be a future here for you at the WSG."

Mica was caught off guard by that statement, thinking the head of security was there to scold her or have her arrested. It was highly unusual to greet a stranger in a moving car and offer her a job after talking to her for three minutes, but on the other hand that may just be his style and he didn't want to create an adversarial situation.

"This is quite a surprise. I will have to think about that one for a while. Will that be all right?"

"Oh, sure. Take all the time you need," Jonathan smiled. "I just didn't want you to think I was going to have you arrested or something like that."

They both laughed.

Gerard and Lionel rode in silence for a few minutes until Meister finally asked about the investigation surrounding Marilyn's murder. He knew more than he let on, but he was interested in Lionel's side of the story. He talked to Ryan Snyder about it in some detail. Gerard had a hidden tape recorder in the breast pocket of his suit coat. A recommendation he took seriously from agent Snyder.

"Well, to be honest, the Bethesda police are trying to pin it on me with some cockamamy story built around bogus evidence. They are trying to trap me, but I got out of the precinct when the investigating officer went to consult with his fellow officers and left his evidence folder in the interrogation room with me."

Gerard shook his head.

"Sounds like they weren't running a very good investigation. Didn't I hear something about a memorial service coming up soon for your late wife?"

"Yes, it's Thursday. I better show up, too, or the police will really be suspicious."

"There is a way around the police being there, you know?"

"What would that be, Gerard?"

"Make it private or for family only. Then the police either have to have a warrant to enter the service or a warrant for your arrest and no judge in his right mind is going to grant that to the police for a private memorial service."

Meister didn't want to add that Lionel was in a very bad place with Hans Richter and the World Solutions Group. Attempting to steal digital information from the WSG or any Swiss based company was a federal crime in Switzerland, punishable by death or a longer prison term than anyone could survive.

Avis was curious, now that Lionel had become CEO of R.L. Thornton Enterprises, where that left Jeffrey. So he asked him after relaying his condolences about his grandfather.

"Well, Mr. Marsden . . ."

"Please call me Avis. I don't even think my father ever answered to Mr. Marsden."

"OK, Avis. My grandfather taught me his business early knowing that someday, one of his heirs would take over. I have an older brother, but he is not mentally capable of being in the business. He is not outcast, just not talked about. He's the family secret. He was diagnosed with a brain tumor when he was eighteen and it proved to be inoperable. He lives in an institution in the Poconos near the family summer home."

"So sorry about your brother."

"Well, thanks, Avis. I also have a sister, two years older, who decided to use her part of the family fortune to buy drugs and men. She *is* outcast," Jeffrey said. "And no one knows where she is. So, my grandfather had me learn the business starting before puberty. I was learning a lot from Wendell Bennett when he died and grandfather, by necessity, had to take over and train me. Then there was the boardroom explosion in 2016 that damn near killed my grandfather so there needed to be a successor as soon as possible."

"So where does Lionel Kittring enter the picture," Avis said. "How did Don know him?"

"A long time ago, someone at the Posse decided that having an FBI agent in the family was a good idea," Jeffrey Olson said, laughing and banging the car seat in front of him. "This story cracks me up. So, the president of GoG, you know what that is, Guardians of the Gate, called J Edgar Hoover and invited him to the house for a drink. And he accepted. At that time, the Posse was headquartered in DC and Hoover was thinking some big case his agency had been investigating was going to get a boost. Grandfather said Hoover was the most arrogant man he'd ever met including FDR and Bernie Madoff, "Jeffrey said, stopping to catch his breath and regain his composure. "Anyway, grandfather met Lionel in London on some sort of joint FBI and MI5 training mission. They used to see who could get drunk the fastest and pick up the most women."

"And they stayed in touch all these years?"

"Grandfather hated the FBI and got out as soon as he could reap some government financial reward and the easiest way to do that was to collect disability. So he shot himself in the leg," Jeffrey said. "Yes, he and Lionel Kittring stayed in touch off and on. They rubbed each other's backs from time to time."

CHAPTER SEVENTY-TWO

The next day, Avis and Jeffrey went back to the airport to get Xing Ma. He was his usual jovial self, but tired, as it was a long flight from Wuhan to Davos with three intermediate stops, the usual delays and plane changes.

"Welcome to the new world of flight, Ma," Avis said, slapping him on the back.

"Thanks. Where's Lionel? I thought he might meet me here. We originally were going to meet in Provence."

Jeffrey looked at Avis.

"Lionel is under house arrest. Hans accused him of masterminding the digital theft and killing Charlene Evans. And since Lionel managed to get the theft charges dropped, Hans wanted some measure of certainty that Lionel would not bounce on him," Avis said. "Did you know that while you were in jail, you broke into Charlene's hotel room and used the toilet and then went over to Lionel's room and used the glass in his bathroom?"

Jeffrey gave Avis an odd look and whispered in his ear.

"Or maybe the other way around!"

They all laughed.

"One of Captain Sansby's officers emailed me about that because he knew I'd been in jail during the time in question. He actually wanted to know how someone could lift my fingerprints and then copy them to the toilet lever and bathroom glass," Ma said. "I told him that not just anyone could do such a thing. It takes experience and painstaking patience. I told the deputy it had to be a person with extensive fingerprint experience and evidence gathering."

"Could Kittring have done something like that?" Jeffrey said.

"Perhaps, but not likely. I would think someone like the medical examiner, Bjorn something or other, or someone from Sansby's office," Ma said. "Someone who did it regularly because it is so tedious, but also someone who wanted to pin it on me and steer the evidence away from who actually did it."

"That may explain why it has taken so long to produce results," Avis said. "Whoever did it was so good that perhaps we'll never find out who actually killed Charlene Evans."

"I hate to say this, Avis, but it's not impossible that Charlene killed herself with the bed pillow. Someone could've slipped her something, the guy from the Summit most likely and then put the pillow beside her," Ma said. "I heard they found a pillow next to her body. She could've rolled over on it."

Terrence Sansby, Bjorn Somer sand Sven Alston were waiting at the WSG offices for Xing Ma, Jeffrey and Avis when they arrived. A large video screen formed the backdrop that could connect them to Beverly Swift, Janet Yellen, George and Gail Evans. The room was arranged classroom style with five rows of tables facing the media center.

Meister spoke first.

"Everyone take a seat and we'll wait until Hans arrives. In the meantime, help yourself to the breakfast buffet."

Hans arrived shortly thereafter accompanied by two assistants wheeling steamer trunk-size transfer cases that they wheeled up to the front table. They began placing their contents on the tabletop. Two other assistants passed out a thick blue book to each attendee.

"Good morning everyone. Sorry to be late," Hans offered. "Thank you for coming. I will be as brief as possible. Please reference the blue books to follow along."

Hans Richter paused and drank some water.

"The WSG has only tried to unite the world with the brightest, richest, most progressive people and companies on earth because they are the ones who can change things, for better or worse, through their actions. People who have no vision or don't think about the problems we face, are jealous or political or perhaps just plain stupid and write or speak or protest about what we do, not because they want a better world, but because they are the ones who are equally jealous and uninformed."

His listeners applauded and a couple stood up and applauded louder. Hans motioned them to sit down.

"I have been accused of using the World Solutions Group as a refuge and shield for large, wealthy companies, billionaires and the political elite. I find this interesting since the WSG was the only place these same people were willing to gather to discuss the issues of climate change, education, healthcare and poverty. These issues weren't created overnight and won't be solved overnight, but we have to start somewhere and the WSG has been a pretty good place to begin. All the naysayers will always be there as long as they have an audience and ammunition, good or bad, to point the finger at someone else."

Hans paused and everyone in the room stood up and applauded.

"I am a social scientist, not a diplomat or a politician and many of my words and declarations have been taken out of context. The statement quoted most often is, 'In the future you will own nothing and be happy' which I said in the context that if the world continues on its current path, you won't own anything because you won't be able to afford it and that over time, people will be happy with that. It attracts more Internet users taken out of context for the people already being paid too much if they scare the hell out of everybody."

Ryan Snyder stood off to the side out of sight to everyone gathered and took notes. He had been impressed with what he heard and was looking forward to putting a name to a face in the form of Lionel Kittring. Gerard Meister missed to introduce Ryan to Lionel at the end of the meeting, so Ryan Snyder was waiting patiently.

CHAPTER SEVENTY-THREE

Reese finally got through to Beverly on the fifth try to her cell phone.

"I know, I know, Reese, I'm sorry, but I just talked to Wyatt's office and he will meet us over there at six o'clock. I have been ridiculously busy today and I had to keep my phone off in order to concentrate. I have been thinking about Q all this time and I was on the video feed to Davos. Things just aren't right with that failed theft, the murders and Lionel Kittring's outrageous behavior." She took a deep breath. "Been a hell of a day! What time will you be home?"

"I can pick you up. We should go by the house and then out for dinner if you want."

"Do that. I need to call Janet if she's still in her office. I need to fill her in on my trip to Connecticut."

"OK. See you soon." Reese said.

Beverly called Janet and she picked up on the first ring.

"How are you holding up, Beverly? Been quite a couple of weeks for you."

"Better, thank you."

They each had their own agenda and Janet wanted to know if Beverly had been on the WSG feed because she missed it and the scuttlebutt was that Hans made a quasi-dramatic plea for his recent actions against the digital breach.

"Yes, I did make the virtual meeting and what you heard is pretty accurate," Beverly said. "I will run the replay for you on Monday, if you like."

"Just send the link. I will be in Canada Monday and Tuesday," she said, "How did it go in Connecticut?"

Beverly smiled.

"Think it was good that I went. Long story short, Lionel Kittring as much as confessed that he intercepted the email message from Charlene to her parents. He forwarded it back to them after they sent it to the authorities in Davos," Beverly said. "I have to go. See you when you get back."

All the lights were on in the Tilden Street house, but there didn't seem to be anyone around. Beverly checked her watch. It was 6:10 p.m. She looked back up the street, but didn't see Wyatt Douglas' car and it wasn't parked in the driveway. They smelled fresh paint when they entered through the unlocked front door. There were ladders and paint trays, drop cloths and paint brushes laying across open paint cans, but no workmen.

"These people left pretty fast because something either scared them or they were told to leave," Reese said, walking into the dining room and then the kitchen. Beverly was right behind him.

She screamed when she looked out to the back porch. A long, blood curdling vetting reserved for pre-pubescent teenage girls watching horror movies late at night. The kind of scream the writer of every horror movie ever made hopes to elicit. Reese stopped short of saying anything when he saw a man in a blue sports coat hanging from the framing of the back porch roof.

"Is that Wyatt?"

Beverly closed her eyes. "Yes. That's Wyatt Douglas."

She took her cell phone from her purse and called 911. After explaining her emergency, she called Wyatt's office and talked to Theresa Hammond. She dropped her phone on the floor when Beverly explained what they found. She was sobbing and mumbling so fast Beverly couldn't understand her.

"Theresa. Theresa. Calm down," Beverly said. "I've called the police, but you must get over here ASAP to identify the body and talk to them when they arrive."

Theresa snuffled hard to regain some semblance of composure.

"Sorry. Have you talked to his wife?"

"No, I haven't. You better call her because she won't know who I am. And besides, I don't have her phone number."

"I will try to reach her. She travels for her job and I'm not sure where she is," Theresa said. "Will you be there when I get there?"

"Most definitely. If you don't find me, ask for Beverly Swift. See you soon."

Beverly heard her gasp.

"The Beverly Swift . . . former leader of the Blaze? Oh, my God. I didn't make the connection before."

"Guilty. I will see you soon, Theresa. Thank you and feel free to give Wyatt's wife my cell number."

"Will do!"

"The police, the coroner and many others are arriving now, but we can talk when you get here."

The police did not move Wyatt's body dangling from a porch rafter until the coroner had a chance to examine him. The coroner suggested that he may have been dead before he was hung, suggesting poison or a lethal drink or possibly strangulation because the only marks on his body of any consequence were around his neck.

"I would say generally we can rule out suicide, unless it was an assisted suicide, because there is no furniture or other objects around that he could stand on to execute this hanging himself" the coroner said. "He could've eased himself through the rafters after tying off the rope, but he would've run the risk of breaking loose when he dropped."

When Theresa arrived, she was carrying a canvas bag. It was her collection of Beverly Swift CD's. Beverly introduced her to the police investigators and the coroner. She identified Wyatt amid sobs and hand-wringing as if he were more than just an employee. She told Beverly that she did reach Sally Douglas and after an initial spat of hysteria, she calmed down enough to say she was in Chicago and would be on the next flight back to DC.

Meanwhile, Reese started through the house looking for anything else that could provide more information about what happened. He went upstairs to remove himself from the confusion and drama in the kitchen that such events invariably bring. The surveillance cameras were mounted in the corner near the ceiling in each bedroom and the hall. On the top shelf of the smaller closet was the surveillance control panel and the audio and video feeds were on for every room downstairs. Reese took a photo of the console with his iPhone and turned the console off.

Lionel gasped and tried to get the video feed back from the controls on his iPad. He called Jeffrey Olson in exasperation.

"Forget it, Lionel, you can't control anything about the surveillance feed from your end. Only the surveillance company and the end user, by turning it off and on, can control it," Jeffrey said. "But, we have all the information we need."

Lionel seemed confused. "So, how did Wyatt die?"

"The same way Wendell Bennett, Ellen Steele, Dr. Eric and Gunther Schmidt died. They were all given lethal doses of a combination of heroin, opioids and Carfentanil, an animal tranquilizer. Looks like Goody's Headache Powder," Jeffrey said. "In the toxicology reports, it will look like an Opioid overdose."

"Sounds nasty."

"Yes, stay away from it. Don't ever let anyone else mix your drinks, be in the kitchen during meal preparation and don't turn your back on anyone around food or drink, especially at a party."

"Good to know," Lionel said. "So, who did kill Wyatt Douglas?"

"Technically, his wife, Sally. She just didn't know it and no one else will either except you and me," Jeffrey said. "She thought she was putting non-dairy creamer in his coffee, but it was our powdered concoction. In a lower dose, it can take four to six hours to work. One of our construction workers put Wyatt in the noose to make it look like he was hanged. In the time it took to discover him, the non-dairy creamer was gone from his body."

"The coroner seemed to figure out pretty quickly that he was already dead when he was hanged," Lionel mentioned. "I think there will be an ongoing investigation."

"Didn't you say something about wanting to talk to Mica?" Jeffrey said. "Where are you by the way?"

"I'm in a very empty airport in Munich," Lionel said. "Unexpected layover. The plan had a mechanical issue. Yes, I do, want to talk to Mica. She's in Davos, right? I have an idea to throw a wrench in Hans Richter's lofty plans for the world and Mica is just the person to take care of it."

"Good. I'll call her room and let him know. Will you arrive tonight or tomorrow?" Jeffrey said. "Speaking of taking care of things, We need to take care of Reese Talbot."

"We're getting ready to board our flight, so I will be there tonight. Let's discuss this later. I think we have other priorities just now."

CHAPTER SEVENTY-FOUR

Ryan Snyder identified himself to Avery Saxton who arranged a hastily called meeting with Gerard Meister, Terrence Sansby, Bjorn Somers, Sven Alster, Avis Marsden and himself to discuss Lionel Kittring. Agent Snyder presented the evidence he had gathered stateside and Sansby and Sommers filled him in on what they had gathered in Davos.

"Is there evidence of a weapon or weapons?" Ryan said. "We all seem to have sufficient circumstantial evidence, but nothing to make it stick in court."

"Have the Bethesda Police searched the house where Lionel and Marilyn lived? I know he has a gun safe and I've seen it," Avis said. "Lionel is a very meticulous person and he may have returned the gun or guns to that safe. We should contact Sergeant Waters."

"Excellent idea, Avis," Snyder said. He called Waters from his cell phone and hung up three minutes later. "They're on the way to see a judge about a search warrant. I think in Lionel's absence, the warrant will be served on R.T. Thornton's legal team."

"Is Waters going to call back after making his search?" Avis said.

"Yes. We just have to wait, Snyder said. "What is the agenda for today?"

Mica woke with a start when Jeffrey rang her room.

"I'll be right there," she muttered automatically. "Give me ten minutes."

Meanwhile, Lionel explained his idea to Jeffrey, who thought it might just work. Jeffrey went back to his room to take a nap claiming an upset stomach just as Mica arrived. Lionel explained to Mica how he needed her help to pull off his next idea to cripple the World Solutions Group and weaken their position on world issues.

"They all think of Hans Richter as some kind of global tech messiah incapable of doing wrong, but you can tarnish that image, Mica," Lionel said in his soothing, 'we're all in this together' voice. "There are a couple hundred websites this message needs to reach along with fifteen hundred corporate sites, all uploaded at the same time. Do you still have those web addresses in your database?"

"Yes. I rarely erase anything from my server." She said with more confidence than ever. "I need to see the messages you have and what time they need to be released. The tricky part is making sure the messages on local servers go out worldwide at the same time."

Lionel tapped the messages he had stored on his phone and sent them to Mica.

The clip shows Klaus telling Eric Schmidt, former CEO of Google, that the WSG has to be careful not to reveal the details of the Great Reset too quickly as people recovering from COVID19 or those low on money or skeptical to start with will not go along with a CBDC (Central Bank Digital Currency), microchips in the next round of Booster shots or continued required mask wearing. The whole social engineering experiment will go up in smoke."

"I have discovered a connection between big oil and the World Solutions Group and the IMF, specifically Hans Richter, Gerard Meister and Yvonne LeStatt. It was a large donation from a cartel of Big Oil firms like Exxon - Mobil, Shell, BP, Standard Oil and some of the biggest banks . . . JP Morgan Chase, Citigroup, Mellon and the like. They were run through the IMF as if being laundered."

"I am increasingly concerned about the America I love," he began. "We no longer take any responsibility for our actions, spending trillions of dollars on wars we can't or don't intend to win only to enrich our war machine and the elites who run them. We pump trillions more into the economy through a slight of hand called 'quantitative easing' that had kept the stock market and the housing market afloat while duping our citizens into believing we're that we're doing just fine," Q said. "We're not doing fine. And if we don't start being accountable for our actions, we are not going to own the world's reserve currency, but will turn it over to the likes of the IMF, the World Bank, the International Bank of Settlements and many others who don't have our best interest in mind, only their own. We continue to blame others for our wrong headedness and divert the attention of our fine citizens with masking, hand washing and social distancing while our environment, money and education systems fall apart!"

"The clips should follow one another and run continuously on each website," Lionel explained. "How long would you estimate this will take you to get this up and running?"

Mica was counting silently to herself.

"Eighteen hours to build it, two hours to test it, four hours to revise it. Twenty-four hours, but I can do it in twenty," she said, smiling impishly. "Three million, half upfront."

Lionel went to the bedroom of his suite and returned ten minutes later. "Check your bank account."

Mica gave a thumbs up and told Lionel she was going back to her room to get started.

"I'll check in with you every three hours and let you know how I'm doing," Mica said. "And update you on my progress." Mica went back to her hotel room to start working on the new Bot. Something was bothersome about this last ditch effort by Lionel Kittring to sabotage the WSG and more particularly, Hans Richter. It was quite obvious that the digital theft had been foiled and the price to pay for that was going to be stiff.

Mica wasn't going to be party to it. She closed her laptop.

'What would a new digital attack prove?"

CHAPTER SEVENTY-FIVE

Beverly was going through emails and text messages in a vain attempt to get caught up when her cell phone rang. I was Jordan Quincy.

"Beverly, I talked with the Los Angeles County DA's office and they told me that the head wound would be circumstantial evidence and not admissible in court without being able to show the face, too."

"I gathered as much not to mention how difficult it would be to prove who it is. Unfortunately, Lionel knows that."

"So, what should I do?"

"There have been some other incidents, internationally, that we think Lionel is involved in and we're trying to smoke him out, so all I can say is sit tight," Beverly said sympathetically. "I'll been in touch."

Lionel waited outside Jeffrey's room for security to arrive. Jeffrey lay peacefully across the bed with no expression on his face. His glasses were on the floor next to the bed and one arm was outstretched like he was trying to reach for something, perhaps the room phone. He was still wearing his shoes. He was dead and Lionel thought maybe he died as soon as he hit the bed. Bjorn Somer spoke up.

"Was he in your room before he came back here?"

"Yes. He's the Executive Chairman of the company I work for and we were having a planning session," Lionel revealed. "He said he was going back to his room to lay down because his stomach was upset."

Bjorn Somer did not like Lionel Kittring, he thought Lionel was too smart for his own good and lied about events and circumstances to have his own way. He bit his tongue trying to remain neutral while he gathered the facts.

"Did he have anything to eat or drink?"

Lionel rubbed his chin.

"We had breakfast in the hotel restaurant. I believe Hillary waited on us," he said. "You can check with her. Then we adjourned to my room and we had coffee while we worked."

"Do you recall how he drank his coffee? Black or with cream and/or sugar?"

"He drank it with cream, coffee mate or something similar, but no sugar." Lionel said.

"The powdered creamer, not milk or cream?"

"Correct."

"Can you show me the package, Mr. Kittring?"

"If the tray is still in my room, sure. Shall we go have a look?" Lionel said, standing up from the desk chair.

The tray had been removed, but Bjorn called the hotel manager and got him to hold removing anything from the tray until he could have a look. Sven Alston knew what Bjorn was after and set the creamer bowl aside as evidence.

"I've got it, Bjorn, in my office. Pick it up on your way out," Sven said when Bjorn called back.

The medical examiner didn't say anything, just disconnected the call. The police showed up and Captain Sansby went directly to Lionel's room. He wanted to arrest Lionel Kittring more than anything but he recalled the admonition from Gerard Meister to not arrest anyone. Meister told him privately that unless they caught someone red-handed, nothing would stick. *'I'd just like to get him in my car. I'm not sure we'd make it back to police headquarters!'*

The three men returned to Jeffrey's room where the body was being removed by medical examiner personnel.

"Anything else, gentlemen?" Lionel said.

"No, but thank you for your input. We'll let you know if we need anything else."

"Very well. Good day, gentlemen." Lionel walked away.

They took the body to the basement, the lowest level, and unzipped the body bag. Jeffrey was gasping for air. He crawled out of the bag on his own power.

"That was close."

CHAPTER SEVENTY-SIX

Lionel urged Gerard Meister to talk to Hans and call a special on-line meeting of the World Economic Forum. Two hours after Lionel's appeal, Hans called him to say he had agreed to the special on-line meeting the following day at three in the afternoon.

Lionel went to Mica's hotel room to tell her the new timetable. Mica had sequestered herself in her room since leaving Lionel the day before. Room service dishes were stacked on the un-slept bed. Mica was working hard at the task at hand. Unkempt and wearing the same clothes from the day before, Mica was like a kid in a candy store with an unlimited budget. Lionel had to knock three times to get Mica to answer the door.

"Everything all right?" Lionel said cheerily.

Mica didn't say anything, but brought Lionel over to her computer to show him her handy work. Mica had actually patched together some old Bots, made certain changes to make them appear new and set up an online code so that they would never arrive at their intended target. Things that Lionel could not discern by looking at the computer screen.

"I just loaded the last of the messages to the WSG member sites and was getting ready to test them," she said. "Care to take a test drive? What's the schedule looking like."

"The on-line meeting is tomorrow afternoon at three, so you have a little more time. Show me the content."

Mica accessed the member only website that contained 2500 email addresses, contact names, physical addresses, phone numbers and other pertinent information to make a complete file. She showed Lionel that it was the legitimate site. With a few clicks of the keyboard, Mica was actually controlling the content, messaging and timing of all the member's log-in information with the content they would see when they logged into their WSG account.

The following message came up first:

"I have discovered a connection between big oil and the World Economic Forum and the IMF, specifically Hans Richter, Gerard Meister and Yvonne LeStatt. It was a large donation from a cartel of Big Oil firms like Exxon - Mobil, Shell, BP, Standard Oil and some of the biggest banks . . . JP Morgan Chase, Citigroup, Mellon and the like. Run through the IMF as if was being laundered."

Charlene Evans

Lionel slapped Mica on the back. "This is perfect."

Mica had mocked up an agenda to test the code. On the first try, the message popped up before the bold letters appeared on screen, so he adjusted the code. The next time, the message didn't appear at all, so she adjusted the code again. The third try was the charm. The program was ready to go. Lionel was impressed and pleased even though he had no idea what he was looking at.

"I'm going to take the content down for now and reload it tomorrow afternoon at one o'clock in plenty of time for the meeting," She said. "Do you know where they will be broadcasting from?"

"I know from previous experience they use a soundstage inside WSG headquarters for security reasons," Lionel commented, rubbing his temples vigorously.

"I get that," Mica said. "I'm going to rest awhile since I've been up all night. I will have everything ready to go in the morning, but I better get room service to pick up this mess."

"Set them outside the door and call them. They will pick it up," Lionel said. "C'mon, I'll help you."

Sven Alston smiled when he hung up the phone and gave a thumbs up.

"You're good to go, Avis," the general manager said.

Jeffrey paid a housekeeper two hundred Kroner to let him put some things in the cleaning cart and accompany her to Mica Hrbek's room. When she opened the hotel room door, she and Jeffrey could hear the shower running. The housekeeper took a couple steps into the room to announce herself.

Jeffrey went directly to Mica's computer and downloaded all the contents to a thumb drive, careful not to leave any prints on the machine. He loaded the contents of the thumb drive onto a duplicate computer he'd brought with him. Jeffrey checked quickly that the new malware that had been preloaded was working.

He stuffed Mica's computer into a leather computer bag and walked to the hotel room door just as the shower quit. He gave the housekeeper another hundred Kroner and left. Mica stepped into the bathroom doorway, dripping wet, wrapped in a bath towel.

"Oh, you're still here. I thought I heard the door."

The housekeeper smiled.

CHAPTER SEVENTY-SEVEN

Mica woke with a start because the room phone was ringing. She was sure it was still Tuesday afternoon and that she'd been asleep a couple hours.

"Mica, are you'll right?" Lionel said in an urgent tone. "Are you ready to go to the meeting?"

"Meeting? What meeting are you talking about?"

"The WSG special meeting. It starts in an hour and a half. Are you sure you're all right?"

"I thought that was tomorrow," Mica said. "What day is it?"

Lionel sighed.

"It's Wednesday, Mica. Have you been sleeping since I left you yesterday?"

"Pretty much, I guess. I thought it was still Tuesday," she said. "I was having this weird dream that Jeffrey was still alive and sitting in the room with me, working on my computer."

"That is weird. We need to get over to the WSG headquarters. How soon can you be ready?" Lionel said.

"I'll be at your room in fifteen minutes."

"See you then."

Jeffrey and Avis were sitting in the WSG auditorium waiting for the fireworks to start. They were talking to Ryan Snyder about what came next. Avis asked Jeffrey if he was confident that his second visit to Mica's room fixed his concerns.

"Yes, the first trip was a bit hasty and I just wanted to know the programs I replaced would work properly," he said. "I'm confident they will work now. I also rigged this timer so I can control when Mica accesses the new programs. Kind of a fail-safe device in case she tries to tinker with the programs before the big show," Jeffrey laughed. "Mica was so zonked I don't think she would've heard a bomb go off."

Avis nodded and checked his watch.

"Mr. Snyder, have you heard anything from the Bethesda Police Department?"

"Yes, but please call me Ryan. Sergeant Waters texted me with a copy of the search warrant. They found several handguns in the gun vault, two of which had been fired recently, in the last three months, and Lionel's fingerprints all over the weapons," Ryan said. "If they can match the bullets with any of the killings, we have our killer. Does the name Tomas Hogan ring a bell?"

"Loudly. Great news, Ryan." Avis said. There was a small stack of papers in his lap that he was reading from off and on between conversations with Jeffrey and Ryan.

"What's that?" Jeffrey said, pointing to the papers in Avis's lap.

"Well, technically it's all the charges that will be brought before a judge here in Davos against Lionel for Charlene's murder, Tomas' murder, and other attempted crimes while Lionel has been here," Avis said as a matter of fact. "Then there are the other charges in the United States for Senator James Quincy, Lionel's wife's sister Adele and Wyatt Douglas. And accessory murder charges for Gunther Schmidt, Ted Swift, Dr. Eric Wade and Eileen Steele."

"Wow! He'll never get out of prison!"

Ryan Snyder smiled. "Amen to that."

"That's the whole idea. You guys better get out of here. I don't think most technocrats believe in ghosts and if Mica and Lionel see you they'll pass out!" Avis chuckled, looking at Snyder. "Can you operate that remote from anywhere?"

"Yes, I'm going over to police headquarters where I do think they do believe in ghosts. I will watch what goes on until I have to be back here for the finale," Jeffrey said. "You want to come with me, Ryan?" He nodded. "One last question, Avis, what do you think Lionel will do when he sees that Marilyn is still alive?"

"I honestly don't know. Lionel has been in a business full of surprises for a very long time, so your guess is good as mine," Avis said. "But, he is quite ill and could do most anything. He could get physically ill and throw up or go on stage to embrace her or he could try to run. Everybody but Lionel, knows he's in a lot of trouble."

Jeffrey Olson and Ryan Snyder barely made it out the door when Mica and Lionel arrived. Lionel waved to Avis and then he and Mica went closer to the stage to take seats there. It was fifteen minutes until showtime and the auditorium was filling up. Many locals came to these events as entertainment and for a way to learn more about the World Solutions Group.

Mica took her seat and opened her computer. It turned-on, but nothing happened. It didn't boot up, flashed briefly and turned off again. She checked the battery which was fully charged. She tried to boot it up several more times. Nothing happened. Mica was beginning to panic. Lionel gave him a strange look as screen messages were beginning to appear over the stage. Avis texted Jeffrey and told him to flip the switch. Mica shut the laptop down and rebooted again and then everything suddenly worked. Her program loaded into the WEF mainframe with thirty seconds to spare. Lionel handed her a handkerchief to wipe her upper lip.

Hans and Gerard took the stage together to thunderous applause as the house lights went down and the spotlight shone on them. Hans stepped forward and raised his hands to let the crowd know it was time to stop clapping. He told the crowd essentially the same thing he'd told the digital theft team after they were discovered, but added some other information that had been leaked to the press and the public about WSG.

The message appeared on the jumbotron overhead:

"I have discovered a connection between big oil and the World Solutions Group and the IMF, specifically Hans Richter, Gerard Meister and Yvonne LeStatt. It was a large donation from a cartel of Big Oil firms like Exxon - Mobil, Shell, BP, Standard Oil and some of the biggest banks . . . JP Morgan Chase, Citigroup, PNC Bank, Mellon and the like. Run through the IMF as if was being laundered."

The crowd booed and Lionel moved around in his seat, suddenly uncomfortable.

"Of course, we have our detractors. None more vocal than this man."

The powerful in-house camera picked Lionel's image out of the front row and shot it to the big screen. He was not laughing or smiling.

This message appeared for all to see. The camera was still on him and he looked at Mica in utter horror.

"How could you do this to me? After all I've done for you?"

Mica swallowed hard.

"What are you talking about? I've never seen that image before and I wouldn't do such a thing to you," Mica replied. "Go fuck yourself."

Epilogue

Avis was sitting in the first row, waiting for the crowd to thin out. He was recording his thoughts into his cell phone's tape recorder.

His cellphone rang. It was Beverly.

"How did it go, Avis?" she said. "What happened to Lionel?"

"Hans and Gerard turned the tables on him, using his allegations and quotes against WSG into a positive spin," Avis said. "The authorities took him away for questioning, but I understand he's been released. Not for long though, Ryan Snyder with the FBI is waiting to nab him. Lionel faces charges as long as his arm."

"Where are you?"

"I am in the WSG auditorium waiting for the crowd to thin out. This room was packed, "Avis said. "I just got off the phone with Richard Dexter, the head of NSA. They've been cleaning out Lionel's office and found hand-written diaries going back ten years. Pretty typical NSA entries until the entries after he was shot. The director told me his whole tone changed, the entries were erratic and very dark. According to Lionel, everyone was out to get him and his plan was to get them first including anyone who got in the way including the White House, the WSG and NSA. "

"That explains a lot and may even explain Charlene Evan's death, Marilyn's sister's demise, Wyatt Douglas, Tomas Hogan and dare I say, James Quincy. I can't think of the rest," Beverly said. "But maybe you'll get a chance to see all the entries."

"You can include Don Olson, too."

"I . . ."

There was a loud popping sound and the back stage door swung open wildly, banging into the rear wall. Lionel backed out of the door dragging a man's body by the collar behind him, his gun pointed at Ryan Snyder. It was Avery Saxton, a.k.a. Wendell Bennett and he had been shot once through the head. Lionel Kittring let the body drop and turned toward the audience like he was the star in the final scene of a stage play. He brandished a gun in his free hand, waving it around like a toy.

"Wendell finally got what he really deserved," Lionel said, just as Captain Terrence Sansby raised his gun toward Lionel. Lionel saw Sansby at the rear of the theatre.

Lionel raised his gun to his ear and pulled the trigger. It was a fatal blow. Ryan Snyder tried to perform CPR, but Lionel was gone. He pushed Lionel's sleeve up as far as it would go, revealing the Chinese alphabet character that stood for the letter 'M'. It was in the middle of his forearm. Ryan felt vindicated and took a picture with his phone.

"Avis, are you all right? That sounded like gunfire."

"It was gunfire. Lionel just killed himself after shooting Wendell Bennett," Avis said. "Somehow it all seems fitting."

"I guess I don't understand the state Lionel was in for these last few months, Avis. What was going on with him?"

Avis took a deep breath and nodded to the last stragglers leaving the auditorium. Sansby and his fellow officers rushed the stage with weapons drawn to ensure Lionel Kittring's demise and to check on Ryan Snyder.

"I think this goes back to the shooting in 2020 that almost killed him, Beverly. He had never been in such a state and true to his personality he sought the fastest remedy, OxyContin and Oxycodone, without thinking through the consequences. For a while it all worked, but then a combination of heavy drinking, he always was a heavy drinker, a spymaster weakness, the pills, the pressure of his work and finally the Glioblastoma," Avis said. "He wanted to keep up appearances on the outside, but inside it was all killing him. He told me about having a dream about killing Marilyn when in fact he actually had murdered Marilyn's sister, Adele. And, now, the diaries bear that out. Some people are constitutionally ill-equipped to seek help. Lionel was one of them."

"Sounds like fact and fantasy were getting confused in his befuddled brain," Beverly said, "Did he kill Charlene and shoot Tomas?"

Avis sighed again.

"One thing that is very strange is that Lionel made up and planted all the supposed damning evidence against the World Solutions Group waiting for someone like Charlene or Tomas to find it and then kill them to divert attention away from him and the digital theft," Avis said softly. "The Bethesda Police searched Lionel's home and found evidence of at least one killing from the guns he owned."

"Oh my God, Avis," Beverly said, sobbing now. "How sick is that? Did he actually write that in the diary?"

"Yes and many other maligning things. Just be sure, it didn't matter to him who discovered the fake news plants because they were just a means to an end. If you or I had found them, he would've tried to kill us, too" he said. "Not that it is any consolation, but just how his mind was working . . ."

". . . Or not working, as the case may be. So, did he kill Charlene?"

"I think he was planning to kill her, it's just that someone beat him to it and I think that someone was Wyatt Douglas and Lionel knew it, helped him escape and paid him a huge sum of money to keep quiet," Avis said. "Don Olson was Wyatt's father-in-law and shortly thereafter, Don was bragging that Wyatt bought his wife a new Tesla . . . The big, expensive one, even though his only real estate deal in the last six month's was yours."

"You mean all the accusations about the WSG were phony?" Beverly gasped.

"Yes. The only one that came close was the one about the Big Oil companies because Lionel was privy to that scenario, but that's not what really happened," Avis noted. "Big Oil was not trying to bribe Hans, they wanted to be part of the WSG, but Hans was hesitant to let oil companies be part of the conversation, so they just kept upping the ante until Hans and Gerard gave in. It wasn't $10 million apiece, it was more like one million each."

"What about Tomas?"

"We may never know who killed Charlene, but Lionel definitely shot Tomas over the telltale thumb drive. In the back, no less. He kept asking me if I knew which hospital Tomas was in and one of the charge nurses told me that Lionel asked to see him when he went to get the MRI for his Glioblastoma," Avis said. "He was becoming increasingly erratic and wrote that he was helping the Trump loyalists plan something in January if Trump lost the election. I'm afraid his next target was Reese, but Lionel dropped that plan."

"Oh, my God! Why?"

"He thought Reese knew too much about the death of Wyatt Douglas, when in fact, he didn't know anything. Again, an imagination gone wild."

Beverly swallowed hard. "What about Q?"

"There is pretty strong evidence from his diary that he may have killed Quincy because Q became a vocal supporter of the WSG which angered Lionel."

"Getting killed for being in the right place at the wrong time is a pretty flimsy excuse to kill someone," she said.

"Not if you're Lionel Kittring," Avis said. "Let me read this to you. It's a text from Jeffrey Olson."

'Dear Mr. Avis Marsden. Lionel Kittring has been relieved of his duties at R.L. Thornton Companies and I have been ordered by the board of directors to offer you the job," Avis said. "Among the perks, a salary of ten million dollars a year, a one million dollar signing bonus, access two three homes, six luxury automobiles and unlimited vacation time."

"Ten million dollars a year is a lot of money, Avis, my friend," Beverly said. "What do you think Fiona will say?"

Avis laughed.

"She will say, 'Do what you want to do. I'm not giving up my day job.' She never waivers."

"What do you think?"
Avis sighed.
"Sounds like a job for someone else," he said. "I don't think I'm up to it."

Made in the USA
Middletown, DE
31 August 2022